Welcome to Chiho's Room!!

*Dramatization. This never, ever happens.

SATOSHI
WAGAHARA

ILLUSTRATED BY 029 (ONIKU)

5

THE DEVIL IS A PART-TIMER!

YEN
ON

NEW YORK

THE DEVIL IS A PART-TIMER!, Volume 5
SATOSHI WAGAHARA, ILLUSTRATION BY 029 (ONIKU)

Translation by Kevin Gifford
Cover art by 029 (Oniku)

HATARAKU MAOUSAMA!, Volume 5
© SATOSHI WAGAHARA 2012
All rights reserved.
Edited by ASCII MEDIA WORKS
First published in 2012 by KADOKAWA CORPORATION, Tokyo.
English translation rights arranged with KADOKAWA CORPORATION,
Tokyo, through Tuttle-Mori Agency, Inc., Tokyo.

English translation © 2016 by Yen Press, LLC

Yen On
1290 Avenue of the Americas
New York, NY 10104

Visit us at yenpress.com
facebook.com/yenpress
twitter.com/yenpress
yenpress.tumblr.com

First Yen On Edition: August 2016

Yen On is an imprint of Yen Press, LLC.
The Yen On name and logo are trademarks of Yen Press,
LLC.

The publisher is not responsible for websites (or their
content) that are not owned by the publisher.

Library of Congress Cataloging-in-Publication Data

Names: Wagahara, Satoshi. | 029 (Light novel
illustrator) illustrator. | Gifford, Kevin, translator.
Title: The devil is a part-timer! / Satoshi Wagahara ;
illustration by 029 (Oniku) ; translation by Kevin
Gifford.
Other titles: Hataraku Maousama!. English
Description: First Yen On edition. | New York, NY :
Yen On, 2015-
Identifiers: LCCN 2015028390| ISBN
9780316383127 (v. 1 : pbk.) | ISBN
9780316385015 (v. 2 : pbk.) | ISBN
9780316385022 (v. 3 : pbk.) | ISBN
9780316385039 (v. 4 : pbk.) | ISBN
9780316385046 (v. 5 : pbk.)
Subjects: | CYAC: Fantasy.
Classification: LCC PZ7.1.W34 Ha 2015 | DDC
[Fic]—dc23 LC record available at
http://lccn.loc.gov/2015028390

ISBNs: 978-0-316-38504-6 (paperback)
978-0-316-39807-7 (ebook)

10 9 8 7 6 5 4 3 2 1

RRD-C

Printed in the United States of America

PROLOGUE

"…Mraaaahhhhh."

The man let out a cheek-stretching yawn as he unfolded from his reclining chair.

At first, simply dozing for an hour or two had made his back and shoulders painfully sore. But now, his body had grown used to the chair's shape, and he never felt tired when he woke up.

"Man. Didn't think I could *ever* adapt to this thing…"

With another stretch, he picked up the cup and toothbrush placed next to the BuBonic-branded computer screen on the desk in front of him, left his small compartment, and headed for the bathroom.

The space was notable chiefly for its high ceiling, wide expanse, and the seemingly endless array of bookshelves and open-top cubicles. It was an urban Internet café, and the only sound was the air-conditioning and the occasional grunt as someone shifted in their seat.

"Ah, the oolong's…" As he passed by the self-serve drinks corner, the man noticed that the warning light was on next to the switch for chilled oolong tea.

"'Sup, Greek."

"Morning, Satou."

"Satou" was there as well, greeting him by his nickname.

"Ooh, bad luck, Satou!" the Greek said. "They're out of oolong tea."

"*What?* For real?!" Satou launched his vitriol directly at the drink dispenser. "Guh, how ominous. Y'know, I had a feelin' today wasn't gonna go well."

"What, because they're out of tea? So what? Just tell the manager guy up front."

"Manager's coverin' afternoon shift today! The only dudes there right now are Kayo and that Vietnamese guy, and I hate talking to 'em 'cause they act all shifty whenever I show up."

"So if you just gave it up and drank some soda, then…?"

The man didn't know "Satou's" real name.

What he *did* know was that his compatriot absolutely refused to let anything besides oolong tea pass his lips. He was watching his sugar and fat intake—or so he claimed, at least.

"Are you nuts? I don't wanna die young! I'll just drink some water and head to work."

Satou filled a cup from the tap and briskly walked off, not giving the man a second look.

"Oh, you got work today, huh? Congrats!"

The warm praise wasn't enough to make Satou turn around, but it did inspire him to wave weakly back.

"…Anyway, soda first thing in the morning is just painful."

The Greek muttered it to himself while he found the bathroom and began brushing his teeth.

CyberSafe, the space he was spending his morning shuffling around in, was fairly famous around the neighborhood for providing a mailing-address service for its regular customers. "Regular," in this case, meant the kind of people who couldn't afford rent anywhere in Tokyo and slept in Net cafés and twenty-four-hour fast-food joints instead. It beat putting "The Streets" in the address box on your résumé.

All he needed for the moment, however, was Internet access and someplace to sleep during the night. Or whenever he was tired, really. By the time one spent as long in here as the Greek did, it grew hard to tell day from night.

He had come to know Satou along the way.

He couldn't surmise why Satou refused to give his real name. "If I gave my name out all the time," he boldly proclaimed the last time he had been asked, "lotta people could make trouble for me, y'know what I mean?"

The man didn't.

Not that he himself ever reciprocated. Satou called him "the Greek," and that was good enough for him. But since he himself was clearly not native to Japan, the man found himself fascinated by how frank and unreserved Satou was, talking to him out of nowhere. An interesting person to observe.

Yet, considering his reticence about identifying himself, Satou was remarkably verbose about his past history.

He came to Tokyo from out in the countryside somewhere, graduated fourteenth in his class from a prestigious university, passed one of the most stringent government-office exams in the country, worked several years in the Tokyo central bureaucracy, then quit to start a dot-com business back when the first bubble was in full swing. It hit big for him at first, apparently, affording him a freestanding house with a lawn in the ritzy neighborhood of Takanawa and a summer retreat in the resort town of Karuizawa, out in Nagano prefecture.

But thanks to his go-it-alone attitude and lack of personal magnetism, his company started to flounder, thanks in part to an employee embezzling angel-investor money from the accounts. The company fell into someone else's hands, leaving him with nothing but massive debt.

That wasn't enough to faze him, though. Not Satou. He took refuge working for a delivery company, using it to pay off every yen of his debt over the following ten years. But just when he thought he was free, a wave of governmental reforms led to a sudden influx of competing firms. One of them merged with his employer, and he was one of the first on the chopping block. Back to square one.

Still undaunted, Satou went homeless for a few months, saving up cash from odd jobs here and there. The Greek ran into him about two months into his "residency" at CyberSafe.

For now, he claimed, he was squirreling away all the money he could, bit by bit, so he could move to a real apartment by next year and start another company.

"How impressive… I sure don't know anyone with balls that big."

Whether that was all the truth or not didn't really matter.

The important thing was that by the standards of this country, Satou was not exactly on Easy Street.

"It's his eyes. Something really alive in 'em, hmm?"

Finished with his teeth, the man washed his face, rubbing it with a towel.

Looking in the mirror, he was greeted with a large frame, bright red eyes, and silvery hair with a bluish tone to it. If it weren't for the I LUV LA T-shirt peeking out underneath his body-length toga, he would be the living embodiment of ancient Greece.

He looked younger, better built, and far healthier than Satou ever did. But:

"The frozen tuna at the supermarket sure looks more alive than *me*, doesn't it?"

Gabriel, guardian angel of the sacred, world-bearing Sephirah jewels that grew from the tree of Sephirot, laughed to himself and shrugged.

"Hmm?"

Returning to his cubicle, he noticed something rumbling next to his computer. He hurried over to pick it up.

"Hello?"

Possessing a cell phone, a device endemic to this world, gave him access to something like a more precise version of an Idea Link.

He was rather proud of that recent discovery, since it allowed him to keep his Heavenly Regiment stationed in Japan, all biding their time at other nearby Internet cafés and a mere phone call away from action. But this call wasn't from any of them.

"Ooh, already? Okay. Yeah, yeah, I blew it. So sue me."

Gabriel shrugged to himself again, his voice completely unapologetic.

"So what, your 'war's' going along dandy, then? ...Oh, that wasn't you? Oh, suuuuure, yeah, I'll buy *that* for a dollar. So where are you? ...Huh? The obelisk? Oh. There, yeah? Hey, uh, if you don't mind me cluing you in a little, that's not an obelisk. Like, people work in there and stuff? So, uh, can you just wait up top? I'll meet you over there."

He shut off the phone, his lack of enthusiasm growing more prevalent every moment.

"Welp…guess I better figure out what I'm workin' for here."

His eyes, supposedly deader than last week's catch in the frozen-food aisle, glinted a little, perhaps in expectation of something on the horizon.

"I *am* an angel, after all. Would kinda like to do some *good*, you know?"

THE
DEVIL
STRONGLY
DEMANDS
TV
PRIVILEGES

People called the structure "the Manor of Roses."

Since time immemorial, the rose has signified beauty, its proud petals garnering it the love of each era's powerbrokers, its place in the annals of time and song firmly ensconced.

Under the name of this queen of flora, the manor, along with its equally elegant and beautiful, benevolent overlord, has quietly woven a tapestry of history over the long years, evolving into a place of solace—one worthy for the great leader they called King to come and rest his weary bones inside.

With its sanctified master and royal guest, the manor's past was just as refined and everlasting as that of the red rose itself. Perhaps it was only natural that the angels themselves, the subject of worship and adulation from all mankind, occasionally deigned it with their presence.

But, despite it all, the Manor of Roses was still an earthly structure. As a reception hall for the divine and heavenly, its confines occasionally proved a mite cramped.

In fact, when last greeted by the awesome light of an angel, the rosy paradise within its walls was marred slightly by an enormous hole gouged into one wall, marking a potentially final twilight to the King's solace.

The King looked up at that wall, the one so helplessly disfigured not long ago. "Feels like we've been out here a lot longer than we actually were."

The King's servant, standing faithfully next to him, was equally transfixed by the sight. "It was not long at all, my liege. We barely worked half the time we planned for."

The cadger that the King reluctantly allowed room and board also chimed in, listlessly: "No complaints from me, dude. Now I don't have to deal with the outside world ever again!"

The cleric, inhabiting the room adjacent to the King's, expressed a profound solemnness instead: "Wherever you hang your hat is home, as they say…and this is starting to look rather homey again, indeed."

The King's able work assistant regarded the manor with admiring eyes: "I'm pretty amazed they patched the whole thing up in four days, though."

The King's enemy ruefully observed the proceedings: "This is crazy. That hole was enormous, and in the space of four days, it's gone without a trace?"

The child who mistook the King and his foe for its parents asked the King a question: "Home all bedduh?"

"…Well, look—I know we all got our own personal takes on this, but there's one thing I *seriously* wanna ask my landlord."

The Manor of Roses, aka Villa Rosa Sasazuka.

Beholding their two-floor, sixty-year-old wooden apartment in the Sasazuka neighborhood of Tokyo's Shibuya ward, Satan, the Devil King who once plotted the wholesale subjugation of the faraway world of Ente Isla—currently doing business as Sadao Maou to you and I—could barely hide his anger.

"Why'd she make us cart all our crap out of there, anyway? 'Cause everything's the exact same as before!"

"There" referred to Room 201 of Villa Rosa Sasazuka, the "Devil's Castle," which was recently ventilated in unplanned fashion by a death beam from the archangel Gabriel.

In the space of just a few days, the cramped, one-room Devil's

Castle looked exactly as it once did—another dilapidated apartment in a lonely corner of Sasazuka watching time pass inexorably around it.

✳

Sephirot is the tree of life. The Sephirah, the treasured jewels it bears, each contain one aspect of the world's core composition. Yesod was one of them.

Alas Ramus, the personification of one of Yesod's fragments that fused herself with the Hero Emilia's holy sword Better Half, became the subject of a pitched battle against the archangel Gabriel the other day. The end result was a hole in the wall that brought the structural integrity of Villa Rosa Sasazuka into serious question, although it was an open question as to whether or not any of the neighbors could tell the difference. The residents were forced to leave temporarily while repairs were completed.

Crestia Bell—the cleric who occupied the room next to Devil's Castle and called herself Suzuno Kamazuki in this world—had some crash space in the apartment of one Emi Yusa, the name the Hero Emilia took on for her new life in Japan. But Maou, temporarily out of a job already due to workplace renovations, was also out of his home.

Thanks to the machinations of his landlord, Miki Shiba, however, he managed to snag a seasonal position at a beachside snack bar and souvenir shop run by Miki's niece. Accompanied by Shirou Ashiya (aka the Great Demon General Alciel) and Hanzou Urushihara (aka the not-at-all-great fallen angel Lucifer), Maou trundled himself off to the coast of Chiba prefecture.

Following soon behind him, as if magnetically attracted in some cosmic fashion, were Emi, Suzuno, and Chiho Sasaki—mild-mannered teen and the only person in Japan who knew Maou's and Emi's true identities and the world they both came from.

The summer job, to put it mildly, did not go as expected. Following the arrival of the Demon Regent Camio—whose wings Maou had entrusted the demon realms to in his absence—the group learned of monumental events unfolding both in Ente Isla and in Maou's former domain, as well as some of the darker secrets that lurked around the lesser-explored reaches of Earth itself.

And—the most important thing to Maou at the moment—the beach house he was expecting to work at for two or so weeks went out of business, and also out of existence, in the space of just over four days.

Between Maou, Ashiya, and Urushihara, the household managed to scrounge up enough pay to more than cover what Maou himself had expected to earn in half a month. But the sudden reintroduction to unemployment was nonetheless difficult to bear.

The partitioning of the demon realms that Camio came to warn him about, and the battle between Ente Isla's peoples over Emi's Better Half sword, weighed heavily on the hearts of both Hero and Devil alike.

It was starting to become clear that Olba Meiyer—Emi's former traveling companion, Suzuno's boss, and top-level cleric in the Church headquartered on Ente Isla's Western Island—was starting to take action behind the scenes.

If anything else negative happened to Maou and his cohorts in Japan at this point, he wasn't sure how he'd put food on the table next month.

That was how things stood in this, the first week of August—a day Maou had expected to spend in Ohguro-ya, serving ramen and yelling at kids to stop tracking beach sand into the shop.

✳

"'Kay, let's do it, Ashiya."

"Yes, Your Demonic Highness. Do not misguide us, Urushihara."

"Dude, all right! Just watch your step, okay?"

A fairly humble set of boxes and kitchen appliances were lined up in Villa Rosa Sasazuka's front yard.

They needed to bring them back into their room, but once he

realized the moving company charged an extra fee for lugging large furniture upstairs, he refused to allow the mere thought of it.

So here they were, Maou tugging at the refrigerator from above, Ashiya pushing up from below, and Urushihara providing verbal guidance from the ground.

Considering the number of times the bearer of the Holy Sword had plunged down these stairs, attempting to cart heavy machinery up them required more heroism than even a Hero could likely muster at this point.

But, to a man, the King of All Demons and his faithful Great Demon General agreed that, if they were to someday enslave the entire world and all who lived and breathed within it, they were gonna have to get that goddamn fridge up there sooner or later.

Chiho craned her head out of the Devil's Castle's second-floor door, located at the top of the stairs.

"I've gotten the apartment pretty much tidied up…but be careful, okay, guys?"

The lighter things—the clothing, the modular shelving, the dishes and such—were already inside and mostly in place, thanks to Chiho's volunteer work. But she wasn't expecting Maou and his friend to actually attempt the heavy stuff themselves. The worry was written across her face as her eyes wavered at them.

"Will you be quick with it? You are blocking my right of way."

Suzuno, meanwhile, turned her irritated eyes upward, offering the demons nothing in the way of pity.

Unlike Maou, her room was laden with furniture and appliances, from the stately wooden chest that held her Japanese-style wardrobe, to the family-sized fridge that was clearly overkill for a woman living alone, to the expertly crafted mirror stand with the cherry-blossom motif. If any of them broke, the mental anguish would almost certainly be far beyond anything Maou could ever drum up for his own junk.

But she, too, breezily refused the movers' offer to carry it all upstairs.

"The men here will help me," she said as she shooed them off. The men would have to bring it all up, starting with the much smaller fridge in Maou's room.

"Goooo, Daddy!"

A little ways away, Emi watched the scene with Alas Ramus in her arms, looking more bored than enthralled.

This was, in all likelihood, a job too delicate to ask Emi to lend a little holy power to.

And—more to the point—common sense dictated that there was no way these two women could have hefted up all of Suzuno's possessions by themselves.

Was this their way of making Maou pay for them saving his hide back at Ohguro-ya?

The mere thought of what would happen if he let any of this premium-looking furniture slip and break in his hands made a chill wind blow across Maou's heart.

"My liege! Why are you just standing there?!"

Realizing Maou was off in his own little world, Ashiya angrily stirred him to action.

"Oh! Sorry. I got it, I got it. Keep it up on your end... Hooph!"

Climbing a few steps, Maou lifted the fridge a few inches off the stairway on his end.

"Here we go... Hnnngh!!"

Grabbing the handles on either side, Ashiya devoted every fiber of his being to pushing the heavy box upward a single step.

"Put the right side up a little, Ashiya. You're gonna scrape the corner. Okay, good!"

As Urushihara scurried around below the stairwell, directing the action from multiple angles, Maou and Ashiya cagily changed position just enough to finally achieve the Herculean task of climbing one step.

They were already covered in sweat.

"Whew! All right! We went up!"

"Y-you sure did! Just keep that pace up for twelve more steps!"

"All right! I'm going up another one! One, two, and...!"

"Harrnnghhh!!"

"Maou, it's gonna hit the wall!"

Screek, whack, thump.

Step by laborious step, the Devil King and Great Demon General pooled their powers together as the refrigerator gradually ascended to Devil's Castle.

"Hang in there, Maou!"

Chiho cheered on from above.

"Dude, three thousand yen more and we wouldn't be going through any of this..." Urushihara groaned down below.

"For once, I actually agree with Lucifer."

Emi sighed as she watched her two archnemeses attempt to will the weight upward by sheer mental force, the refrigerator bobbing precariously in their hands. She turned to Suzuno's furniture.

"You aren't seriously gonna make those guys help you, are you, Bell?"

Suzuno shook her head.

"I very much doubt that, no. If Chiho would be kind enough to spot for me, I can handle this much by myself."

If two grown men were being creamed by a fridge nobody could ever describe as particularly large, how could a spindly-armed, small-sized woman handle an industrial-sized model alone?

"Yeah, true."

But Emi didn't betray a sliver of doubt.

After an extended battle, though, Maou and Ashiya finally managed to ferry their refrigerator up to the second floor walkway without dropping it once.

In the early August heat, this attained for them the appearance of two lemons with the juice squeezed out of them.

"Duuuudes? We still got the washer to do, remember? No resting yet."

Urushihara's voice from below was ominous.

"Almost there, Maou! You hang in there too, Ashiya!"

As always, Chiho remained the pair's sole ally in the affair.

"Hey, Chi, can you bring some flattened boxes over?"

She came back with two broken-down boxes, borrowed from a nearby supermarket by Ashiya to pack their clothes in.

"Ashiya, bring it up a little bit… Okay. Put this back there."

The feet of the refrigerator dug into the cardboard on the walkway.

"Okay, I'm pulling it in. One, two…"

With that, he began dragging it up to the front door, using the cardboard like a sled to avoid damaging the bottom panel and/or his floor.

After a few moments, the two of them were in front of Room 201 once more, summoning whatever fumes of strength remained to lift the fridge over the door frame and place it in position.

The moment they plugged it back in, it began whirring happily, defiantly generating cold air in the face of the sweltering malaise around it.

"Whew. Well, we didn't break it…"

Maou gave the door a tender caress and turned toward his sweltering shell of a companion.

"C'mon. We got the washer next. Emi and the rest're gonna yell at us if we stop."

"Y-yes, my…my arms are shaking…"

Ashiya wiped the sweat from his brow as he turned to leave the room. He didn't get far.

"Agh! S-Suzuno?!"

He heard Chiho shouting from the walkway, accompanied by the sound of something heavy thudding against the wooden floor.

"What's up, Ch…i?"

Maou refused to believe what he saw.

The Devil's Castle washer, until just a moment ago, was sitting on the front yard downstairs.

Now it was poised next to the drain outlet along the outer wall.

Next to it stood an utterly astonished-looking Chiho, along with Suzuno, her face cool as she held her hands outward.

"At *your* pace, the sun will set before we are done."

Her voice was cheerful, her eyebrows low against her slightly damp forehead.

Maou and Ashiya, faces peering out the doorway, looked at the washer, then Suzuno, then back at the washer.

"Y-you did that…by yourself?"

"Yes. What of it?"

"'What of'… I mean…"

Maou's mouth hung open, unable to string any more words together. Ashiya instinctively hid his quivering arms behind him.

Neither of them could imagine Suzuno, the gangly-armed, flappy-kimono-clad little woman in front of them, lifting up a washing machine by herself and tugging it up the Villa Rosa Sasazuka stairway.

"S-Suzuno just… It was just, like…*zoop!* Just, 'up we go'!'"

Chiho, in a rarity for her, had trouble finding her words as well.

"There is nothing that surprising about it, Chiho. To Emilia and me, the feat is hardly of special note."

Walking past the dumbfounded masses, Suzuno went back downstairs, her wooden sandals clacking the whole way.

Urushihara was there, eyes just as saucerlike as the others', and as he watched on, Suzuno approached her own refrigerator…

"…Oof!"

And hefted it up like a piece of packing foam.

"Devil King! Alciel! Bell can't walk down the hall if you keep standing there! Get outta the way!"

The two dumbfounded demons obediently shuffled back into their room at Emi's guidance.

Chiho edged back, little by little, at the refrigerator bobbing its way upstairs.

"Excuse me, Chiho. Would you be able to open my door?"

"Um…okay…"

The refrigerator gave a polite bow as it entered Room 202, a small woman in a kimono following behind.

"Hey, you know…"

Maou muttered to himself as he watched on.

"When she first came here, she was carrying that huge box of udon noodles around like that, too, wasn't she?"

"Perhaps she is rather more…MMA material than she looks, my liege."

"I can hear you! Such insensitive demons!"

Suzuno popped out of Room 202, her embittered face stopping the hushed conversation in its tracks.

"It is a simple application of holy magic to my muscular structure. Surely you were not unaware of such power."

"N-no, but…"

Holy doping, in other words. Though not as blatant as Emi's Heavenly Fleet Feet magic, perhaps, given how that let her freakin' *fly*.

It was originally casted by Church-affiliated doctors and the like, harnessing it to boost patients' strength during treatment and ensure their safety during intricate operations.

This wasn't a case of "if a little is good, a lot is better," though. Attempting to infuse more holy energy than a subject was capable of retaining was a waste of strength, and a single misstep in the related incantations could have adverse side effects as well. You couldn't use it to, say, turn a common foot soldier into a musclebound behemoth.

It would take someone like Suzuno, a high-level cleric and wielder of the Light of Iron warhammer, to toss holy energy around like that.

Taking this power, one revered as a miraculous blessing from up high in Church culture across the Western Island, and using it to move household appliances upstairs made Maou wonder a bit about where this cleric's priorities were these days.

"Wait, can't *you* do that, too, Maou? With your demon hocus-pocus and stuff?"

"Not anymore, he can't. If he could, he wouldn't have nearly drowned in the sea back in Choshi."

Emi sneered upward, her right hand holding Alas Ramus and her left easily holding up Suzuno's microwave.

Maou sneered at her, but:

"Daddy looks all mean!"

Alas Ramus's guileless observation made him drop the retort and heave a sigh instead.

"Alas Ramus is *so* gonna resemble her mother someday..."

"What's that mean? What's wrong with that?" Emi didn't let Maou's lifeless parting shot go unnoticed while Urushihara sidled upstairs and walked toward Devil's Castle.

"Means what it sounds like. None of us live in that big a place, shouldn't you keep her from listening to all that trash talk?"

Emi wanted to bite back at Urushihara, but he had a point. She sheathed her verbal sword, choosing to seethe at the demons upstairs instead.

Alas Ramus was about the only subject Urushihara treated with any level of seriousness. Both Emi and the rest of the gang found that offputting.

"W-well, okay, but that just means Maou used up all his power to keep Japan safe! You know?"

Ashiya nodded sagely. "Well put, Ms. Sasaki. So very understanding!"

"And you said it yourself, right? You said you were partly responsible for the whole Malebranche thing."

"Ngh..." Emi fell silent at Maou's point.

"So it's partly *your* fault, too, that we had to spend all afternoon lugging our crap up here!"

"Are you crazy?! That's something totally different!"

"No, it's not! Besides, you guys have, like, some kind of 'infinite holy power' cheat going on all of a sudden! Which strategy guide did you pick *that* trick up from? When we use *our* force, we tend to go through a lot of it fast, all right? Think about that a little!"

The Devil's Castle denizens were still unaware of the existence of 5-Holy Energy β, the heaven-blessed energy shots Emeralda Etuva—Emi and Suzuno's friend on Ente Isla—was sending them a steady supply of.

"So? Wouldn't that make you feel sad at all? Using your demonic force on something like this?"

"Oh, what, Suzuno can but *I* can't? Besides..."

"Anyway!!"

Just as Maou and Emi were about to embark on another of their pointless verbal tirades against each other, a paulownia-wood dresser stepped in between them.

"You are both in the way."

"Oh, whoops."

"S-sorry."

"And not to parrot Lucifer, but it is said that a child exposed to its parents' verbal sparring faces developmental issues later on in life."

The oddly talkative dresser floated between the stunned Emi and Maou, lightly whizzing its way into Room 202.

"R-right! So let's just get along, okay?"

Picking up on the thread Suzuno left behind, Chiho spoke up, either failing to correctly read the atmosphere or reading it all too well.

"......"

Maou and Emi gave each other an awkward stare and turned their backs, attempting to end it there.

"Mommy, Daddy, no fighting!"

But in the end, it was Alas Ramus's completely carefree intervention that marked the real finale to the great Devil's Castle / Suzuno Move-In, despite how uncomfortable everyone felt about it afterward.

Maou surveyed the room once more.

"...Man, though. It's all exactly the same."

Sitting around the low table in the middle were Maou, Ashiya, and Chiho. Urushihara had taken position in front of the window-side computer, hydrating with a glass of cold barley tea.

Emi, Suzuno, and Alas Ramus were having tea of their own in Room 202. The idea of everyone stopping in Suzuno's place for dinner self-imploded sometime during the afternoon.

With all the people walking in and out on a regular basis these days, four people in Devil's Castle almost made the place seem empty.

"Not exactly, Your Demonic Highness." Ashiya pointed out the kitchen sink. "They fixed the leaky kitchen tap. No matter how tightly I closed it, there would still be a drip. It was driving me up the wall, so I am enormously grateful for it."

"...Oh."

That was the only answer Maou had. It was hard to tell how serious Ashiya was being.

"Don't you think they repainted the walls, too? They probably had to, with the hole and everything," Urushihara added.

"Hmm? Really?"

"Rilly rilly. I think it was a lighter shade of green before, but now it's more lime colored, you know? They must've repainted it to match the new wall."

"Huh... I didn't notice."

Chiho was right. It seemed like the indoor walls were a little more brightly colored than before.

"Well, the rent ain't going up, so it's not like I was expecting too much."

"Oh, absolutely! I want you guys to stay nearby for a while to come, so I wouldn't like to see your finances suffer, either."

Chiho phrased her reply to sound like a perfectly natural rejoinder to Maou's statement. Still, it jarred him.

"Why's that, Chi?"

"Huh? Well, I mean, if you had to go someplace farther out instead, I wouldn't want that, you know? In fact, I thought that was what'd happen just a few days ago. I was kinda scared!"

"Well, I'm not going anywhere. Not like we got anyplace to move to. Or the money for it."

Ashiya nodded his agreement to Maou's humdrum reply.

"...Well, good."

The "That's not what I meant" was loaded up in Chiho's mouth, ready for deployment. But she never quite pulled the trigger.

"...It's always the main dude involved who notices last, huh?"

Urushihara, ever attentive to the conversation (although he rarely betrayed it), nobly sat up and checked the battery level on his laptop. It must have been time for a recharge. He plucked the charger cable out of a nearby box and connected both ends to the computer and the wall.

Then he noticed something unfamiliar.

"Huh?"

Every room in Villa Rosa Sasazuka had five electrical outlets—two in the kitchen for the fridge and microwave and so on, one on the outside for the washer, and two general-purpose plugs on the wall facing the backyard.

Urushihara normally reserved one of the general-use ones for his PC stuff, but in addition to the usual two sockets on the wall panel, there was another connector.

Before its recent renovation, this outlet had been blocked by a pair of tiny screws, preventing its use. No one gave it much notice, since no appliance in the Devil's Castle needed it. But now, before Urushihara's eyes, the connector had transformed, a wholly different beast from back in the pre–Ohguro-ya days.

"Hey, is this…"

It was a round connector.

The screws were gone. In its place, a round, white protrusion with a few pinholes bored in it.

The next moment, something went off in Urushihara's mind.

"Dude, no *way*!"

The sudden exclamation made Maou, Ashiya, and Chiho turn toward him, eyes wide.

Urushihara ignored them as he practically flew out the door.

His voluntarily leaving the room was akin to Jabba the Hutt leaving his crime lair and becoming a triathlete, but before Maou had time to comprehend what was going on, Urushihara was down the stairs and looking up at the apartment's roof.

What he saw convinced him for good.

"There it is…!"

When he returned, his face was so stern that the other three, still clueless, all thought it best to wait for Urushihara to open his mouth and explain.

It wasn't long before the purple-eyed fallen angel stirred.

"Maou, this is nuts."

Maou gulped unconsciously.

Then, giving them a look sincerer and more diligent than anything they had seen, Urushihara proceeded to floor the Devil King and his faithful general with one stroke.

"Villa Rosa Sasazuka's...got an HD hookup!"

A beat. Chiho failed to see why Urushihara found this so urgent. It was not the case for the other two.

"Uh?"

"Wha...?"

Then, in unison:

"*Whaaaaaaaat?!*"

"Agh! Ow, guys!"

"What is all that racket?! Do you want to wake Alas Ramus?!"

"What's going on? Someone attacking us?!"

The demons' harmonic scream was loud enough to make Emi and Suzuno leap out of their own room...and seriously weird Chiho out.

※

From the fridge to the washer, from the computer to the bicycle, the Devil's Castle crew had made more than a few infrastructure investments over the past year and change. But they still had no television set, for several reasons.

They could never find enough free funds, for one. That, and when Maou and Ashiya first fell into Japan, they didn't even understand the concept of "watching TV" in the first place.

By the time they understood its use as a news source, weather forecaster, and font of colorfully inane advertising, they already had many other ways to gain that information.

Most of all, however, the greatest source of hesitance for the Devil's Castle was the fact that Japan switched over to full digital broadcasting a while ago.

The antenna connectors in Villa Rosa Sasazuka were all from the analog era. There was nothing in the rental contract about providing for HD broadcasts, either.

They examined their options a bit, only to find that (a) signing on for an individual plan could put them on the hook for antenna construction costs, and (b) putting up an antenna by themselves could send the MHK man their way, demanding a television license fee and spelling yet more doom for their monthly budget.

So, to the demons, purchasing a single TV required the bravery and resolve of an Acapulco cliff diver. But they were too afraid to discuss it with the landlord. She could always seize upon the topic to put up an antenna herself and jack up the rent on them.

Besides, Japan was bubbling with other information sources. Compared to the fridge and washer—two essentials for keeping the demons clean and fed—a TV was far from first priority.

"Oh, well, you can get news and weather from the Net and your phone and stuff these days, so…"

"Something about *you* telling me that really pisses me off."

Something about the smug way Emi, fellow newcomer to Earth, put it rankled Maou.

"Indeed. I, myself, have only just begun to comprehend how to obtain information on my cellular phone via the Internet." Suzuno took out her Jitterphone 5, a basic Dokodemo model meant for the elderly and other Net newbies, to strike home the point.

"Yeah. If you really want to, you can watch TV on your phone, besides. It kind of kills the battery, so I usually don't, but…" Chiba's flip phone, meanwhile, had a screen you could flip around so the main screen was facing outside instead of in when folded.

Emi sighed. "We've gotten a lot of inquiries lately about batteries, actually. It depends on how you use your phone, of course, but… yeah, I wish they lasted longer, too. If you're using a smartphone, I tell people they pretty much gotta have a portable charger with 'em at all times."

Emi worked full-time as a customer service agent for cell phone giant Dokodemo's main call center. Since her bosses began introducing thinner and more lightweight smartphones, there was a clear uptick in complaints about batteries and why the hell they didn't last so long.

In practice more a portable computer than telephone, these devices' battery lives varied wildly depending on how much users took advantage of their data packages and fancier features. But compared to Suzuno's and Chiho's older models, they almost always went dead more quickly.

Maou glumly interrupted the three women's cell phone confab.

"Uh, girls, you think I'm living so high on the hog here that I can afford a phone to watch TV on?"

"Wait'll you get a load of this… The King of All Demons has a phone with an extendible antenna."

"Huh?!"

"Wha?"

"Pardon?"

Urushihara's poetic turn of phrase made Chiho gasp, Emi gape, and Suzuno tilt her head in confusion.

"Yeah, well, I only have to recharge it every other day."

"Whaa?!"

"Every other day?!"

"Is that long? Short? What are you trying to say?"

That was enough to even surprise Emi. Suzuno remained confused.

"Right after I showed up here, I just asked for whatever cost the least money, and I got this."

Maou removed his phone from his pocket as he spoke.

It sported a few scratches, but looked fairly well taken care of. But even compared to Chiho's and Suzuno's models, it was clearly from another era.

"Ooh. My dad used to have one of those."

For someone like Chiho, growing up in the digital age, a cell phone was a device whose constant presence around her was a given. Even she could tell with a single glance that Maou's device was a modern relic.

"…Who made that?"

The carrier name on the back of the phone was something Emi, who worked for a phone company and had at least a passing knowledge of the competition, had never seen before.

"Your mail address is from AE, right, Maou?"

Maou nodded.

"Yeah, my phone bill comes from AE. But when I bought this, they kept yappin' at me about base costs and data plans and stuff. I kept telling them that all I cared about was talk and text, and they gave me this."

"Just talk and text… Wait, is that a Joose'd Mobile phone?!"

Joose'd Mobile had its heyday a while back, selling cheap prepaid plans and no-money-down phones to millennials with flashy in-your-face advertising. The original service died long ago, merging with AE—one of the Big Three in Japan's carrier scene—a few years back.

"Yeah. The phone was free, it's easy to use, and I figure I'm not paying more than what I use it for, y'know?"

Maou's reply was indifferent. But in this era where even the so-called next generation of cellular devices were now old hat in the wake of all-purpose smartphones, sporting a Joose'd phone—one that ran on a network that didn't even exist any longer—wasn't exactly common.

The fact that Joose'd devices could even run on a modern carrier infrastructure was a miracle in itself. And as their old TV slogan "All Talk. All Text. No BS" hinted at, there was no web surfing going on with Maou's handset.

"S-so…like, Maou, how do you know what the weather's gonna be like, even?!"

"Huh? 177."

The reply offered little explanation to Chiho's disbelieving ears.

"'Course, I still wind up calling the voice-time number by accident every fifth time or so…"

"Emilia, what does '177' mean?"

"You call that and a computer voice gives you the weather. You get the time by dialing 117, by the way. I think you need to dial some kinda special prefix if you're calling from a cell. During training, they just kinda touched on it as something I'd never, ever use, so I forgot about it."

Emi's response belied her customer-service experience. Quick and to the point.

"I had no idea anyone *used* it, though. I mean, a lot of people have the weather on their lock screen these days. ...And if you misdial it all the time, why don't you stick the number in your directory?"

"Yeah, well, that ain't the first time he's tried to palm off crappy tech on us." Urushihara dejectedly shook his head, eyes fixed upon his computer screen.

"Wh-what about the news, then?" By Chiho's judgment, Maou never seemed too far behind at work when it came to current trends and topics. He seemed to have a working knowledge of politics, the latest scandals, sports standings, that sort of thing.

"Well, we have a PC here ever since Urushihara showed up, so... Plus, they have those video screens at the rail stations with news and stuff, right? I like to hang out at the bookstore magazine rack, too, so keeping up ain't too hard."

"......"

Chiho, a child of the information age, couldn't make head or tail of it.

"Besides, what's it matter what kinda phone I have? It's not like I'm missing out on anything, and I'm not planning to upgrade anytime soon, either. But...hmm. We got an HD antenna now, huh?"

Maou gave a thoughtful look to the antenna hookup, then to the outlet occupied by Urushihara's computer. He scowled.

"Hey, Ashiya."

"Yes, my liege?"

"Wanna buy a TV?"

It almost sounded like Maou was talking to himself.

"Hahhh?!"

"Why *that* reaction?" Maou started quizzically at Ashiya, who sounded like someone had run a cheese grater over his throat.

"I simply reasoned from your conversation, Your Demonic Highness, that you didn't see the need for one... You stated a moment ago that you needed no television to know the ways of the world. We already have a computer! And the Internet!" Ashiya frantically pointed a finger at Urushihara.

"Dude, could you stop pointing at me like my computer's the only reason I deserve to live?"

"Hmph. I will admit, you are at least capable now of serving food to people. A living, breathing vending machine."

"Yeah, see? I had dudes *lining up* for me. Beat that."

The conversation between the two was not quite Great Demon General material.

"I think Alciel has a point, though. I've had a TV in my apartment for a while now, but it's pretty much always off. I watch a few minutes of the morning news, maybe a drama or samurai show at night, then the weather, and that's about it. I don't see any major pressing need of one for you guys, just because your landlord installed an antenna."

"You aren't showing Alas Ramus any educational TV or anything?"

Maou turned to face Emi. She glared back. Alas Ramus, who spent the late afternoon napping in Room 202, was currently fused within her.

"Oh, what, you forgot already? The show at Tokyo Big-Egg Town? Shows like *Sunflower Street* and cartoons pretty much bombard kids with colors all the time. I don't want her having another episode, so I'm trying to keep her away from TV as much as possible."

"Huh. Gotcha."

The live-action ninja-ranger show the three of them watched at Tokyo Big-Egg Town a while back was filled with color-coded warriors of justice bounding around the stage. The experience caused Alas Ramus to have something resembling an epileptic seizure.

She always had a pretty deep relationship with colorful things. The ninjas, and the enormous tree they somersaulted around, must have reminded her of the great life-giving tree Sephirot and the multihued Sephirah it bore, each governing over a different color and a different aspect of the world.

As of right now, nobody in the room knew anything about the Sephirot apart from what they heard elsewhere.

None of them could say for sure that the sacred tree had any lasting effect on Alas Ramus. But after that harrowing incident, Emi tried her best to avoid reminding the child of anything resembling Sephirot as much as possible.

"Thing is, though...there's been one time before when I kinda wished I had a TV in here." Maou's voice took on a bitter tone as he thumbed through his memory banks. "It was before Chi joined me at the Mag. You know our Jolly Meals? The ones that come with toys and stuff?"

"Um, yeah, sure."

"Well, the toys are always either really hot, or really cold, in terms of popularity. This one time, we were doing these Pocket Creatures—y'know, Pokétures—toys, and this kid who couldn't have been much older than eight or so comes up and orders a Jolly Meal. So I asked him which toy he wanted, and he was like..."

Maou bunched up his eyebrows.

It was a look of anguish, one not even Ashiya had seen in several months.

"Gimme the one that goes 'croak-a-loak'!"

The sudden scowl, followed by the otherworldly cry, bewildered the rest of the room.

"Yeah! You see? I felt, like, *exactly* what you must be feeling right now. What the hell's this kid mean, the one who goes 'croak-a-loak'? I didn't even know that every monster in the game had their own unique cry like that, so I was totally clueless. And of course we had, like, ten different toys to choose from, so I couldn't really spend the time guessing."

The others, unsure what the point was to this ripping yarn, could do nothing but sit tight and listen. Surprisingly, it was Urushihara who broke the silence.

"I tried searching for it. Turns out it was from one of the movies,

Decahelios and the Path to the Sky King. Decahelios is the mythical Pokéture in that one, and his basic *chibi* form is Dekalo, and *that's* who makes it. He's this little frog guy who lives in a bog somewhere, and eventually he evolves into a dragon."

"You are speaking in tongues, Lucifer."

To Suzuno, not very versed in modern Japanese subculture, Urushihara's speech must have sounded like a runic inscription on the tomb of a long-forgotten ruler.

"But, my liege, if his cry was 'croak-a-loak,' that would imply to me that the correct creature would at least look *somewhat* frog-like…"

"Yeah, Ashiya, but you say that because you've been here on Earth for over a year now. Do the chickens say 'cock-a-doodle-doo' back in the demon realms?"

Every language on Earth had its own unique ways of rendering animal cries and other bits of nonlanguage. The only person who had the right to take someone not native to Japan (or this world) to task for not knowing that *croak* was shorthand for "frog" was Mayumi Kisaki, Maou's manager at MgRonald and a woman oblivious to his past.

"So anyway, these Pokétures were mostly movie tie-ins who first got introduced in the plot, so at the time, all you knew about 'em came from the maybe five seconds they showed up in the trailer. The kid didn't remember the name of that Dekalo guy or what he looked like. So I had no idea, and his mom was like 'Oh, Shocksqueak is *fiiine*, son…'"

Shocksqueak was the most well-known of Pokétures, a constant presence across the entire series and its merchandise.

"The problem, though, was that Shocksqueak was the most popular toy and we had already run out of it. So his mom wound up leaving with this freaky toy that looked like a jellyfish with a bunch of magnets stuck to it."

"Jellyfish with a bunch of magnets stuck to it" provided little in the way of new insight to Maou's audience of Pokéture neophytes.

"…Okay," Emi impatiently spoke up. "So what's the point of this story?"

"The point is, if I had a TV—if I saw some of the preview ads and knew at least a little bit about what we were selling to kids—I could've given that li'l guy what he wanted. It's not my fault we were out of Shocksqueak, but we had all the other ones."

"...Took you long enough." Urushihara eloquently summed up what everyone else was thinking.

"But how does that connect with purchasing a TV?" Chiho asked. "Not to take Ashiya's side, but you could still look that stuff up on the Internet if you wanted to."

Maou nodded at her.

"Yeah, but I'd never see that kinda stuff unless I actively searched for it. I mean, failure breeds success and all that, but if I'm failing to avoid mistakes I could've easily avoided if I cared a little, that's not a mistake so much as sheer laziness, right?"

"And that, my liege, is precisely why the Internet is there! That is as wide a net as anyone needs to cast. The news is no different between the Net and television, is it?"

Maou grinned bitterly at Ashiya, whose fervent desire not to blow their budget on a TV purchase was oozing out of every pore in his body.

"Lemme put it in a way you'd understand. Let's say you heard ground beef was cheap at the supermarket, so you go out expecting to make some burgers for dinner, but when you show up, you notice that the sliced salmon is actually a lot cheaper. So you decide to change the menu to buttered salmon and use the extra change to buy some bean sprouts to flesh out dinner a little. You ever have that kind of thing happen?"

"Um? ...Well, certainly, yes. If you put it that way." The sudden topic shift to household errands perplexed Ashiya.

"So instead of buying buns or ketchup for the burgers, you buy some butter for the salmon. And from that point forward, you know how to whip up a meal of buttered salmon and bean sprouts for really cheap. That kinda thing."

"Yes... Indeed." Suzuno, who cooked for herself just as often as Ashiya, could empathize.

"But that's the thing about the Net. You can't *learn* stuff like that online. If you search for burgers, you get hits about Worcestershire sauce and barbecue grills and upscale burger chains and Wagyu beef and maybe Hamburg, Germany, too, I dunno. But you aren't gonna get anything about buttered salmon with bean sprouts. You don't get that kind of happenstance going on."

"Happenstance, huh…?"

Urushihara sat up a bit, uncharacteristically attentive.

"Of course, things spread in all kinds of ways, so you can't say that about everything. But with the Internet, once something loses your interest, you don't go back again, right? You don't need to."

"Yeah. I suppose you wouldn't. But TV's the same way, isn't it? You don't like it, you turn it off."

Maou shook his head at Emi, the only extraterrestrial with a television.

"But with TV, there are things you don't care about *now*, but might care about later. It's not just an on-or-off thing. With the Net, meanwhile, all you see are the things you want to see. And you need a guide for that sort of thing, right? For things you don't actively want right now, but might come in handy later."

"…Your Demonic Highness, how did you come to know so much about television in the first place?"

"Oh, that was back when we just arrived here. I had this temp job where we all congregated at a soba noodle place for lunch, and they had a TV in there. It was playing the news, and they were advertising this piece about how the temp agency I was working for was under investigation for something or other. So I waited around for the piece, but then another customer changed it to some stupid variety show. Man, that pissed me off."

"I know now's a different story but, Maou, you *are* another world's Devil King, right?"

"Enough of that topic, Chiho. All it would do is serve to depress me even further," Suzuno interjected. "The Devil King, going on about noodles and tuna and hamburgers… It disgusts me."

In many ways, Maou's enemies seemed far more concerned for his future than he was.

"Anyway. I just figured it'd be nice to have some play, you know? Some more exposure to unintended discoveries like that. I know the Net's easier and you can look up anything you want and stuff, but in terms of creating chances to take an interest in something new, I think TV's still a lot more vital. Then, if I want to examine a topic more in-depth, I can hit up the Net for that."

"Yeah, true," Urushihara admitted. "A lot of people brag about never watching TV, but if you look at search term rankings and trends and stuff, TV still affects them a lot."

Maou, uncharacteristically, nodded his approval at Urushihara's point. "I don't need a 3D set or a blue-whatever player or anything fancy like that. I'm just saying, if we can have this media device that plays a major role in human society, I think that'll help us later on. Help teach us about the human world, and help us once we're ready to conquer it."

"Hmmm..." Ashiya grunted as he weighed Maou's thought in his mind.

"And..." Now Maou turned to Emi. "TV gives you live reports on accidents and disasters and stuff, right? Like, flood warnings and so on."

"Yeah. So?"

"If something happens, that could help me take action faster."

Maou used the index and middle fingers of both hands to form makeshift claws in the air.

"...!"

Emi knew what he meant. The Malebranche, the demons they fought over in Choshi.

"That's kind of a secondary reason, but still, if some kind of major incident happens that makes no sense by human standards, we could at least check it out to see if someone from the other side's messing with us again."

That was a concern on everyone's mind. Downtown Tokyo had been the site of several angel/demon duels by now. They barely fended off a full-scale demon invasion off the Choshi coast a few days ago, too.

They had managed to keep casualties to a minimum so far, if only by the skin of their teeth. But there was no guarantee their luck would continue.

Where they stood in Japan, forced to deal with crises as they reared themselves, having as many information sources as possible—the way Maou framed it—seemed to make sense.

"Yes...but..."

Ashiya was in a deep mental conflict with himself.

Part of him agreed to his master's proposal. He wanted to give his assent, if he could. But their budget, and the presence of several alternative tools, dragged at his mind.

Urushihara put Ashiya's anguish into words for him: "We'll have to pay the license fee to MHK, too..."

"...All right. Let me propose you this, my liege." Ashiya lifted his pained countenance upward. "I am in complete agreement with your feelings, but our budget presents us with certain very real obstacles. So perhaps we could begin by conducting a marketplace investigation."

"Investigation?"

"First, we should visit the real estate agent to see how the new antenna affects whatever sort of license fee we would have to pay. If it falls upon us as tenants to pay the fee to MHK, I fear this simply will not work."

"Everything except the utilities are included in my place, but..."

"Do not interject with your babbling, Emilia! I truly do not want to buy this, deep down!"

"That's kind of mean of you, isn't it, Ashiya?"

Maou and Urushihara just nodded, well used to Ashiya's occasional outbursts whenever money was the topic.

"But *if* we are lucky enough to have the MHK fee included, and *if* our rent does not increase as a result, we can then visit an electronics store to examine prices and features. I understand that flat-screen digital televisions are notably more expensive than their analog counterparts. If the baseline prices are too high for us, then once again, I fear it will not work out."

"Jeez, that's rough…"

"Of course it is! All three of us were supposed to be working at that snack bar for half of August! And, yes, we were remunerated well—more than half a month of your MgRonald wages—but we are not flush enough that we can lavish money on expensive home appliances on a mere whim!"

Ashiya had his reasons for playing the spoiler so much: With their jobs at Ohguro-ya gone, Maou was de facto jobless until the remodeling work at the Hatagaya-station MgRonald was complete.

The three great demons were safe from the specter of homelessness, but considering what they could expect in wages next month, Ashiya was hell-bent on surviving the rest of August with the 150,000 yen the three of them had earned for their time at Ohguro-ya.

Maou's wages for July would be deposited in their checking account on the twenty-fifth, of course, but it was not the kind of payday that easily allowed for purchasing a TV all by itself.

"Yeah, but I think the smaller ones go for pretty cheap these days, no? If you don't care about the brand, I don't think you'll have to pay too much."

"Ms. Sasaki… Please…"

Ashiya, capable of hurling a constant stream of hatred at Emi, was far weaker against Chiho.

"…?"

Emi, meanwhile, looked disbelievingly at Chiho, wondering why she said *that* all of a sudden.

Just a moment ago, Ashiya shot down her attempt to advocate for the TV purchase. She didn't expect Chiho to take up the banner again.

"Well, judging by Emi and Chiho, I think we have a pretty decent chance of buying one. So, Ashiya, assuming we clear the MHK and rent hurdles, how much you think we can afford?"

Ashiya needed little time to respond.

"Considering what we made at Ohguro-ya, I can take ten thousand yen from each of our wages. So, thirty thousand yen. *Maybe* thirty-five thousand. No more than that."

"Whoa, dude! That's *my* money you're taking!"

Urushihara blurted out his honest surprise at the demon's calculation. Ashiya fired back, his face like the mask of some mythical monster.

"I have every right to garnish your entire paycheck to make good for all the wasteful spending you've done, you!"

"Heh-heh-heh! Thirty-five thousand! You said thirty-five thousand, didn't you?"

Maou, meanwhile, had a cheese-eating grin on his face.

"Ashiyaaaaa, don't you think you're forgetting something?"

"Mm? What?"

Ashiya involuntarily shuddered at Maou's smile, now beyond cheese-eating and venturing into the realm of demented.

Maou shot a finger toward the refrigerator, grin still plastered on his face.

"Where'd we buy that fridge? Where'd we buy the washer outside?"

"The fridge…?"

The two most expensive items in Devil's Castle. Maou had blown through nearly all of his savings to buy them earlier in the year.

Both quite a bit more budget friendly than what Suzuno had in her own room. But still.

"That…that was at the Socket City in Shinjuku, my liege… Ahh!"

It finally dawned on Ashiya.

As he watched, Maou produced a plastic wallet from somewhere and ripped open the Velcro keeping it shut.

Then, as if trying to make this as mentally tortuous for Ashiya as possible, he slowly, dramatically removed a silver card from it.

"Finally noticed, huh?"

Like a well-honed sword, the card glinted in the air as Maou thrust it at Ashiya's face.

There was the familiar Socket City logo, the phrase POINT CARD below it. At the bottom. 6239 POINTS was printed over the silver film.

"This... How?!"

Ashiya found himself floored, literally brought down to tatami-mat level by the unexpected shock.

"You wanna know how we made it this far without using any of these points, right? I can see it on your face, man! You wanna know?! Well, look around you! Count all the consumable goods we have that you'd buy at an electronics store!"

When it came to consumable goods you'd buy at an electronics store, lighting and batteries were usually the first to come to mind.

But Devil's Castle was illuminated by fluorescent lighting, with no other lights besides the bulbs in the bathroom and by the front door. The former bulb had burned out once, but otherwise, nothing since Maou bought the fridge and washer.

The only thing around the Devil's King domain that used replaceable batteries was their emergency flashlight. Urushihara's old computer, and the digital camera–printer combo Maou used to record every aspect of Alas Ramus's life, were purchased on different occasions at discount shops in Akihabara, meaning no Socket City points were ever sacrificed.

The printer was also old enough that not even the larger stores bothered to carry official ink cartridges any longer. They replaced the red cartridge once after tracking down an off-brand version.

Some of the big-box electronic shops also carried food and other household items, but never at much of a discount. It was never worth traveling all the way to Shinjuku for that, considering all the deals they could find locally in Sasazuka.

So, throughout the whole summer, the only thing they used these points for so far was a single lightbulb.

"Thirty-five thousand yen?! Hah! Don't make me laugh! Add these points in, and we can raise that limit all the way up to 41,239 yen! And if we have forty thousand, we don't even have to get the crappiest one they got, either!"

"In...incredible!!"

"Bah-hah-hah-hah! You miss one hundred percent of the shots that you don't take, Ashiya! That's one more obstacle between us and a TV out of the picture! Now I'm *really* looking forward to visiting the real estate guy!"

"Heh…heh… Ha-ha-ha! But, Your Demonic Highness, failure to plan is planning to fail! There is no guarantee that our rental contract won't strike a lethal blow upon all of us! As long as there remains even a slim chance of them pinning the license fees on us, you promised we would drop this entire line of thinking, remember?! Then the points mean nothing! Nothing! Prepare yourself for a hearty meal of crow and humble pie shortly, my liege!"

"You're on! I'm gonna march right over to the real estate office right now and get this show on the road!"

"Very good, Your Demonic Highness! I would very much like to see your face when you realize the folly of ignoring the common-sense pleas of your humble servants!!"

The others in the room might as well have excused themselves out while the Devil King and his Great Demon General bickered at each other about a point card.

"…I'm sorry. I'm ashamed of these guys, too."

All Emi and Suzuno could do was nod their agreement to Urushihara.

But Chiho watched Maou and Ashiya's somewhat misguided arguing intently, an oddly serene smile on her face. "You wanted a TV that much, huh, Maou?"

Emi shrugged, exasperated. "Yeah, well, he mentioned he goes to movies and stuff, so he must've been interested in one for a while…"

Suzuno, still living quite comfortably thanks to her travel prep, had other things in mind:

"…Hmm. Perhaps I could consider one of my own, if the fancy strikes me."

✳

With the completely clueless and arguably witless Maou and Ashiya off to the real estate office and all of the major moving work complete, Emi and Chiho said their good-byes and left the apartment.

"It's pretty nice, though, isn't it?"

"What is?"

The pair struck up a conversation along the warm summer path.

"I mean, all of them making it back to Sasazuka, despite everything," Chiho continued. "Maou and Suzuno and everyone having their apartments all fixed up. Everything feels kind of normal again."

"Normal, huh…?" Emi grumbled. "I think I'm starting to lose my grasp of what 'normal' even means any longer."

"I think it's nice, too, how Maou and Suzuno both wanna get a TV."

"Oh? Why's that?"

Suzuno was one matter, but having another appliance in Devil's Castle indicated that, at long last, they had a little breathing room.

And having a little breathing room was all the reason Emi had to feel on edge.

They needed to team up just to carry a refrigerator a little way, and Emi had just watched them yelling about point cards like a pair of elderly retirees. But they were still arch-demons, tyrants who once made an entire world shudder in fear.

And—as she continued rolling the thought around her mind—even if they *did* have a little more breathing room, there had to be oodles more things they needed to buy ahead of a television.

Emi had learned just other the day that during those few days Alas Ramus was at Devil's Castle, they were having her sleep on the bare tatami-mat floor with a rolled-up towel for a pillow. She gave all the demons a good slap on the head for that.

"I mean, now that Ohguro-ya's gone, they're jobless, right?" Emi protested. "But they're still acting like that they have a bunch of money to spare."

"I guess so," Chiho admitted. "Our location doesn't reopen until the fifteenth, either…"

MgRonald wouldn't open for over a week. It was a tad difficult to imagine Maou and Ashiya vegging out in front of the TV that whole time. Urushihara, sure, but not the other two.

"But if I know Maou, I'd say he's got something in mind. There's still a lot of day labor–type stuff out there."

"Hmm… Maybe."

If Maou had any great ideas in motion right now, that made Ashiya's opposition all the more bizarre. Ashiya had a habit of playing the "we're so, so poor" card too often, but he was usually pretty tolerant when it came to sensible investments.

Emi arched her eyebrows upward. "Well, it's fine by me. Not like it's my problem if they spend themselves into a hole."

There's no need at all for me to worry about their financial situation. Why am I going on as if I care about what happens to the Devil's Castle?

Maou mentioned several good points when he defended the TV purchase, but it wasn't like a TV was a perfect font of constantly useful information.

To Emi's mind, a lot of it was just celebrities she'd never heard of chatting with each other, or comedy bits that she hadn't lived in Japan long enough to understand. Or home-shopping shows selling the kind of junk you only see in home-shopping shows and nowhere else. Gossip about this or that big name that had absolutely no bearing on your own life at all. Programs that Emi had no idea what the creators were trying to say to the world were all over the airwaves, often across every channel at the same time.

That was just the take of one alien visitor, of course, and the samurai dramas she preferred were no less time wasters than any other show format. But it wasn't like obtaining a TV was a meaningful step in the demons' plans for world domination.

Chiho, seeing all this complex thought written clearly on Emi's face, chuckled to herself and opted to reel in the conversation a little.

"…But either way, if Maou and Suzuno are buying TVs, I guess that means they're staying in Japan for a while, huh?"

"What do you mean?" Emi tilted her head a little, not understanding what she was getting at.

"You saw all those demon guys at Choshi," Chiho began.

"Demon guys" made them sound friendlier than they deserved, but Emi nodded regardless.

"I was kinda scared that everyone would go back to Ente Isla because of that," Chiho continued. "If they hadn't shown up offshore like that... Like, if it was in the middle of Shinjuku instead—that would have been a huge disaster. At the time, I thought to myself, what if you and Maou had said, 'We can't put all this burden on Japan anymore!' and took off?"

"I wasn't *not* thinking that..."

The words fell from Emi's lips. Chiho flashed a carefree smile.

"I don't think a TV's something you buy just because it's cheap. You buy one because you're expecting to use it for a while to come. So if they want one, I just thought that meant that you're all gonna be in Japan for the foreseeable future."

"Well, I appreciate the warm welcome, but aren't you afraid at all?" Emi had to ask.

"You've thought about it, right? If things ever go south, so to speak, all these angels and people and demons... We won't be afraid to hurt this country if we have to. You've already faced death once, Chiho."

Thanks to a human, not a demon, and one of Emi's former companions, to boot. She still felt guilty about that.

"Mmm... I'm not all that afraid now. It was kind of a shock at first, but you and Maou have always been there to protect me, so..."

Whether she understood Emi's feelings or not, Chiho's reply was surprisingly straightforward.

"I don't know very much about Ente Isla, but both of you—the strongest human in that world, and the strongest demon anywhere—are protecting me. It'd be kinda rude if that *didn't* put my mind at ease."

"Oh... I see."

Logically, she was right. Chiho was about the only girl in the universe to enjoy close ties with both the Hero and Devil King. There were elderly clerics in the Church who could only dream of such powerful connections.

"...And I haven't forgotten, of course, that you and Suzuno want to defeat Maou at the end of it. I know you could never forgive those guys for what they did to Ente Isla. So I'm always thinking about it. Thinking about how I can take all these people who're really dear to me and have them all be happy."

"Can't be done."

"You didn't need to reply *that* fast…"

Chiho gave Emi a playful scowl. She knew to expect that from her; Emi made her outlook clear enough on a regular basis.

Chiho turned her eyes to the large shoulder bag the other girl was holding. "I know this is just a personal request and I don't really have any right to ask you this or anything, but can I count on you guys for Alas Ramus, at least?"

"…That *is* an issue, I'll grant you that." Emi shrugged, reluctant to discuss the topic.

"Is she still asleep?"

"Yeah. If she doesn't get up, maybe I should just take the train home before I bring her out."

Alas Ramus was still fused with Emi as she enjoyed her afternoon nap.

That was the rule Emi stuck to outside of the nighttime hours. That way, she didn't have to worry about the stifling summer heat inside Villa Rosa Sasazuka.

Still, she always carried diapers, water, a sippy cup, and a bunch of other gear in her shoulder bag. The whole "mother" thing was starting to seem familiar, even normal to her.

"It's kind of a different thing, now that she's fused with my holy sword. If she still thinks the Devil King's her dad, I can't really fight him with my sword. I can't have her kill her own father like that. But…I know how children help bind the family together and stuff, but I gotta draw the line somewhere, you know?"

"Yeah. I'm sorry."

Chiho bowed a bit to apologize for bringing it up.

"…That, and I'm not really in a position to go back home right now anyway. As long as the Devil King doesn't get bitchy about the TV and decide to return to Ente Isla, I'm not going anywhere."

"Not in a position to? You?"

This was the first Chiho had heard about this, but Emi shook her head softly. Chiho opted not to pursue it further, and the pair continued on in silence until they reached Sasazuka station.

"Well, guess I'm off."

Emi gave Chiho a light wave as she approached the turnstile.

But then her eyes widened as a lightbulb went off in her mind.

"I'm sorry, Chiho, can you wait there a second?"

She made a beeline for a nearby instant-photo booth. Chiho could guess why—and, in a few moments, Emi emerged with a sheepish grin and a stretching Alas Ramus.

"She insisted on saying good-bye to her big sister."

"*Nffhh*...aye-bye, Chi-sis..."

Her pronunciation wasn't quite all there this early on from her nap, but she lifted her heavy eyelids high and waved a pudgy hand at Chiho.

The sight made Chiho relax her facial muscles.

"Bye-bye, Alas Ramus! Let's play together again soon, okay?"

"Mnh... Let's go splish-splash again..."

"Sure! Maybe we can all go to the pool together."

"...*ooofgh*..."

"All right. Maybe you can nap a little more at home, okay? ...I'm gonna have a hell of a time trying to go back into work mode tomorrow. Have a good night."

Emi readjusted her hold upon Alas Ramus, already journeying back into dreamland, as she nodded at Chiho and made her way toward the turnstile.

With the child out in the public eye, there was no fusing her back into her body now. Chiho grinned as she watched them go, the memory of Alas Ramus's face and hand bringing the warmth back into her face.

"Oh, hello! My, you're home early today."

When Chiho made it back home, her mother, Riho, was at the door to greet her, apparently about to leave herself.

"Where are you going, Mom?"

"Oh, just over to Shinjuku for a spell. An old school friend of mine's in town, so I'm having some tea with her. I'll be back for dinner, so could you start up maybe half a bowl of rice in the cooker for me?"

"Okay. Just half? Dad isn't coming home today?"

"Who knows? He hasn't called, anyway. If he does, I'll just whip up some instant ramen for him or something."

A police officer's hours were generally pretty well set in stone, barring major incidents. But whenever disaster reared its ugly head, returning home could be a major challenge.

Her father had a bad habit of not keeping his wife informed about whether he needed dinner or not. But as she waved good-bye to her mother, Chiho resolved to fill the entire cooker with rice. *Dad deserves more than instant ramen, at least.*

As she stepped inside, she was greeted by a blast of cold air from the AC, still lingering after her mother turned it off.

"Maybe I'll just chill for a bit and take a shower. I don't need to cook that rice until later anyway."

It was just before three PM. No work, no club activities, and—for a change—no demon-related errands to run. Chiho wandered into the living room and blithely picked up the TV remote.

"I wonder what Maou's gonna watch once he buys a TV, though. I bet he'd be into game shows and documentaries and stuff."

Her mind conjured up an image of the three of them fighting over whether they'd watch a game show, a cooking show, or anime. It made her laugh out loud.

"Oh, brother... They're always so serious about everything, too."

Chiho watched a fair share of TV herself. Dramas and music shows gave her something to discuss with her school friends, although her personal preferences leaned toward travel and documentaries. There were one or two weekly quiz shows she never missed, too.

The influence of Emi and Suzuno on her life had driven her to give samurai dramas a try recently. Maybe talking about TV with Maou could make life more fun for them. Thinking about it that way, things didn't seem entirely bleak going forward.

"Anything on…?"

Chiho picked up the program guide lying on the living room table and skimmed through the listings.

"Oh, they're rerunning *Quaking Mad* in a sec. The news is on, too. Maybe I'll turn on MHK first and switch to *Quaking Mad* later."

She pointed the remote toward the TV set and pushed the power button. The two-second time lag between pressing the button and getting an image passed without incident.

Then:

"…Huh?"

The moment the screen turned on, the Sasaki residence's living room was bathed in white light.

✳

As the lurching train jostled her around, Emi recalled the Idea Link phone call Emeralda gave her right after returning home from Choshi the day before.

Alas Ramus fell back asleep soon after waving good-bye to Chiho, dozing away in her arms.

"The pool, huh…?"

She stared out the window at the cityscape offered by Sasazuka station's elevated platform. The Keio express train she rode blasted past the following station, Daitabashi, as it headed for the next stop at Meidaimae. From there, Emi would change to the Keio Inokashira Line on her way back home. Her home in Japan, that is.

"How long is this 'normal' gonna go on for…?"

If it kept going, was that good for Emi, or not? It was impossible to tell from her tone of voice.

Emi couldn't have known the answer herself.

Unlike the usual updates she gave Emi regularly, this last call from Emeralda had a sense of serious urgency to it.

It didn't surprise Emi, though. After everything that happened in Choshi, she was prepared, in a way, for unforeseen events.

*   *   *

The call from Emeralda Etuva had arrived the previous day, the evening after she had returned home from Choshi.

With Villa Rosa Sasazuka ready much earlier than expected, Emi answered the call just as Suzuno was preparing to cart her belongings back to her apartment.

"Looks like we're gonna have a pretty big war over hereeee. I think you better not go hooooome for a while, Emilia~."

As Emeralda put it, the Central Continent was starting to see more demon sightings, and Efzahan, the empire that dominated the Eastern Island, had just declared war on the Federated Order of the Five Continents and every member country in a move to seize the central island. Even more surprising, there were apparently demons among Efzahan's armies.

The presence of demons among humans, of course, reminded Emi of what the Devil Regent Camio had told her: of Barbariccia, leader of the demon realms' most potent forces...and of Olba, who drove him to the battlefield.

Emi warned Emeralda of it all: the possibility that Olba was involved with this sudden declaration and how Efzahan might have beefed up its warpower with the Malebranche.

The name Olba stopped even Emeralda cold for a moment, but the Malebranche seemed less of a shock to her. Apparently, they had already confirmed that on their side.

"But why can't I go back? There are demons among the Malebranche just as powerful as Malacoda, the general from the Southern Island."

Emeralda had a ready reply for the question.

"Well, isn't it ooooobvious? Because this war still hasn't involved aaaanyone apart from human parties yet!"

There were demons among the Eastern Island armies, yes. But the war was carried out under the name of the empire of Efzahan and the Azure Emperor who ruled over it.

"Thaaat, and with our savior officially dead, if you started fighting for one side or anotherrrr... Even if you won, all the nations would

start fighting again over you, so they could procure saaaafety for themselves."

"What am I, a nuclear bomb?"

"Newkewler?"

"Never mind."

"The Azure Emperor's a slyyy one, too. They're after the Central Continennnt, but—and I don't know whyyy—but they want your holy sword, toooo."

Emi saw that coming to some extent. And if they just proved that Olba and Barbariccia were involved, her sword probably mattered a lot more than the Central Continent anyway.

"They're after your sworrrd, and they brought deeeemons over to do it, too. Can you guess whyyy?"

Emi pondered over the riddle for a moment.

The Azure Emperor ruled over a nation riddled with civil strife and conflict, but he was still emperor.

Efzahan was part of Emi's route as she journeyed to slay the Devil King. Some areas were dirt-poor, and some were in open revolt against the emperor, but there were also rich and bountiful cities, populated by vast crowds of citizens loyal to the leader.

It was a sign of the influence the emperor wielded over his vast land. And now he was commanding a demon army as he took on the rest of the world. What was driving him?

"I don't know who came up with the idea, but whoever did must be rotten to the core."

"Oh, did you figure it oooout?"

"If they win, it's all good. Even if they lose somehow, it was all the demons' doing, not theirs. That sort of thing, right?"

"You guessed it!" Emeralda's light chuckle came across loud and clear.

Efzahan's strategy went something like this: If they could seize the Central Continent and bring the knights from the Northern, Western, and Southern Islands under their sphere of influence, they had nothing to worry about. Victory for Efzahan, fair and square.

But even if they lost, thanks to Emilia the Hero or some other

unforeseen element, they still had an out. *The demons made us do it! Those monsters took over our minds, our country.* Ente Isla hadn't lost its fear of the demon hordes yet; any attempt to demand restitution from Efzahan or prosecute the Azure Emperor as a war criminal would lose steam fast.

Besides, the other islands hardly functioned as a cohesive unit. Any one of the Northern, Western, or Southern Islands could betray their allies and side with the East. If Emi whipped out her holy sword and joined the fray then, she'd be branded a traitor. The Hero Emilia, drawing her bow against her fellow humans! It would fatally damage her legitimacy as a savior of mankind.

"All right. I get it. But you be careful, all right, Eme? Heaven and Ente Isla and the demon realms… They're all getting crazily intertwined with each other. It's hard to see who's friend and who's foe any longer."

"Oh, I'll be fiiiine! No matter what happens, I'll always be there for you and Albert, okaaay?"

Walking—more like casually strolling—to the beat of her own drum, as always. It always distressed Emi a bit, somehow.

"…Hee-hee. You're right. I'll bet."

"But you neeeever know when you might need the tools in your disposal, riiiight? I may want to borrow you sooner or later, Emiiiilia. For now, thoooough…just keep fighting as 'Eeeemi Yusa.'"

"Sure. Thanks."

"Oh, you're wellllllcome! I need to thank you for that vaaaaluable information, too. Say hello to your darling husband and child for meeee!"

"…Emer."

"Ah-ha-ha! That was on purrrrpose."

Unfazed by Emi's voice, low enough to flash-freeze lava, Emeralda laughed as she hung up.

Soon, Emi relayed the entire phone call over to Suzuno.

Word of Efzahan's menacing moves, and the possible presence of Olba among them, made it hard for Suzuno to hide the shock, despite her previous conference with Camio. But the conclusion she came to was the same as Emeralda's:

For now, Emilia must avoid a hasty return to Ente Isla.

Turning away from the box she was currently packing, Suzuno turned to Emi, her bunched eyebrows belying the clear danger she felt they were in.

"Do you think, Emilia, that…that we face a danger unlike any before? That fate will ask us to do something completely the opposite of our appointed mission? That…we may have to protect the Devil King, with our own hands?"

"Huh? Where'd *that* come from?"

Emi's eyes opened wide at the absurdity of the idea. But Suzuno was deadly serious.

"Think about it—the events in Choshi revealed to all the world's demons that their lord is alive and well. And Olba is aware of the Devil King's presence in Japan, is he not? Even as he serves to tie the demon realms together with the Eastern Island, for all we know?"

"Yeah…"

"One wrong move, and the Devil King could be whisked away, back to his realm!"

"Whaaat?!"

"Bmhh!"

Emi's shout at the sheer ridiculousness of it all made Alas Ramus murmur her approval in her sleep. The Hero put a panicked hand to her mouth as the child turned over and began lightly snoring again. When she spoke next, she took pains to keep her voice down as much as possible. "…What do you mean, whisked away?"

"Remember what Camio taught us. Why did the demon realms face such a monumental rift after its armies were destroyed? Camio, who trusted in his master's survival, strove to lay low and preserve his nation's strength. But Barbariccia and Ciriatto attempted to take up the Devil King's flag and conquer Ente Isla anew. What would happen if the Devil King suddenly stepped into that chaos?"

"What would happen…?"

"Camio returned home because he was convinced the Devil King's rightful place for the moment is Japan, did he not? Which suits our purposes fine. But Barbariccia is different. If he knows the Devil King is alive, plainly he will try to bring him back in order to prop up and rebuild their forces. Their main force has merely detached itself from the local rule, following a political struggle. Their loyalty for the Devil King has never flagged."

Emi nodded.

"If you put everything Camio said together, then I suppose, sure."

"Now think about Efzahan's rampage. Efzahan has never truly believed in diplomacy as a solution to anything. The situation at its borders has never been anything less than volatile. The Azure Emperor is rumored to be a tyrannical despot, one who uses brutal oppression to keep any insurgencies from boiling over. But we should not let this cloud our judgment. It may sound like a ready-made excuse if they are ever defeated, but perhaps the Azure Emperor truly *has* fallen to the demon forces led by Olba and Barbariccia. Perhaps they are manipulating his mind after all."

"M-maybe…"

The idea seemed plausible to Emi. But given how she all but assumed the Azure Emperor was engaged in a simple, brazen power grab for the Central Continent, she was still loath to agree.

That was the difference between Emi, the consummate frontline soldier, and Suzuno, the politician in the smoke-filled room.

Regardless of his methods, I will gladly praise the Azure Emperor for his political acumen. No regular man could govern a land as wide, and wild, as the Eastern Island without at least a modicum of talent. He has ruled for over twenty years, and I understand he is busy grooming his successor at the moment."

"…You do *that* much research for your missionary work?"

"Of course I do. When one sets off for a foreign land to proselytize, one needs to know what local policymakers will think of your religious efforts. I can say with full confidence that there is not a single inch of Ente Isla whose political situation the Church is not intimately familiar with."

Suzuno's face indicated she felt this was as much common sense as knowing how to cross the street.

"But that is the reason I feel the Azure Emperor might actually be under the demons' spell. That lengthy reign of his."

"Oh?"

"Back when the Devil King's army was in full force, which general was it who conquered the Eastern Island?"

"Oh."

Even Emi could pick up on it by now.

"Yes! He may be a shadow of his former himself, little more than a bickering househusband, but he was the only Great Demon General that there is no record of the Hero Emilia having ever defeated in combat. Alciel took over the Eastern Island not long after the Devil King's army made its first appearance. If the Azure Emperor still has dark memories of those dreadful days, there is every chance he would kneel before them once more to protect his nation, his life. And that's not all. If Barbariccia can successfully bring back not just the Devil King, but Alciel as well—a demon well versed in governing the entirety of the Eastern Continent—that could easily gain him a beachhead from which he could invade Ente Isla once more."

"……"

The more she thought about it, the more ominous things seemed to her.

"But…I don't…I mean, I don't want to sound like I'm complimenting the Devil King or anything…but if Barbariccia did that, don't you think it'd piss him off?"

Suzuno briskly nodded.

"He would be angry, yes. The fact that we are fighting together with him in this world—on the surface, at least—is in no small part thanks to his astonishingly generous, easygoing ways. I do not wish to admit it, but I must."

"……True."

Emi didn't want to admit it, either. But the events of the past few months flew in the face of her gut feelings.

"If Barbariccia were to make any such bold moves, it would enrage the Devil King. He would want to punish him, no doubt. He is still King, a fact he proved well enough in Choshi," Suzuno added.

"King?"

"If he was pressed hard enough to make a decision, he would never abandon his people, his former close officials. And then…he would never return to Japan again."

"…!"

Emi gasped. The idea was starting to seem entirely likely now.

Maou acted like he was whiling away his youth, going through the motions as he tried futilely to keep his family in the black. But the way his mind worked never changed. Multiple times before, he proclaimed to Emi's face that he'd return to Ente Isla.

And all the countless demons who longed for their one true king… Could he ever just set them adrift like that?

What other reason would he have for forgiving Ciriatto, the demon who turned away from Camio and attempted to carve out his own Devil Kingdom in Maou's name?

That, and:

"…Ohh."

The groan from Emi's lips echoed quietly.

Maou, returning to his world, as Devil King.

Emi was shocked. Shocked that, in response to that mental picture, the first thing that came to mind was, *That'd sure make Alas Ramus sad.*

"What? N-no! I don't…"

And it'd be even harder on Chiho.

"N-no! That's… I mean, it's not *not* true, but it…"

After everything everyone's done for him, he'll just run off without repaying that?!

"That's not the issue here!"

"Nnuhh… Fff…iihh…"

Emi's verbal sparring with herself made Alas Ramus quiver as her eyes opened. A rude awakening for her, it seemed. Her face began to contort itself.

"Ah, uh, s-sorry, Alas Ramus, I didn't mean to scare you…"

"Hie-yaaaaahhhhh-aahhh!"

She started crying anyway. Emi picked her up, trying frantically to calm her, but her mind was too frazzled to form a coherent strategy.

That came across loud and clear to Alas Ramus, who showed no sign of stopping her bawl-fest.

Until the child finally grew bored of the tirade and went back to sleep, Emi could do nothing but cradle her as reassuringly as she could.

Eventually, dabbing her tear- and snot-stained face with a wet tissue, Emi softly laid her back down on her bed.

"…Ughh…"

The fatigue came like an avalanche. She put her face down on the bed, next to the child.

Then her mind returned to the issues at hand.

"I refuse to let the Devil King reform his army. He…he is the murderer of my father, the enemy of my people…"

"Are you reading that from a script?"

Emi could feel Suzuno snickering behind her.

"Shut up a second. …I'm still kind of in a state of shock, okay? You don't have to butt in."

I am the Hero, and he is the boss of the demons. Peace for the world and her fellow humans was on her mind, of course, but more than anything, she couldn't forgive how his armies shattered the tranquil, quiet life she had had with her father.

There was no way she ever could.

And yet…

It took a disturbingly long time for her to recall that, nowadays.

I haven't worked through my feelings or something, have I?

There's no way I ever could.

"There's no…way I ever could…"

Emi whispered it to herself weakly.

Then, while there was no way she meant it on purpose, Alas Ramus turned over and placed a soft hand on Emi's head.

Almost like she was trying to comfort her.

"…*Oooooogh.*"

Emi felt the sadness take over, her lips tight as her head flopped onto the bed again.

"If Alas Ramus never sees the Devil King again…it would make her terribly sad." Suzuno's words hung quietly in the air. "And it would make Chiho sad, as well. I doubt it would ever be the same between her and us, either."

"……"

"That, and the denizens of Devil's Castle owe us a great debt. Until we collect on it, it would annoy me greatly to see them fly off somewhere."

"You're reading my thoughts, aren't you? That's cheating."

Now Emi was lashing out at anyone, anything, she could.

"Not at all. I just think we are of similar minds here. But what follows after that…is something that is not Emilia. As a cleric, I am bound never to allow a child to kill her own parent for reasons beyond her own control. No matter what. Even if that parent is the Devil King. Thus…"

The sound of fabric against fabric told Emi that Suzuno was standing up.

"For now, to prevent the worst from happening, we must protect the Devil King from the demons of his own realm."

"This is just…so hard. I can't take any more of it."

"I am not asking you to handle it all, Emilia. I am still his neighbor, after all, and nothing would make me happier than to set the table for the Hero to slay the Devil King. That, at least, I will take responsibility for. As long as another archangel or Malebranche chieftain does not rear its ugly head, I can handle things well enough by myself."

"...One word of warning: Staking them out is the most boring thing in the universe." Emi didn't bother lifting her head as she spoke, evoking a very un-Hero-like sense of lethargy.

"Alciel runs the place like a military school to keep them under budget. Lucifer just taps, taps, taps away at his computer day and night. The Devil King works, eats, and sleeps. That's it. Smile on his face the whole damn time. Keeping a constant vigil over them made me feel like some kind of creepy celebrity stalker."

"Yes, but MgRonald is closed for the moment, is it not? We should remain cautious, at least for now. Once the restaurant reopens, Sariel will be running interference for us as well. The demons will be loath to take major action."

Across the street from Maou's workplace off Hatagaya station, there was a Sentucky Fried Chicken franchise managed by the archangel Sariel.

Thanks to his falling head over heels in love with MgRonald manager Mayumi Kisaki, Sariel had been kissing up to Maou to an almost embarrassing extent.

The two of them were on rather poor terms, it was true. But Barbariccia would hardly be foolish enough to attempt to kidnap the Devil King while he was literally under the nose of an archangel.

"...Huh. Suppose so."

Emi could barely summon a whisper in response.

"...Listen, Bell. You know why I like samurai dramas so much? And not the ones about wandering *ronin* or peasants rising up to fight injustice. I'm talking *Vice-Shogun Mito* or *Maniac Shogun* or... Well, I've taken a liking to *Samurai Inspector Hyouzo* lately, too, but..."

"Um? No..."

Suzuno blinked, having trouble surmising Emi's intent.

After a moment, Emi finally lifted her head off the bed.

"Because they're about people in high positions fighting for truth and justice and all that. If there's a villain who won't listen to reason, he'll beat them up until they see the error of their ways. Everything works out; everyone's happy. Even if it's all made up, I like seeing good win out so...*completely* like that. Clean and simple."

"I see. The slings and arrows of outrageous fortune, one could say."

"What?"

"Something I read in a book recently."

"Oh."

With a groan, Emi stood up. Suzuno pretended not to notice the slight red twinge in her eyes.

She sniffled and shook her head.

"...If only..."

"Hmm?"

"If only they had AC in that apartment..."

"The savior of our world has has grown soft indeed."

It was uncharacteristic sarcasm, coming from Suzuno as she caressed Alas Ramus's hair.

Emi bunched up her face and looked down upon her.

"How much is the rent over there?"

"Forty-five thousand yen, if I recall."

"'Cause this place has more than a few problems, but I got it for fifty thousand."

The price quote drove Suzuno to take another look around Emi's room.

"Could that be the case...? Truly?"

A large closet. Two rooms, each about 150 square feet. With air-conditioning, a bathroom, a fully electric range, and an autolock down in the lobby.

"No. This cannot *possibly* be fifty thousand yen per month."

"Well, I mean, there's a *lot* of backstory to that, so... Ah, well. I guess there's a lot of empty space over there, still. I'll have to make up my mind someday."

Where was "over there"? When was "someday"? Suzuno decided not to ask.

"Oooogh...Mommy..."

Just then, a pudgy hand placed itself on top of Suzuno's as Alas Ramus babbled in her sleep.

Patting her soft, adorable skin, the cleric found herself smiling.

"I do not so terribly mind, shall we say, the lukewarm bath I find myself in."

"Huh?"

"How else could I describe our current situation? As long as the Devil King remains in Japan, he will be the perfect picture of hard work and diligence. We sit here, living in the most glorious civilization we have ever known, surrounded by caring friends and confidants, allowing the days to leisurely tick away. But how much..."

Suzuno gently picked up Alas Ramus's hand, running a towel up to the shoulder socket.

"How much longer can we live like this?"

It was question neither Suzuno, nor Emi, nor the Devil King could ever know the answer to.

"Mommy, when will we go splish-splash next?"

By the time Emi returned to her condo in Eifukucho, Alas Ramus was wide awake.

"I wonder," Emi replied vaguely. "If you're a good girl, Alas Ramus...if everything stays as it is, I bet we can go real soon."

"Let's go! Splish-splash peep peep!"

Whether she was aware of Emi's feelings or not, Alas Ramus picked up on "go real soon" and nothing else, eyes shining with glee.

Recalling her conversation with Suzuno last night, Emi found it suddenly difficult to look Alas Ramus in the eye.

"...All right, Alas Ramus. You've been sweating a lot today, haven't you? Let's go take a bath together."

"Bath! Splish-splash!"

One never had to drag Alas Ramus into the tub.

The outings to the public bathhouse with Maou, back when she lived with him, apparently left a positive imprint on her mind. Whenever the subject of a bath came up, Alas Ramus would faithfully spring into action.

It took until now for Emi to realize that it probably had little to do with her genesis. This was just a little girl who loved playing in the water, was all.

A lukewarm bath might be just the thing for tonight. Too hot wouldn't be good for her. And in this summer heat, it'd make for a delightful soak.

"Okay, I need to get a few things ready. Can you be a good girl?"

"Okey!"

Alas Ramus raised her hand in the air, trotted to the living room, took off the hat she was wearing, placed it on the table, and sat down on a chair. She picked up the papercraft birdcage on the table and began spinning it around, keeping a careful eye on Emi.

It was her way of saying *I'm being a good girl!*

Emi nodded, face considerably lightened, and tossed her shoulder bag toward a corner of the kitchen before heading to the bathroom. Draining the water she used for laundry purposes in the morning, she took up a sponge to give the tub a quick scouring as she reached for the shower valve.

"Mommy! Whirr whirr whirr!"

Then she spotted Alas Ramus at the bathroom door, not being a good girl at all, the smartphone from her shoulder bag in her hand.

In fact, judging by the screen, she had already answered the incoming call, hadn't she...

Must've brushed a finger the wrong way when she took it out of the bag.

Emi was crestfallen as she took the phone away. Whoever called must have heard the child shouting across the room at her.

"Um, hello? Hello? Emi?"

The voice from the speaker, along with the name screen, filled Emi with a profound sense of relief.

"Well, thank you, Alas Ramus. But don't touch Mommy's cell phone without permission, okay?"

"Don't?"

"Emi? Helloooo?"

"Oh, but thanks for bringing it to me, though."

"Ee-hee! Okeh!"

Emi patted her on the head. The little girl gave a ticklish grin in response and trotted back to the living room.

"Emi, are you there?"

"Hello? Sorry, Rika. Alas Ramus picked up my phone for me."

It was Rika Suzuki, Emi's friend and cube mate at her workplace. She didn't know about Ente Isla and everything surrounding that world, but she knew Maou, Chiho, and Suzuno well enough. She also knew Emi was watching a toddler named Alas Ramus.

"Whoa, that was close. If you weren't there, she might've decided to call up Saudi Arabia and give you a massive phone bill!"

"Yeah, sorry, I'll be more careful with it. What's up?"

"Oh, um…"

Rika uncharacteristically clammed up.

"Hmm?"

"Hey, where are you, Emi? Your voice is kinda echo-y."

"Huh? I'm in the bathroom. I was just about to scrub the bathtub a little."

"Ohhhh. Okay. Well, if you're busy, it doesn't have to be right now or—"

"What? Wow, what's up with you today, Rika? Is this gonna go for a while, or…?"

Rika couldn't have sounded more reluctant. Compared to her usual sunny self, it was hard to imagine.

"No, no, nothing that long, but… Oooh, how should I put it? Maybe it kinda will, actually."

"Rika…? What's up? Something going on?"

Emi stiffened her voice a little. *Something troubling her, maybe?*

Depending on how you gauged it, this might be Rika acting agitated over something. Whatever it was had to be serious.

Emi sat down on the edge of the tub, preparing for an extended chat.

"If something's on your mind, just say it, okay? You called because you wanted to talk to me, right?"

She could feel Rika agonizing over something across the line.

"…Well, don't laugh, okay?"

That relieved Emi a little. If Rika was afraid it'd make her laugh, it couldn't have been too much of a doggie downer.

"I won't, I won't. So what's up?"

"Um… So, like, I know it's really weird to ask somebody this…"

"Yeah?"

"But I don't have anyone else I can ask, so…you mind if I bend your ear for a little bit?"

"Sure, go ahead. What's on your mind?"

Emi tried her best to squeeze it out of her. If her friend was in trouble, she wanted to help if she could. She'd done so countless times in the past, and Rika also helped her out of a pinch more than once.

If she was pussyfooting around the issue this much, it must have been tormenting her pretty badly.

"Okay, so…"

Rika, her voice more resolute now, took a deep breath.

"Um, what kinda clothes do you think Ashiya likes?!"

"……………………………………………………………………………"

Emi, seated on the bathtub, mobile phone firmly planted against one ear, froze.

"…Emi?"

Rika took Emi's lack of immediate response with a hefty dose of suspicion.

It wasn't enough to release Emi from her shackles.

Whenever someone runs into a completely unexpected set of circumstances, they try to harness their past experiences, tossing all of them into the wind in a mad attempt at a solution. Much of the time, though, all those past experiences offer little more than a lot of wishful thinking.

There was no better way to describe Emi at that moment. Which was why the answer that finally dribbled out in the end was:

"Something…cheap, maybe?"

"Cheap? So, like, no fancy brands or anything?"

"Y-yeeeaaahhh."

Emi was still frozen, her voice bereft of emotion.

"I've never seen him wear anything besides stuff from UniClo. There's no way he'd be wearing those cheapo shoes because he *likes* them…"

"Huh? *Whoa, whoa, Emi, that's not what I mean. I'm not talking about what kinda stuff he likes to buy for himself.*"

"…What *do* you mean?"

Emi's face began to twitch a little again.

A dark foreboding spread across her mind. She could literally feel her organs squirm uneasily in her chest.

"*I mean… Oh, you know what I mean, Emi! I'm talking about what kinda outfit you think he'd find cute on a woman!!*"

It must have taken a lot of courage for Rika to ask the question.

Of *course* she couldn't have brought it up with anyone else.

The only women who knew Ashiya before Rika were Emi, Chiho, and Suzuno. But as far as Emi knew, Rika wasn't chummy enough with the other two to ask them questions like *this*.

She and Chiho had gotten closer, certainly, thanks to the whole Alas Ramus thing. But this was a more intimate issue. Really, asking someone what to do in order to make a man pay more attention to you was the same thing, 99 percent of the time, as confessing you have a thing for him.

"Can…can I ask you a question before I answer that, Rika?"

"*Wh-what?!*"

Emi, for her part, was shocked to the point where she thought her heart would stop and she would remain a statuesque figure on the bathtub forever. But across the phone line, it was clear that this coming-out party was sending Rika's internal temperature off the charts.

"Is there something with you and Alc…and Ashiya?"

If there *wasn't* something, Rika wouldn't be asking any of this.

She *did* notice, when they had both run into Ashiya in front of the Hatagaya Sentucky Fried Chicken, that Rika acted a bit odd around him. Not quite herself, somehow. Did they have a chance to interact with each other after that?

"N-no! Nothing! Nothing, I swear! But, it's just that…um…"

Emi could picture Rika flailing her hands in the air.

But her voice trailed off as it continued on, down to a barely audible whisper as it proceeded to bring Emi's body down to absolute zero.

"Ashiya…invited me…to go shopping with him…"

Emi's vision went black.

THE DEVIL EXPLAINS HUMAN RELATIONS

"Dude, I should've known you were still in Japan. What're you here for? If it's Maou, he's out right now."

Urushihara didn't bother removing his eyes from the PC screen.

The floor that Chiho took the time to clean up for him was already littered with empty plastic bottles and snack wrappers, forming a kind of magical barrier that seemed to naturally spring from the ground wherever Urushihara decided to lurk.

The summer sky was blue as blue could be, the sun's rays pounding mercilessly upon the town of Sasazuka as Urushihara took a sip of barley tea from a nearby cup.

"Oh, I *know*. I was watching. I'm here 'cause I wanted to talk to *you*! The Devil King's confidant and his next-door neighbor were nice enough to go away for me, too, so…now or never, y'see?"

"For what."

Urushihara kept his back to the voice.

"My word, though, this room is *hot*! How can your computer operate, or you move around? As I recall, it's bad for computers to run in such heat."

"Not really. It's not like I'm overclocking it or anything."

"Oh no? Well, that explains why your desk is right by the window,

I s'pose. Guess you got the barest excuse for a breeze that way, mmmm?"

"Dude…"

"In any event, it sure is hot. This chocolate mint from Len and Mary's is deee-lish!"

This, finally, was enough to make Urushihara stir. He turned around, the annoyance writ clear on his face.

"Can you just say what you want? Otherwise, I'm gonna call Maou on SkyPhone and tell him you stormed in, raided the fridge, and ran off, Gabriel."

Facing him was a large angel who was, as he spoke, about to bite into an ice cream bar he had just casually helped himself to from the Devil's Castle refrigerator.

"Ooh. Sheesh. He's got you *that* tight on a budget, mmm?"

"Dude, just stop it. *I'm* the one he's gonna get pissed off at."

"Oh, don't be such a grouch! What's so bad about a loaf of ice cream, a jug of barley tea, and *moi*?"

"Nobody asked for you, dude. Just tell me what you want and get outta here. Don't blame me if they burst in and whine at you to pay for the wall you knocked down."

"Hey! That's not exactly how *I* remember it. It wasn't me who knocked it down, exactly. It was that Alas Ramus girl who punched me through it, remember?"

"Yeah, and who made her do that?"

Urushihara was impervious to this game.

Gabriel couldn't have known that their landlord covered the entire wall repair, but he did appear to feel at least slightly at fault for the unplanned Devil's Castle home renovation.

"Wow, though… *You're* the one he's gonna get 'pissed off at'? Reeeeeally?"

Gabriel grinned a smarmy grin as he greedily licked at the bare wooden stick that once held his purloined ice cream bar, tossing it into a side wastebasket.

"That box is for plastic. The regular trash can's next to the fridge."

"Oh, who are you, the Grand Pooh-Bah himself? Come onnn…"

"No! No 'come *onnnnn*'! *I'm* the one he's gonna yell at, all right? Just go away! You're driving me crazy! Why are you even *here*?"

Even Urushihara was nearing his limit now, no longer bothering to hide his irritation.

"Y'knowww…"

"What?!"

"You were the golden child. The archangel closest to Mr. Big himself. And now you're griping and moaning about some bozo getting angry at you? Now *that's* rich. And you actually care about separating the garbage. This's too surreal. I can't even find it in me to laugh."

Gabriel knew exactly what he was going to do with this topic.

But Urushihara betrayed no sign that it riled him any more than he already was. "Yeah, sorry. That was then, this is now. 'Sides, you were the one who talked about how important image is to us. If you're gonna call yourself an angel, you could at least try to recycle."

Urushihara sniffed derisively and focused his attention back on his screen.

Gabriel paid it no mind.

"Why're you even with that young demon wannabe anyway? I mean, I know everybody's saying how much of a wimp you are right now compared to your glory days, but I kinda wasn't around for those, you know? So I'm just wondering, what were you thinking? Like, sue me for asking, but what drove you to shack up with the demons over in their world…?"

"It's 'cause I was bored."

"Bored?"

There was a chuckle lodged in the response.

"Yeah. And it's fun here."

"Fun? Sitting in this sweat lodge, watching Web videos, cowering in fear that your new lord's gonna chew you out for tossing a bottle in the wrong bin? Not to rub it in, bro, but I'd take the Internet café *I'm* staying in any day over this pigsty."

"It's fun. And at least it's not—"

"Whoa there, tiger! No making fun of Internet cafés."

Urushihara's purple eyes made their way through the overgrown hair covering his forehead on their way to staring Gabriel down.

"At least it beats staying up *there*. Staring into space for hours on end until it finally drives you insane."

"Yeaaah, and your little escape's *kiiiind* of becoming a huge pain in the neck for me."

"Helps pass the time, right?"

Gabriel declined to answer. A huddled mass of cicadas swarmed around the trees in the backyard, making the heat and humidity feel even worse with their incessant cries.

"I hung out with Satan 'cause I had nothing to do, dude. I was so devoid of anything to occupy me that it was freaking me out. No other reason besides that. So, we done here? If that's all you needed, the door's that-a-way."

"Ah, *there* he is!"

"Uh?"

Just as he was about to shoo him outside, Gabriel stopped him cold.

"I slogged my sorry hide all the way down to beautiful sun-soaked Sasazuka because I wanted to ask about that Satan guy."

"So? Ask him about himself. It's not like Maou's out on a trip or anything. He's somewhere in Shinjuku."

"Ahh, but he's not gonna tell me anything *now*, is he? Plus, he's still pretty young, yeah? Not like you. I just thought asking the likes of *you* would save us all a lot of headache."

This manner of coercion was familiar to Urushihara. He had heard enough of it up in heaven.

"Plus, the way I see it, instead of asking someone with nothing but secondhand knowledge, asking someone who knows the guy directly would give me much more accurate intel to work with, am I right?"

"Huh?"

This made little sense. Sadao Maou was the Devil King Satan himself. There was nothing secondhand about him.

Gabriel wagged a chiding finger at Urushihara.

"What I'm trying to *tell* you, Lucifer, is I'm talking about some-one *else*. The 'Satan' that *you* were playing around with. Not the greasy-haired social dropout you're bumming crash space from."

Urushihara's eyes immediately stiffened into a sneer. Gabriel gave an equally jeering smirk in response.

"I'm talking about the Devil Overlord Satan. You know him."

"Oh. Is that it? Dude, you made me sneer at you for nothing."

He sighed, as if disappointed at the revelation, and turned back toward the computer screen.

"Heyyy! What d'you mean 'is that it'?! If you didn't notice, I was *trying* to make this into a serious conversation! Was that not *clear* enough to you?"

"I'd be a second-class bum if I cared."

"Oh, what, do you have any perks for being a first-class bum?!"

"No. No perks, but nothing really bad, either."

"Well, maybe that's how *you* think about it. 'Cause if I had to give it to you straight, I'd say you're wasting your life away, aren't you?"

"If I cared about what other people thought about me, I'd stop being a bum right there. That's total bush-league bum-ness."

"If you're planning to be *that* much of a bum, aren't they gonna kick you out before too long?"

"Dude, getting kicked out is, like, less than third-class bum. A first-class bum has to toe the line. You can't make an effort to suck up to whoever it is you're leeching off of, but you have to make sure you don't drive him to do anything rash, either. It's kind of like a sport."

"That's one sport I *really* don't want to visit the Hall of Fame for, I reckon. Where is it, the bathroom at the thrift store? Also, how is that *not* caring about other people?"

"It's totally not. I'm just gauging how much my opponent can stand and working within those rules. That's different from car-ing. Sometimes the rules get rewritten and I have less space to work with, but that's gonna be the same in any world, isn't it?"

"……"

"A true bum isn't afraid of death. He needs the resolve, the bravery to continue with his social-dropout lifestyle every waking moment of his life. If I broke a rule and he kicked me out, I wouldn't be bumming anymore. I'd just be homeless."

The way Urushihara framed himself as a sort of religious practitioner, despite constantly snapping whenever his roommates mocked him for his bum-ness, gave an insight into exactly the sort of mental gymnastics he tackled every day.

There were few less appropriate times to be busting out poetic epithets like "not afraid of death" or "with resolve, bravery."

Even an archangel from another world could agree with the rest of Japanese society on that front. His face was blank, confusion giving way to grim resignation.

"Whatever it is you're trying to convince me of, it's not working, do you hear me? It wouldn't convince anybody of anything."

This was just the sort of response Urushihara relished the most.

"You don't have to be so pedantic, Gabriel."

"Huh?"

"If it wasn't for what happened, you, me, everyone else…we all woulda been bums. Up there."

"…!"

Gabriel gasped a little, not expecting this.

The grin on Urushihara's face grew a shade darker.

"See? You *do* care. Second class, second class."

"…Listen."

Realizing he was being taken on an all-too-familiar ride, Gabriel lightly shook his head, attempting to regain control.

"We're departing from the subject. I wanted to ask you."

"After all that high-and-mighty crap you gave me? Good luck."

The full bore of the archangel's eyes was upon Urushihara.

"If you know anything about the Devil Overlord Satan's lost treasure, I want you to tell me."

"What's that? 'Zit worth anything? 'Cause I want the money. I'd probably have the all-time mother of inheritance taxes to pay, but…"

"That isn't what I asked you. It…it's not that kind of thing anyway!"

"So what is it?"

"I don't *know*. That's why I'm asking!"

"If you don't know, how do you know it's not worth anything?"

"Do the demon realms even *have* a currency system?!"

"No."

"Do you *want* to make me angry?!"

"Ughh… This is such a pain in the ass…"

Urushihara stood up from his seat, stretching out his cramped legs.

Then he took out a memo pad and a pen from the prefab bookshelves and started to scribble something.

"Okay, here it is. The treasure of the demon world, as much as I can remember. Enough to make people up there's eyes explode."

"You call this handwriting?" Gabriel blurted out without thinking. He could be forgiven: It was the scrawl of a five-year-old, and in capital letters to boot.

"NORTHUNG…Nothung? The sword of Gram, hmm? That's not it. What's this? Ader… No. What's ADERAMEKINPEAR mean? Is this all one word?"

"That's 'spear.' The spear that was with Adramelech's tribe back in the Age of Myths."

"The magical spear Adramelechinus! Can you at least learn how to write lowercase letters for me? And they invented spelling for a reason too, you know."

"Screw that. Too much to remember."

"Feh…FALSGOLD…? Oh. Alchemy. The story of how they created brass in an attempt to create false gold, hmm? ESTRLJEM, parenthesis, LEMBRENBE… The heck…?"

"Lhemberel Levherbé. A magical beast the Demon Overlord kept. Rumor says it's still alive somewhere in the demon realms, wearing a collar with an astral gem—an arcane jewel crafted by the Overlord himself. Hey, maybe it's one of your Yesod fragments, huh?"

"…You really want me angry, don't you?"

The look on Gabriel's face was severely embittered. The look on Urushihara's was hurt surprise.

"What? I'm trying to be pretty serious here!"

"Even back then, people named Satan tended to be pretty poor, all right? He was the Demon Overlord, and he was still cheap enough to try tricking people with fool's gold! I don't remember him leaving any weapons or technology worth a rat's ass when he died, and I wrote down pretty much everything right there, okay?!"

"Pfft… And who knows how much I can trust this, even…"

Gabriel wadded up the piece of memo paper and threw it into a trash bin.

"But I don't have any way of *making* you talk. So whatever. I'm outie."

"I told you, that's the recycle bin…"

"Don't forget, though, I'm practically doing you a favor right now."

"Huh? Favor how?"

Gabriel turned unexpectedly stern as he looked upon Urushihara, currently pouting to himself as he fished out the paper wad and ice cream stick from the bin.

"The Observer is coming. And depending on what he decides, it might not be 'doves' like me paying house calls any longer."

That marked the first time today that Urushihara showed any major change in expression.

"The Observer?!"

"Why're *you* acting all shocked? Sariel, the Evil Eye of the Fallen, was teamed up with him, and now he's outta the picture. You had to know he was gonna show up sometime?"

"How could we know that, dude? And why're you expending all this effort on us *now*, after millennia of bumming around? Oh, and don't give me that 'dove' crap, either. You're like a shoebill or something. I have no idea *what* you're thinking."

"Yeah, thanks for that compliment. What's a shoebill, anyway?"

As he spoke, Gabriel took a piece of paper out from his robe.

"Anyway. If you remember anything else, call me on this number. Not that I'd expect you to."

"Like I ever would."

There was a cell phone number on the business-card-sized paper Gabriel flung onto the floor before turning around to put his sandals back on.

"By the way, though…"

"What?"

"If you're trying to find Satan's old crap, then what happened to your search for Yesod fragments? 'Cause Emilia just got a new one."

It was the one crudely embedded into the hilt of the jeweled sword Camio brought over for them. But not even Urushihara knew what Emi had done with it afterward.

Fusing with Alas Ramus was enough to power up her sword and Cloth of the Dispeller to the point where Gabriel was helpless against her.

Bringing another Yesod piece into that picture could help make more of her Cloth materialize. Or not. But if it did, that created issues for both the Devil King's army and Gabriel.

That was the intent behind Urushihara's question, but Gabriel reacted with no measurable surprise.

"Those? Yeah, that's kinda on the back burner for now. I mean, the Observer is coming, so try to read between the lines a little, okay? I got taken off the front lines after the assorted managerial screwups we've had, so if *that* fragment is with Emilia, then fine by me for now."

"Hmm? Well, okay, but…"

"Thanks again for the info! If you see Emilia, tell her I'm not gonna lay a finger on 'em for the time being, you hear me? So take care of that baby."

With a lazy wave, Gabriel stepped out of the door.

Once his footsteps faded way, and the aura of his holy energy had finally disappeared from the Villa Rosa Sasazuka environs, Urushihara returned to his computer.

He began typing away, the cicadas providing him with a little seasonal background music.

Then, in a rare display of emotion, Urushihara began humming to himself as he browsed through his preferred video site.

"Amaaaaazing graaaaace…how sweeeeeet the soooooound… Hell yeah."

✳

The call center for the Dokodemo cell phone provider was shrouded in a strange sort of tension.

There was always something of an unnatural aura surrounding Emi Yusa, the cheerful yet thick-skinned customer service representative whose skill in foreign languages made her one of the phone bay's star players.

She was there, just as always, handling the callers other agents were too helpless to handle.

If you went up and spoke to her, she was the same old Emi Yusa.

But.

When she wasn't speaking with anyone. While she was waiting for a call to come in. In other words, whenever she was alone—

—her face was scary. At least, she *looked* scary. Anxiety and anger over something that couldn't quite be put into words were etched across her features.

She was clearly worried about something, and clearly, it was distracting her.

It had no effect on her work duties, but today in particular, Emi was hard to approach.

"Um, Ms. Yusa, I..."

"...Yes?"

"Uhm. Oh. Um. Never mind. I'm sorry."

The woman seated next to Emi excused herself, picking up on her state of intense concentration.

Emi brought a hand to her forehead, wondering if she really looked that fearsome.

Rika didn't have a shift with her that day. Instead, on the opposite side of where she usually sat, there was Maki Shimizu, a college student who had joined Dokodemo after her two cube mates.

She acted fairly reserved most of the time, but in a call-center job that required dealing with irate old men and whiny complainers on a daily basis, she had a remarkable resilience for her age. She was a fairly valued member of the force, in other words.

"...No, it's okay, Maki. What's up?"

Maki was in her second year of college, which meant that Emi was, by Earth standards, actually younger than she was.

But the accumulated history they had both experienced, coupled with the aura the two of them generally emitted, made Emi seem far older.

This gave Emi some level of respect among other people in the office, who treated her like a multiyear veteran of the call-center trenches.

"Um, you...you're looking scary."

The straight appraisal made Emi even more self-conscious.

It must have been the face of a tormented monster. And as Emi thought about it, the sight of this hardy customer-representative soldier—never daring to flee at the sound of yet another irate pensioner who couldn't read the manual—having difficulty facing up to her proved that the problem was fully on her own end.

"Um, I'm sorry if this is a weird question, but..."

"No, no, what is it?"

Maki's voice, while hesitant, was perfectly clear.

"Did you have an argument with Rika or something?"

"Huh?!"

Emi was shocked. This was not at all what she expected, and so clearly, from her mouth.

"Wh-why did you think that?"

"Oh, it's not...? Well, that's good, anyway."

"I'm not arguing with Rika about anything. What gave you that idea?"

Mika softened a little, the look of sheer surprise on Emi's face calming her.

"Well, I got to work the same time as Rika yesterday. I took my lunch break later than usual, but just when I went out to get something, someone called Rika on her cell phone."

Emi could feel her stomach churn a little. She knew what that phone call was.

"After that, Rika was acting weird the entire afternoon, so...I think she called you once she got off duty, so I just thought maybe something was going on."

"Ohhh... And since I was looking all angry, you probably thought we were fighting, huh?"

Emi expelled a deep sigh.

The call Maki mentioned was probably the one Emi had picked up in her bathroom the previous day. As for that other one…

"Though looking back…I guess she was kinda all over the place. I'd spot her grinning to herself, then she'd start looking all troubled. It's like her mind wasn't on her work at all."

Maki grinned a bit herself as she sought Emi's appraisal.

"Do you think Rika found a new guy or something?"

"Gnnh!"

The groan was perhaps louder than Emi meant.

"M-Ms. Yusa?"

"Oh, um… It's noth—"

At that moment, the scene in front of Sentucky Fried Chicken played back in her mind.

"No! Stop stop stop stop! Cut me a break!"

"Ms. Yusa?!"

Ignoring Maki's surprised yelp, Emi placed her head on the desk.

Chiho, she couldn't do much about. She had already been intimately familiar with the demons by the time they met. But Rika joining the fray would make Emi's stress levels accelerate to the stratosphere.

"Why's it always on a day like this…?"

"Oop. …Thank you for calling the Dokodemo Customer Support Team! This is Shimizu. How can I help you today…?"

"Yes, hello, thanks for calling the Dokodemo Customer Support Team…"

"Thank you for your phone call today! Are you there, sir…?"

"Why do I have to be so busy?!"

Emi felt like she wanted to cry.

The calls came without a break from the moment her day started.

The morning roundup e-mail mentioned that all feature phones and smartphones equipped with digital HDTV support were facing issues with signal reception today.

"Ugh, this is the TV company, people! It's not our fault!"

"Ms. Yusa…?"

Maki covered the mike on her headset and frowned.

That must have been loud enough to be audible. Emi winced and brought her hands together in apology. Another call came onscreen.

"...Hello, and thank you for calling the Dokodemo Customer Support Team. This is Yusa..."

Another complaint about TV reception.

The common thread among the complaints was that the screen flashed white whenever users launched the TV app.

That, and this flashing ate up the phone's battery like wildfire.

It didn't happen wherever there was a weak cell signal.

The phenomenon tended to happen to everyone at generally the same time.

And, while it didn't particularly matter, a strangely large number of people reported it happening when they used the TV app inside their own homes.

"If you're at home," Emi muttered to herself, "just watch your own TV, you freaks."

Dokodemo HQ's operational team had yet to give the call center any guidance about the cause, so all Emi and the rest of the staff had to offer customers were their profuse and heartfelt apologies.

It could have been a lot worse, at least. Anything involving people's voice, text, or Net connections would have been murder. Most users, by comparison, didn't bother with TV on their phones that often—not when even the biggest screens didn't offer more than a small, occasionally choppy image. In an era where people could record multiple HD broadcasts at the same time, mobile-phone TV was mostly a toy unless you absolutely had to have the current live broadcast on your phone.

It was to the point where the TV-reception hardware was gradually being phased out of phones in Japan to make room for improved voice, Net, and app performance.

In other words, even though Dokodemo still offered a full line of phones with TV reception, the number of complaints for the current outage was still slow enough that Emi had time to trouble herself over Rika.

When the company had a Net outage a while back that made texting unavailable for a mere thirty minutes, that was enough to knock out the phone systems of every call center nationwide, a disaster epic enough in scale to make the national news.

"TV, though, huh…?"

Emi's talk with Rika the day before made her mind blank out for a moment, but as the conversation went on, she learned that Ashiya apparently had asked Rika for advice on purchasing appliances.

She had no idea why Ashiya had Rika's contact info, but apparently Rika promised to give Ashiya some advice on buying a cell phone not long ago.

That ongoing issue fell by the wayside with Maou's Choshi trip, only to be rushed back to the forefront by Rika's somewhat hushed voice over the phone.

Emi wavered, unable to dissuade Rika from avoiding Ashiya for reasons she couldn't reveal. Instead, she advised Rika to just "be herself"—about the most slapdash, generic advice one could give at a time like this—and hung up the phone.

Then she immediately placed a call to Suzuno, who reported that—as expected—Maou had come storming back from the real estate agent, supreme victory written on his face, with Ashiya behind him looking like the sky was falling directly on his bank account.

The rent remained the same, they owed nothing for the home repairs, and since the MHK television fee was paid by the landlord on a collective-housing contract, it was already factored into the rent.

"And as I discussed last night, I intend to join them on the hunt. I thought this might perhaps be a fine opportunity to purchase a television of my own."

That report lightened Emi's heart a little. Just a little. A wiped-down kitchen counter in the frat house party of her life.

Rika wasn't going alone with Ashiya. Suzuno and Maou would be with them.

"…But is that gonna be all right?"

"M-Ms. Yusa?"

Stress and talking to herself went hand in hand with Emi, who was too lost in thought to acknowledge Maki's concern.

Rika sees Ashiya as a regular young man. There was no point trying to pretend otherwise.

With every ounce of willpower she could muster, Emi attempted the grueling act of picturing Ashiya for who he was. Shirou Ashiya: Well-built, muscular, and tall. Hair that just barely escaped taglines like *shaggy* or *unkempt*. And a face taut and wizened by ages of dealing with poverty. To an impartial observer, he probably looked like a forlorn liberal-arts major with a background in the—

"Rghh."

It made Emi sick thinking about it, but that was the conclusion a lot of people would make.

And beyond that, he was polite and amenable around others, never came off as arrogant or cocky, but was still strict enough to upbraid his master Maou for his mistakes and spew venom at Urushihara all day for...being Urushihara.

His main minus was his near-total lack of income, but that was chiefly by his own design. If he completed the steps necessary to find a job, he would no doubt excel at whatever he tried his hand at. As a demon, he was just as much an expert with languages as Emi was.

And since his dirt-poor lifestyle left him with next to no money for entertainment, you never had to worry about excessive drinking or smoking.

And he could cook, clean, and do laundry. *Perfectly.*

Chiho Sasaki, by modern teenage standards, was so exceptional that she ought to be classified as a national monument and preserved for generations to marvel at. But looking at it this way, Emi had to admit—as a man, Ashiya was pretty prime pickings, too.

Maybe Rika fell in love at first sight. She couldn't do much about that.

"Does Rika know...Bell and the Devil King are coming along?"

Now a different sort of frustration began to make itself known— not from the Hero Emilia, but as Emi Yusa, Rika Suzuki's friend.

Over the phone last night, Rika sounded like she was trying (and failing) with all her heart to hide her embarrassment...and her excitement.

She never used the word *date*, but Rika must have known that Ashiya recognized her as a special woman in his life.

But...

"Is that registering with any of them...?"

This shopping trip involved buying a TV for Devil's Castle. Rika, Ashiya, Maou, and Suzuno coming together seemed natural enough.

Given how fiendishly well organized Ashiya always was, he might have let Rika know about that by now.

But Rika must have had some kind of faint...expectation in mind, at least. Nothing strong enough to call hope, but it was there.

The expectation that she'd be alone, out together with Ashiya.

And Rika knew, in her own way, that Maou and Suzuno would be there, but she still saw that as a disappointment...

"...No! That's wrong!" Emi shouted.

"Wh-what's wrong?!" Maki, awaiting a call in her booth, shivered in surprise.

But Emi had no time to worry about her.

Where did Emi go wrong?

Ashiya is a demon. He just looked human right now because he was drained of his malevolent force. There was no way Emi could allow a demon like him to ever be alone with a valued friend of hers.

Ever since the previous day, her mind had been going off in all kinds of odd directions.

There was an uneasy truce between her and the demons, but it was one they were both forced into. From head to cloven hoof, they were the enemies of all mankind.

And with Suzuno around, she could protect Rika if anything happened. And Ashiya. And Maou.

"...I don't *care* about the Devil King and Alciel!!" Emi pronounced aloud.

"Eep!"

Maki, next door, sounded close to tears.

Then a large shadow appeared behind Emi as she rubbed her head and squirmed in disgust at herself. Emi didn't notice, but Maki looked on like a woman saved from the gallows at the last minute.

"……"

Fifteen minutes later:

Emi was plucked out of the office by the floor leader managing the call-center crew.

She was normally a hard worker, one who had pretty good relationships with everyone on the staff, so she avoided a serious reprimand. But:

"Are you tired or something? You can just head home today. Having you around is messing up the workplace atmosphere."

It hit hard. Enough so to darken Emi's face considerably. But it was true. She was preoccupied with so much today, it was getting hard to function like a normal human being.

And she was rough on Maki for no good reason. She'd need to apologize later.

Emi looked at her watch.

It was three in the afternoon. She was being sent home a good two hours earlier than usual.

She might as well use that time for her own needs, then.

Judging by what Maou and Ashiya had said the previous day, the four them were somewhere in Shinjuku right now.

She turned on her cell phone to contact Suzuno or Rika…but stopped herself. It took all her remaining strength.

"…It'd be too weird."

Rika had approached her with this news just yesterday. If Emi showed up while she and Ashiya and the others were out shopping, that would put Rika in an incredibly awkward position.

Tailing the four of them unnoticed wasn't an option, either. Emi's past few months of experience told her that Ashiya would never be anything but a perfect gentleman toward Rika. And if Maou noticed Emi following after them, he'd never let her hear the end of it for the rest of her mortal life.

Given the current situation, trying to follow them and getting spotted could even potentially cause cracks to form in her and Rika's friendship. The idea offered no benefit to Emi.

"In which case," Emi whispered to herself, "maybe I should work toward my own goals every now and then…"

She could no longer simply walk up to Maou and slay him. Not with Alas Ramus fused into her holy sword.

Even if Suzuno's hunch was right and someone decided to kidnap the Devil King and his general, that didn't mean Emi was obligated to stick by them at all times. Until something actually happened, it'd be unwise to approach Rika, either.

Which opened up other opportunities.

Emi unfastened a pocket in her shoulder bag, inserted a finger, and plucked out a small, stone-like object.

It was a Yesod fragment, misshapen and smaller than a marble.

It had been embedded in the sword held by the Devil Regent Camio. Maou had tossed it over to her on the way back from Choshi, claiming he didn't need it.

Remarkably enough, Alas Ramus didn't offer much interest when shown it.

This was the first time Emi had obtained a fragment by itself, but considering Alas Ramus's behavior and past, she assumed the child would extract whatever power the stone had and merge it with her own, or something. Just as Emi's Better Half inadvertently led her toward Alas Ramus in the Devil's Castle on Ente Isla. Just as the fragment on the other side of Ciriatto's Link Crystal led his horde to the holy sword.

And…

Emi was trying to hunt down another Yesod fragment she was pretty sure existed in Japan right now.

At the time, she hadn't noticed it as such, but later Maou had named it a Yesod fragment.

The jewel with the power to return Alas Ramus to normal. Carried by a woman who knew Alas Ramus's name. A woman in white who approached her at Tokyo Big-Egg Town back on that day, wearing a ring festooned with a purple jewel.

Could she be…?

"…I better just leave it at that in my mind for now…" Emi shook her head, chiding herself.

This was a person who shouldn't have been here at all. A person she knew only through what other people told her. Someone who crashed with friends for days at a time, but never showed her face to Emi. It might have been her.

"I can't go breaking out my holy sword in public, either…"

Ever since she obtained the fragment in Choshi, Emi had been putting together a way to make use of it.

Yesod fragments were naturally attracted to each other.

But the only ones Emi had so far were the Better Half, Alas Ramus, and her Cloth of the Dispeller.

No matter how much she toned down her holy force, the sword would never shrink down beyond the size of a knife. Once her energy fell below a certain level, it would disappear entirely.

She considered using the fragment in the sword's scabbard, but that would require her to materialize the Better Half anyway. If the woman in white was in an urban area somewhere, Emi and her unsheathed weapon would be reported to the police in an instant.

With Alas Ramus, though, the Yesod fragment that formed her core essence was apparently the crescent-moon design that occasionally appeared on her forehead.

If she used that fragment to attract other Yesod fragments to her, that'd require her to carry a baby around with a light-up forehead that looked as if it should be firing death lasers at giant movie monsters. It wouldn't be very inconspicuous.

The Cloth of the Dispeller wouldn't work, either. She didn't know where the core of it was in the first place.

Given the alternatives, taking a fragment the size of a pebble on the street and walking around with it in her bag was not a problem at all. She could camouflage it in any number of ways, too.

There are tons of light-up key chains and other dinky little accessories these days, besides.

The only concern that remained was the potential for this Yesod fragment to bring Gabriel and his heavenly cohorts upon her if she used it. But the chances of that seemed slim.

Emi had unleashed the full force of her Cloth and Better Half over in Choshi. But despite the fact that Gabriel picked up on the woman in white and Alas Ramus immediately, there was no sign whatsoever of him showing up this time.

The fact there was one cheerfully hewn into the jeweled sword that Olba gave to Camio was odd, too.

She didn't know who was on the other end of Ciriatto's Link Crystal, but neither this mystery person nor the Yesod fragment that person presumably had showed any sign of drawing near her, either.

They might just be stringing her along, waiting for the right moment to strike. But even if they did, Emi was fresh from defeating Gabriel. She liked her chances against well near anyone right now.

"...I wanted to do this smarter. I wanted some peace in my life."

As she left the building that housed her workplace, Emi regretted speaking to her coworkers like a bratty teenage bully as she headed for Shinjuku station.

There would normally be a stairway directly in front of the building that led to the subway. However, Olba and Urushihara had collapsed the tunnel through some method or another, and it still wasn't back open yet.

It annoyed her for several reasons, not the least of which was because heading down there would bring her back to air-conditioning sooner. She stewed over that as she avoided the nearby eastern entrance to the rail station and headed for the New South exit, home to Shinjuku's long-distance bus ticket counter.

Proceeding under the pedestrian bridge and passing by the eternally-under-construction southern exit, she passed by the stairs to the New South exit and walked on through the automatic doors of Takashima-daya, the high-end department store.

She breathed a sigh to herself as the cool air caressed her skin, ignoring the brand-name handbags, shoes, and other accessories lined up on the shelves as she dove deeper inside.

Then, before her unfolded a space quite different from the previous oasis of luxury—one done up in a deep green, with a great variety of merchandise crammed into a large number of aisles.

This new space was separated from Takashima-daya by the escalators, and while it was still in the same building, it was completely its own beast.

It was the Shinjuku branch of Tokyu Hand, a do-it-yourself store the size of a small city. When it came to anything you could call a tool or an accessory, there was practically nothing it didn't have.

The selection began with wood and machine tools before moving on to construction equipment, clocks, leather goods, stuff for the outdoors, metals, project kits, party goods, character merchandise, and almost anything else they could get their hands on.

Emi rode up the escalator, heading for the floor where they sold a variety of crystals, minerals, and fossils. It wasn't long before she found what she was looking for: a small bottle with a cork, meant for exhibiting crystals with. She also stopped by the accessory-kit section for a ball chain and a few other metal bits and bobs.

From there, she proceeded a very short distance to the Yoyogi Dokodemo Building. Evocative of the Art Deco skyscrapers that dominated the US cityscapes way back when, it housed the Yoyogi office's primary business departments and communications hardware.

There was a Muddraker's burger place on the first floor, which Emi swung into for some tea and a chance to lay out her goods on the table.

"...There we go."

A Yesod fragment inside a corked bottle with a chain attached looked like nothing but a somewhat quirky key holder. She didn't need to have it lit up 24/7, so as long as she could make up a quick story about it when anyone asked, it was all good.

It definitely beat carrying her unsheathed holy sword around, or showing Alas Ramus's glowing forehead to the entire world.

The restaurant was largely deserted. Lunch was over, and it was still a tad early for the dinner rush.

Emi put her completed key chain back in her bag, then, taking a moment to ensure nobody was looking, infused the fragment with just a bit of her holy energy.

The Better Half, the Cloth of the Dispeller, and Alas Ramus all acted in concert with this infusion, making the fragment grow in strength.

She took pains to regulate the flow, remembering the dazzling glow her sword had emitted when she had set foot within Ente Isla's Devil's Castle.

Then she gave a light pump of her fist with her free arm.

"...Yes!"

The Yesod fragment inside the bottle began to glow a faint shade of violet, just like her sword and Alas Ramus's head. Then, after realigning itself within the bottle, it shot a straight beam of light in a certain direction.

The beam was cut off by the inside of Emi's bag, of course. But all she needed was the directional guidance.

The light was pointed southwest of Yoyogi.

One potential location immediately sprung to mind.

"...Ugh, Sasazuka?"

It was pointed right at the zone of Tokyo where Emi and Maou spent most of their lives.

"But...hang on a sec. It might not be there at all. Maybe it's *past* there, even. ...Might as well take this as far as it goes, though."

Sasazuka would need to be on her list, of course, but all she had to go on right now was a general southwestern bearing. There was no guarantee this light wouldn't guide her all the way down to Okinawa.

One thing was already for sure, though. The fragment in Emi's bag, the Better Half, the Cloth of the Dispeller, Alas Ramus—and something else: There was another Yesod fragment in this world. Emi stepped out of Muddraker's, a new sense of confidence fresh in her mind.

"...Which way would this thing turn if it's reacting to something on the opposite side of the world, though?"

✳

She knew the whole time.

That was what he had told her, after all. Having this be anything else would certainly not be her preference.

The other end of the relationship didn't seem too conscious of its existence. And, looking back, she clearly acted out of sorts whenever they were together.

But…

"I was just thinking, you know…*what if*, am I right?"

"Pardon me?"

"Nothing, nothing."

Rika grinned to herself, remembering that Ashiya was standing right next to her.

After agonizing over how dressy she should be for the big day, she opted for a tunic-style top, some short pants, and a well-worn pair of mules. Nothing too fancy, just your basic going-out gear. It proved to be the right answer.

Ashiya *was* standing next to her, yes. But in front of them was this guy, Sadao Maou—Rika still wasn't quite sure if he was Ashiya's friend, or ex-boss, or what—and Suzuno Kamazuki, Emi's pal.

Maou and Ashiya were decked out in UniClo from top to bottom, not much different from before. They were reasonably coordinated, at least. Suzuno, meanwhile, was in a kimono as always.

Going full volume with her fashion choices today would've made the men in the group stand out like a pair of sore thumbs. Rika's wardrobe was just barely casual enough to make the entire team look remarkably well balanced.

Upon meeting up at the western turnstile at JR Shinjuku station, the four of them took an underground tunnel to the Socket City in front of the station's main bus terminal.

Rika had brought along nothing but a purse just large enough to fit her phone, her wallet, and a few cosmetics. Now, though, she was carrying a large, solid-looking plastic bag with one hand.

It was a set of *tsukudani* simmered fish from Choshi. A souvenir from Ashiya, who told Rika by phone about their trip beforehand.

Offering a selection of saury, mackerel, and European pilchard, it was nothing more, and nothing less, than a souvenir. The sort of thing you purchased robotically at the gift shop when you remembered you needed to bring *something* home.

"...Well, it works for me." Rika grinned to herself, feeling a tad warmer for reasons besides the summer heat.

It was a very Ashiya-like present, to say the least.

And for someone living alone like she did, Rika would never turn down something to fancy up dinner a little.

She wasn't a child any longer, besides. She was mature, and her emotions matured with the rest of her. In a distressing way, she was all grown up.

Rika turned toward Maou and Suzuno to shake off the bad vibes.

"So, what are all of you lookin' to buy today, anyway?"

"I am merely here to purchase a television set. These other two, I cannot say."

"Uh, hello? I need a TV, too?"

Maou shot it back at Suzuno. Rika looked up at Ashiya, who clearly wanted to voice his dissent.

"What about a phone?"

"...Perhaps, once we gauge the TV prices..."

"A phone? What's that about?"

Maou turned around, picking up on their conversation.

"Well, I *told* you, I promised I'd help Ashiya find a cell phone for himself. It's the twenty-first century, and he told me he didn't have one."

"When did you get to talking about *that*?"

Maou never knew—was never made aware—that Ashiya, Rika, and Chiho had been tailing him at Tokyo Big-Egg Town. That was why, just like with Emi, he had no clue why Ashiya and Rika were so suddenly friendly with each other.

"I dunno how much I can help you with buying a TV, though. I got an HD screen at home, but it's not like I know a whole lot about them or anything."

"Oh, not at all, Ms. Suzuki. The fact you own a television at all is vital to us. You made the purchase yourself, right?"

Rika's apartment in the Takadanobaba neighborhood contained a flat-screen LCD set. It was the first major purchase she made with the money she saved up from working in Tokyo.

"Yeah, it's from Toshina. It was pretty much one of the first HD-compatible models, so it's kind of old, but it's a twenty-sixer and it has all the component video and HDMI connectors and stuff. I just added a DVR and Blu-ray player to it not long ago."

Rika found herself stared at by three pairs of eyes, all telling her that they had no idea what she was talking about.

"Um...?"

Suzuno cleared her throat. "I...imagine this may be difficult for you to believe, Rika...but our knowledge of home electronics begins and, sad to say, ends in the era of rabbit ears."

"For *you*, maybe."

Suzuno let Maou's jab go unanswered.

"It was kinda the same thing when I bought a phone," Maou continued, "but you're talking as if we've got all the basics down pat already. It doesn't really mean much to me if this or that's installed on it if we don't know what 'this or that' even is."

"Yes," Ashiya agreed. "And, Ms. Suzuki, I was hoping you might be able to teach us about all of this."

"Ohhhh...kay?"

"So, this Toshina. Are they a well-known electronics manufacturer?"

"We're starting from *there*?"

Ashiya's question all but floored Rika. She stopped walking.

"Okay. Let's rewind a bit. I think going to the electronics store right now might be *just* a little dangerous."

Rika paused for a moment to think.

"Uhmmm, have, have you guys eaten yet? 'Cause how about we all have some lunch and I can at least tell you the bare minimum you all need to know?"

Maou nodded as he wiped the sweat from his brow. "Oh…yeah, it's about time, huh? It's been so hot lately, I haven't had much of an appetite at all."

"I have not eaten either…" Suzuno grinned and raised an eyebrow at Ashiya. "But the real issue is whether this compulsive miser here would allow a trip to a restaurant."

Ashiya protested hautily. "Suzuno Kamazuki…you see me as nothing more than a close-fisted skinflint, do you?"

Then he turned to Rika: "As long as we can restrict it to three hundred yen or below per meal, I am prepared to make the outlay."

"……"

Maou and Suzuno found themselves unable to respond.

Five hundred yen would be understandable enough, but at the three-hundred level, the pickings started to get slim. That would be just enough, maybe, to eat something off the main menu at MgRonald or a beef-bowl chain joint.

But Rika looked unfazed as she began walking forward.

"Okay, let's do it. Mind if we go someplace I know about? It's right near here."

"Um, you know someplace we can eat at for three hundred yen?"

"Yeah, well, I kinda predicted he'd say that. I dunno if it'd be enough to fill up a full-sized man, but we'll see."

She brimmed with confidence as she climbed back up to the surface streets, guiding the other three to the front of a mixed-used office building.

Suzuno was the first to spot the sign.

"'Manmaru Udon'… What? Udon noodles?!"

Manmaru Udon was an udon chain that got its start in Kagawa prefecture, the birthplace of the thick *sanuki* udon noodles that dominated much of Japan these days. They were known for their self-service bar of side dishes and toppings, and—more relevant to today's proceedings—they offered high-quality noodle dishes that started at 105 yen.

"U...udon for a hundred five yen?" Ashiya, predictably, demonstrated the most shock.

He wasn't deliberately trying to be difficult, but not even he expected a restaurant to offer anything below his quoted number.

"Huh... I heard about this, actually. This is Manmaru, eh?"

Maou, being a fast-food employee, at least knew the name, although this was his first actual visit to one.

"The small-size plain noodle bowl goes for a hundred five yen, and if you add a couple of toppings to that, you can keep it under three hundred and still fill up a little," Rika added.

"Do... Are you a frequent visitor, Ms. Suzuki?" Ashiya inquired.

"No, just sometimes. The broth that udon gets served in around Tokyo is too thick and spiced up for me, but it's a lot plainer here, so I like it more. Kinda easy on the wallet, too, huh?"

"Yeah, no kidding."

"So anyway, we can eat here and I can clue you in about TVs a little before we hit the store. I'm not a huge expert or anything, but seriously, you'd be asking for trouble if you walked in there right now."

Rika stood in the front of the line, showing the rest how to order. Behind her were Ashiya, Maou (still pondering over Ashiya and Rika's apparent chumminess), and Suzuno, each wrapping up their order in sequence.

"You're going with plain udon, Suzuno?"

Rika couldn't help but ask. Even Ashiya and Maou topped their 105-yen bowl with some sweet-potato tempura and fried fish sticks, but Suzuno, surprisingly, went with plain old noodles and broth.

"I need to test this first. One small udon, as is, will suffice."

As is, in this case, referred to the not-too-cold, certainly-not-too-warm temperature Manmaru typically sold their noodles at.

The chain's 105-yen price point was more than just cheap for cheapness's sake—it was devised to encourage more people to give *sanuki* udon a try. A sign of the franchise's confidence in their goods, in other words.

"I never shy away from a fair challenge."

"...A fair what?"

The four of them sat at a table and took out their chopsticks, Suzuno sizing up her bowl as intently as a samurai preparing to strike with his sword.

"'Kay, well...dig in, everyone." Sounding the bell like a cafeteria lunch lady, Rika watched as Ashiya and Maou dipped their chopsticks into the broth, both thinking over their own private matters.

"...Let us begin."

Suzuno shot her eyes open and brought a load of noodles to her lips.

"!!"

One bite was enough to make her face change color.

"This...is...!"

"Uh, hey, Suzuno?"

Maou's voice clearly did not register with Suzuno as she quickly went in for more noodles. As the other three watched, she finished up the entire small bowl of plain udon in under a minute. The sheer zeal she brought into her eating performance mesmerized the group. She gave a light exhale as she wrapped up the final mouthful, but after a few seconds, her shoulders began to visibly shake.

"Why...why...?"

"Wh-what's up, Suzuno? Didn't like them too much?"

The bizarreness of Suzuno's reaction gave Rika genuine cause for worry. But Suzuno responded with a gruff stare, her voice low.

"Why...is such splendid udon a mere hundred and five yen?"

"Huh?"

"The thickness, the body, the mouth feel, the salt level, the finish...all absolutely beyond reproach."

"Yeah...? Well, great, but..."

Her eyes remained stiff and resentful, but Suzuno now looked more like a gourmet restaurant critic as she stood back up, bowl in hand.

"...Another order!"

"Yeaaah, have fun," Maou muttered into his noodles as Suzuno stormed back to the counter. "I know they're good and all, but *that* good?"

Ashiya looked up for a moment from his bowl. "Yes, well, Ms. Kamazuki is something of an udon aficionado, I believe. Perhaps something in it struck a chord with her."

For some reason, the observation caused anxiety to shake itself into existence within Rika's heart. Why would Ashiya know about Suzuno's favorite foods? She knew they were next-door apartment neighbors, but were they friendly enough to know about each other's eating habits?

"...Aha..."

Rika shook her head rather than take the thought any further. There was nothing strange about it at all. Even Rika had at least a vague idea of what people around her ate on a regular basis. And Suzuno became acquainted with Ashiya long before Rika entered the picture. If they lived that close to each other, he was bound to find out somehow.

As if to quell the anxiety once and for all, Rika opened wide and took a large, crunchy bite out of the *kaki-age* tempura fritter over her noodles.

"So getting back to the TV for a moment... Did you have an idea of what kind you wanted to buy or anything?" she asked.

"If I can watch TV with it, I'm good to go," Maou replied.

"Well, yeah, but—"

"You said earlier that you owned a Toshina something-or-other that was 'a twenty-sixer,'" Ashiya began. "Is that the model number or some such part?"

Maou's phoned-in preferences were as unexpected as Ashiya's earnest question.

"N-no, no, it's twenty-six inches. That's the size of the screen...or of the TV itself, maybe. One of the two?"

Rika had trouble remembering which was correct, but reasoned that it didn't enormously matter either way.

But this was far more than simply not keeping up with the latest models.

Rika was no gadget guru, but televisions and video recording already existed by the time she was born. Her DVR wasn't any thornier to use than any video device that came before it.

"Huh. So if twenty-six is normal, then I guess we're maxing out at twenty-nine, maybe?"

"What?"

Rika's eyebrows bunched together at Maou's continued nonsense.

"I'd like to keep it on the bigger side, though. Like, twenty-seven or so. Twenty-four would be too small, so I'd want to go for twenty-six or twenty-seven…or twenty-eight if I can."

She kind of understood what Maou was getting at as he rattled the numbers off. They indicated that this wasn't going to be easy for her.

"It doesn't work like bicycle tires or anything…"

"No?"

"I mean, the newer ones, if they're meant for the family room, they come in thirty-two inches even at the low end. If money was no object, you could even pick up a fifty- or sixty-inch screen right now—like, about the size of a tatami mat if you laid it on the floor."

"What the heck would you watch with something *that* big?!"

Maou—on this issue, at least—had a point.

"Mmm, movies and stuff, I guess? Some people are really picky about video and audio quality with that sort of thing, so…"

"Would regular programs show up that large as well?"

Ashiya's trembling question created a mental image in Rika's mind.

"You know, maybe that wouldn't be so nice, huh?" she admitted.

Movies and nature documentaries would be one thing. But watching a normal news broadcast, the national legislature in session, or some inane comedy show in massive, high-resolution perfection seemed pointless. Rika chuckled at the idea of the top half of a newscaster's body projected across her entire living-room wall.

"But that's gonna be way out of your budget anyway. My twenty-six-incher's probably about…this big, I guess?"

She drew a rectangle in the air in front of her to illustrate.

"They're all gonna be flat-screen models these days, so you just have to worry about the width when you're deciding where to put it. How much money do you have to work with?"

"Forty-one thousand, two hundred thirty-nine yen."

Maou's response was instantaneous.

"Why so exact?"

"He's never *not* exact with our budget." He motioned to Ashiya.

"No, I am not. So, do you think we'll be able to purchase a television with…41,239 yen?" The nervous tension was clear in Ashiya's voice.

"I performed some preliminary investigation over the Internet earlier, but all I could find on the low end was used goods, shady-looking store sites, and things like discount offers if I signed up for a new broadband provider. I'm afraid I failed to get a clear picture of what a TV would cost by itself."

"Well, if you're buying a home appliance like this, it's probably better to get hands-on with it first anyway…"

Rika nodded slightly.

"But if you don't mind going down to twenty inches or so, you could probably squeak under the forty thousand mark, I think."

"Hell yeah!"

"Wha…!"

Maou's fist pump was accompanied by the blood draining from Ashiya's face.

Suzuno chose that moment to return, fresh bowl of noodles in hand.

"Upsized a bit, huh?"

It was another plain udon order, this one in a bowl easily twice the size of the first.

"Even their largest size is only four hundred yen. How could they possibly earn a profit at these prices…? The state of Japan's food security never fails to mystify me. Have we returned to the subject of television yet?"

She was already slurping away as she spoke, her face softer now. Apparently she calmed down enough that she could think about other things besides noodles again.

"I could provide a budget of up to seventy thousand yen if needed. Would that enable me to make a purchase?"

"Oh, you could get a pretty good one with that budget, I'd imagine. We've got less than a year before Japan switches over to all-HD broadcasting, so some of the older models are starting to get really cheap these days."

"Is that the state of things...? Curse you, HD broadcasting... A thorn in my side to the very end..." It was unclear where Ashiya was targeting his grudge, but his chopsticks were about to snap in his hand.

"Beyond that...if you hit up the thrift shops, you could get an old picture-tube TV for less than ten thousand if you wanted, but there wouldn't be much point to that once they stop broadcasting in analog."

"So why're they even selling those?"

"Well, apart from changing your antenna, you can get HD broadcasts from a cable company, too. Then you'd have to rent a tuner, but that would let you watch digital TV on an analog set. There's a lot of people who don't want to throw out a perfectly good TV, you know?"

"Hm," Suzuno muttered. "Would that grant me access to a vacuum-tube and transistor-model television?"

Rika shook her head at Suzuno's oddly impassioned query.

"I...dunno about that. I mean, I've heard of transistor radios, but..."

"Ah. I merely thought that, considering how quickly things evolve in Japan, people would be all too ready to sweep away with the old to bring in the new. But hearing of this technique to connect yourself to the past... It gladdens me, a little."

"Hey, um, I've kinda been wondering about this, Suzuno, but did you maybe grow up in a foreign country like Emi or something?"

"Hmm?"

"I dunno, you just like saying stuff like 'In Japan it's like this,' 'In Japan you do that,' that kind of thing."

"...Ah. Yes. Um, yes. I come from a religious family, and we were stationed overseas..."

The unexpected question threw Suzuno uncharacteristically off balance.

"You're lettin' the udon get to your head."

The muttered remark earned Maou a kick under the table from the blushing Suzuno.

Rika did not seem particularly suspicious, however. Suzuno wasn't lying, after all.

"Oh, one of those missionary things? Wow, I guess there really are people like that, huh? Like, I saw on TV once about this priest in Japan who went deep into Africa to spread Christianity. Kinda made me think about what a big world it is, y'know?"

"There...are people like that in this country, as well...?" Suzuno looked at Rika, eyes wide. "I had thought the Japanese held little interest in religion."

"Oh, no way! I mean, you wouldn't see all those horoscope and fortune-telling apps on phones if we didn't."

"Oh? I can call someone on my phone to have my fortune read?"

"It's not the automatic time hotline, Suzuno."

"......"

Rika didn't mean to bring it up, but it still put Maou in an embarrassed silence.

"But...yeah, you see miniature Buddhist shrines inside IT firms and stuff. That, or some big electronics firm will hire a priest to drive the evil spirits away from a tract of land so they can build a new factory on it. I mean, pretty much everyone's picked up their fortune on a piece of paper at a temple at least once in their life. I forget if I told you that our family lived right where our business is, but there's a little shrine in the office, and in one corner of our workshop there's an *inari*, too. I had to keep that nice and dust free as part of my chores as a kid."

"Was this an *inari* sushi production plant?"

Suzuno's eyes instinctively turned to the *inari* sushi—balls of rice wrapped in fried tofu—on offer back in the self-serve side dish bar.

"Wow, Suzuno, I think the udon's eating into your brain."

"Huh?"

Maou shook his head at his quizzical lunch companion.

"Gah-hah-hah-hah!" Rika burst out laughing. "No, no, I told you, we manufactured parts for shoes. But, oh, I guess maybe you didn't know if you didn't grow up in this country. I'm talking about a little shrine. It's meant to commemorate the god of foxes in the Shinto religion."

"Oh! Oh, yes, of course, of course. Yes. I apologize... Urgh! Devi— Sadao! Why did you not speak up sooner about that?" On cue, Suzuno lashed out at Maou in self-defense, turning red.

"*You're* the one from the religious family. Ain't that kind of a problem, you not knowing that? And you were totally clueless about that *mukaebi* thing, too... Why don't you quit the whole missionary thing and just open up an udon restaurant back home?"

The critique was as accurate as it was scathing. Suzuno visibly shrunk in her seat...

"Ow!"

...and delivered another kick with her wooden sandal-befitted leg. The results almost bought tears to his eyes.

"Hee-hee... Aw, I'm sorry I laughed at you. I sure don't go to Sunday mass or pray before meals or anything, but you'd be surprised. Japanese people have just as much respect and thankfulness toward the bigger things in life as anyone else would. We kinda spread it around in a lot of crazy directions, but it's not like we're the only ones, I suppose."

"Thankfulness?" Suzuno asked.

"Yeah. Though I guess if I was a missionary like your family, I'd have to be a lot less casual toward it all than that, I bet." Rika remained cheerful as Suzuno mulled over her words. "But Jesus said to love thy neighbor and all that, right? If your god told you to kill anyone who didn't listen to what he said, that wouldn't be much of a god at all, I don't think. Instead, all the religions just kind of get along in Japan, and I think that's how it oughta be."

"...!"

Suzuno let out a light gasp at Rika's observations. It went unnoticed.

"Mm? That some kinda argument?"

Maou pointed toward the front door, where a customer was having a loud verbal exchange with an employee.

"Um, sir, I'm afraid that I..."

The employee, a woman young enough that this was probably a part-time job to put her through college, was frantically trying to explain something in words and gestures. The message didn't seem to be getting across.

"Ahhh..."

Which it probably had little chance of. They listened in, but the customer didn't sound Japanese.

The employee, realizing that English was this person's mother tongue, was at her wit's end trying to figure out what to do.

A little help from her coworkers would have been appreciated, but the long line at the register precluded any immediate aid.

Maou stood up.

"Here, I'm gonna help out a sec."

"Whoa, don't you think you should leave 'em alone...?"

Rika stopped him. The customer was on the tall side, about as much as Maou. He was wearing a large, tacky pair of sunglasses, and the voluminous Afro he was sporting gave him a convincingly punk image.

Given his continued shouting, this didn't appear to be a calm exchange of opinion.

"It's fine, Ms. Suzuki."

It was Ashiya who stepped up to reassure Rika. Maou acknowledged both of them with a nod, then walked in between the employee and her customer.

"Um, can I help with something?"

"Huh? Erm..."

The employee, about to break down in tears, all but latched on to Maou's arm. Clearly she was in no position to give a collected account of what happened. Her eyes had that *I don't even know what I don't know* look he saw in a lot of the rookie part-timers who haunted his MgRonald. So he decided to deal with the man instead.

"<Um, hey, man. I think she's having trouble figuring out what you're asking for. What'd you need?>"

"Whoa, Maou can speak English?!"

He could hear Rika's blurted-out surprise from across the restaurant. It gave him a little jolt of glee.

"Uhhh…" The man sized up Maou and the employee for a second, then finally addressed Maou.

"<Yo, anyone got a fork in here?>"

"<A fork?>"

"<Those chopsticks're about as useful to me as drumsticks. There ain't no law saying I can't eat udon with a fork, is there?>"

The man looked at Maou over the rim of his sunglasses as he spoke. Maou raised an eyebrow in response to this attempt at intimidation.

"<I don't think so, but if you don't cut down on the volume pretty soon, I think they might kick you out of here.>" With a grin, Maou turned to the employee to explain the situation.

"Oh! Y-yes, I'll bring one right out!"

She scurried behind the counter, forgetting to take the man's order entirely.

"<Nice. Hey, thanks. You're a pretty cool guy for bein' so young.>"

The man, now notably friendlier, gave Maou a playful jab on the shoulder and joined the line for the self-serve bar.

This puzzled Maou a bit. He understood how the system worked, apparently. So why couldn't he tone down his behavior a bit?

"<No problem.>"

He turned his back to the man, still a bit confused, and returned to his table.

"<Yeah, it was nothing too big in the—> Oh, whoops. Sorry."

There, he found Rika staring at her in befuddled amazement.

"You people are, like, total mysteries. Why are people like you and Emi sticking to part-time work, anyway?"

"Huh?"

"Oh, nothing. But, hey, if we're all done here, let's get going. The store's probably gonna get crowded soon."

"Uh, sure."

Taking another look, Maou realized that Ashiya and Suzuno had finished up their lunch while he was dealing with the other customer. In a restaurant this small, they couldn't tie up their table forever. It was time for him to fulfill the day's original goal. But before they could reach the exit:

"Um, sir...!"

The employee Maou rescued chased them down.

"Hey, um, thank you so much for helping me out! The, uh, my manager wanted you to have this..."

She presented him with a ticket, 1 SML PLAIN printed on it. Maou would've eagerly accepted it any other day, but this time he shook his head.

"It's fine, it's fine. And I know it's easy to get in a panic if someone doesn't speak your language, but he's only human, too. If he doesn't understand you, you gotta do what you can to make him get the picture."

"Y-yeah..."

"So the next time someone who doesn't speak Japanese shows up, just try to figure out what he's trying to say and give him whatever help he needs. He'll come around sooner or later, so..."

"R-right! Um, th-thank you very much! Come back soon!"

The employee bowed deeply at Maou's back as he briskly left the building. Ashiya strode on proudly, as if he was the one behind the whole event, while Suzuno watched on suspiciously. Rika, meanwhile, was still in a state of disbelief.

"So! Leaping to the rescue of any damsel in distress you see, then?"

Maou turned around at Suzuno's snort.

"It's nothing like that, okay? It's just that, if that kept going, it'd ruin the whole atmosphere in that place. Who wants to be uncomfortable while they're trying to eat?"

Rika jumped to Suzuno's defense.

"Then at least accept the free meal ticket, why don'tcha? I'm kinda surprised you turned that down."

"Yeahh, I probably didn't need to do that. But, you know, when I go someplace like that, I always end up feeling for the staff."

"Huh?"

"That girl just now reminded me of Chi when she first started.

And now that I think about it, when I first met her, *she* was getting tripped up with language issues, too."

Maou smiled a wistful smile.

"I really don't want new hires to get in the habit of having their boss give out free food vouchers to smooth everything over. Then you don't really feel like you did anything wrong. You don't learn anything from it, other than there's this escape valve you can tap anytime you want. So I guess I didn't think it'd be good to take it."

"Indeed. I considered it a terrible waste, but if those are your wishes, I see no reason to question them." The sigh emanating from Ashiya's lips indicated just how much of a terrible waste he thought it was.

"All that, and you don't even know any TV brand names. So weird..." Rika crossed her arms in thought.

"Well, I mean, sympathy by itself doesn't help much, does it?" Maou went on. "That's not what *I'd* want, next time I'm in the hot seat. And you mentioned 'love thy neighbor' just now, too. As a fellow fast-food lifer, if both of our joints can grow and attract more customers, maybe this episode'll help that girl become a serious sales demon someday."

"You are making little sense to me. Love thy neighbor, so she can be your enemy someday?"

"Well, let's call it 'frenemies,' okay? The Mag and Manmaru are both pretty huge companies. There's enough space for all of us."

It wasn't entirely clear how serious Maou and Ashiya were being with their conversation, but something about it caused Suzuno to raise her head up.

"Ah. Yes. Rika! I wanted to ask you. If it was not a god, what *would* it be?"

"Huh? If who's not a god?"

"If a god told you to kill anyone who didn't listen to what he said isn't any kind of god, what is it, then?"

Rika needed nearly ten seconds to grasp the intent behind the question.

"Oh! Oh, you mean from earlier? Eesh, I totally forgot... Well, it's pretty obvious, isn't it? It's people. Who else would try to pin their god's name on whatever evil they're doing?"

"Hello? Hey."

Right after the guy with the sunglasses and the Afro left Man-maru Udon, he took out his cell phone and made a call.

Suddenly, he was speaking fluent Japanese.

"Look, I picked English 'cause it was supposed to be the most commonly understood language in this world! Nobody's getting me at all over here! And if you knew I was going to end up here the whole time, why didn't you have me learn the language they actually *use* here?! I'm like a walking embarrassment to myself! I'm sick of it!"

The person on the other end of the line must not have been very apologetic. Behind his sunglasses, his eyes were filled with rage.

"...I don't *care* if it's spoken by a billion or so people! Because right now, I can speak to exactly *no* people! I knew I never shoulda trusted you!"

He stamped his feet and removed his sunglasses so he could have something to whip around the air in his fury.

"Huhh? Yeah, yeah, I'm full. Fine and full of energy. My schedule's kinda full, thanks to a certain *some*one I could name, but whatever. Ugh, this drives me nuts."

His eyes, as he looked up at the bright summer sun in frustration, were purple—a good match for his counterculture fashion choices.

"Right. Sure. Okay, so I got my second job left to do today. I thought I had a good thing goin' yesterday, but it just picked up on this girl from a normal family. Like, why do I even have to *do* all this by myself?"

The man shut off his phone, continuing to mumble to himself as he navigated the crowds of the city.

The only person he had been able to communicate with so far in this world completely failed to notice the single streak of purple in his Afro.

✳

Just ten minutes of walking was all it took for the light beam to change direction.

As she walked down the hill next to the police station that faced the western exit of JR Yoyogi station, Emi felt a faint hope that her target was closer than expected.

Come to think of it, Tokyo Big-Egg Town—where Emi ran into the woman in white before—was situated in Bunkyo ward. It seemed unlikely that her target was wandering across the country with no destination in mind. Maybe she was sticking to the central area of Tokyo after all.

There was no way she could be traveling around Japan with a Yesod fragment just for giggles. If the light's direction changed this dramatically after a few minutes' walk, just a few steps could alter how they were aligned with each other.

In other words, she was close. Real close.

"Up ahead's…Meiji Jingu, I think."

In between the JR Yoyogi and Harajuku stations was the Meiji Jingu shrine, an ancient edifice surrounded by an equally primeval forest. The approach to the shrine followed in parallel with the train tracks, allowing pedestrians to travel between the two stations in about fifteen minutes.

Emi was aware of this because she had visited Meiji Jingu once after hearing about a famous, if totally mythical, "power spot" that existed within.

She came not long after reaching Japan, hoping to find a way to refill her holy force. What she found was a simple well, not a single atom of power streaming out of it—a fact seemingly ignored by all the visitors in search of mystical inspiration.

"Oh, it's not Meiji Jingu?"

But as she reached the bottom of the hill and checked the light again, she found it pointing not at the shrine forest, but down an underpass cutting through the Shuto Expressway.

She followed the light, half curious about where it led, and gradually it switched angles on her again.

"…Oh, no way."

It was a hospital.

Emi found herself hesitating in front of the building. SEIKAI

University / Department of Medicine / Tokyo Hospital was printed in large lettering on the front.

She walked from one end of the building to the other. The light dutifully changed its angle to match, constantly pointing inside.

"What's *that* about?"

Having a reaction this close by was a surprise in itself. Having it be inside a hospital simply added to the confusion.

Putting everything that happened to her together, it seemed plausible enough that the woman in white worked inside.

Angel or demon, everyone had to work to live in Japan. Sariel, the Evil Eye of the Fallen, was now dutifully managing a Sentucky Fried Chicken. Even Gabriel apparently had the cash, somehow, to shop at convenience stores.

Another logical theory was that she was in the hospital, or at least visiting, due to injury or illness.

Emi had at least a general idea of who the woman in white was. If she was right, though, she wouldn't necessarily be in this hospital under *that* name.

She focused a bit, but try as she could, she didn't feel any holy, demonic, or otherwise nonnative energy nearby.

Thus, she began pondering over how to get in. She could pretend to be visiting a patient...but if someone spotted her, it could affect her entire social position in this world. For a Hero, she was being awfully indecisive.

"Um... Is that you, Yusa?"

The sudden voice from behind made Emi's heart skip a beat.

"Wh-wha?! ...Oh."

"Oh, it *is* you! Well, this is quite a coincidence. Are you going inside, Yusa?"

It was no one Emi ever would have expected.

"M-Mrs. Sasaki?!"

It was Riho Sasaki—Chiho's mother.

Why was she here—and leaving the hospital, too?

"Oh, I haven't told anyone yet, either... You work near here, if I recall, yes?"

"Um, yeah, I... Yes."

Emi vaguely nodded, unable to tell the truth, but even she noticed something odd to what Riho said.

"But...uh, what haven't you told anyone? Is something up?"

Riho reacted with a disquieting shake of her head—like she was deeply troubled, or about to cry. It put Emi ill at ease.

"Do you have a spare moment, Yusa? I was wondering if you wouldn't mind stopping in for a moment."

Watching Riho venture back toward the hospital, for some reason made Emi's sense of foreboding amplify itself in another direction.

Passing right by the front desk, Riho gestured Emi to join her by the elevator. She was wearing a visitor's name tag, something Emi only noticed just then.

As they boarded the car, Emi suddenly realized she had forgotten to shut off her cell phone, as was customary in Japanese hospitals. She peered into her bag.

"......"

Inside, the light beam from the bottle was spinning like a disco ball.

The Yesod fragment was on the hospital grounds after all.

"Over here."

Emi's anxious pulse very well could have been racing faster than when she stormed the Devil's Castle on Ente Isla.

There was a "Sasaki" nameplate on the door to the room Riho guided her to.

Inside, the space was divided into four quarters by a set of curtains. Riho walked up to one of them, gestured for Emi to come closer, then slowly lifted a drape.

"...!!"

Emi gasped.

✳

The main Socket City location by Shinjuku station's west exit was just about five minutes' walking from Manmaru Udon as well. It was a huge electronics superstore bordered by the Keio long-distance bus depot.

The eastern exit was once dominated by Electronics Bazaar and its selection of themed storefronts, but they all closed a while ago, with places like Lovelace's and Eggman fighting for mindshare in its place. On the other side of Shinjuku, though, Socket City had a near monopoly.

There were other electronics stores nearby—smaller ones, usually specializing in cameras or other enthusiast goods. But Socket City was the eight-hundred-pound gorilla in the neighborhood.

Maou, of course, swaggered in like he owned the place.

"Hah! This place is fit for a King, man!"

Purchasing a washer and refrigerator, then using their gift points to pick up a lightbulb, did not proffer ownership of the entire store. But there was no doubting that Devil's Castle held a hoard of store points by now—the equivalent of 6,239 yen in cash, by Socket City's reckoning. It'd be only human to want to squeeze as much shopping value out of that as possible.

It was a siren song, the perfect way to guarantee repeat customers. No wonder cashiers in stores worldwide were bothering customers to sign up for their own cards. Woe be to the hapless customer caught in their grasp. Until you wrung them dry, there would always be a little voice inside of you, nagging at you about not using those precious, precious points.

"Hey, Ashiya, you think there's anything in the Devil King's army we could point-ify?"

"Now is no time for such fruitless endeavors, my liege. Focus on the purchase before you."

Ashiya, eyes fixed upon the store fliers in his hands, wasn't interested in playing along. The ad-speak in Socket City and every other outlet's circulars—"We will not be undersold!" and "We honor all our competitors' sales for the same item!" and so on—caught him hook, line, and sinker. The moment he spotted it, he ran all the way over to Shinjuku station's east exit by himself in the heat to snag fliers from the rest of the stores.

"Dang, Ashiya, you sure aren't playing around."

Rika chuckled as she looked on.

"But the prices aren't gonna be that much different from outlet to outlet, will they? You didn't have to go that far…"

"Nah, I think Ashiya has the right idea."

Rika took Ashiya's side, even though Maou didn't see the point of fretting over an extra one or two yen.

"If that's the offer the stores are giving, it's up to us to make 'em live up to their end of the bargain, y'know?"

"…Well, logically speaking, yes. But it just seems kinda greedy to me…"

"See, *this* is what's wrong with people in Tokyo. They actually think that's being greedy."

"Huh?"

Rika crossed her arms, a bit too deliberately to be serious about it, and began to plead her case.

"Shopping is all about bargaining, you know? I want to buy something as cheap as I can get it. The stores want to sell it for as much as they think they can get away with. It's a game you play with them—how much the store is willing to compromise, how much customers can make the store compromise for them. That's what doing business is all about. And to do that, you need to be informed."

"Bargaining, huh…?"

"That, and people in Tokyo think that's being greedy because they think haggling's simply about making the other guy go down on the price."

"Are you from the Kansai region or something, then?"

"Oh, didn't I tell you, Maou?"

She pointed at herself.

"I was born in Kobe."

"What's the nickname MgRonald has over there?"

"I've already had Tokyoites ask me that question a million times…"

It was a thousand times more important to Maou than Rika.

"But I mean… How to put it? Haggling is kind of like negotiation. You're seeing how this relationship is gonna go, moving forward."

"How it's gonna go?"

"Yeah. For example…"

Rika pointed out a pair of customers in the TV section.

"You see that couple in their fifties or so? With the salesguy?"

Maou nodded.

"That salesguy's really good. He's breaking up all the difficult terminology into easier-to-digest chunks for them. You're in the customer-service business, Maou. That kinda thing makes a good impression on people, right?"

"Yeah. You can't do that without some product knowledge and at least a little hospitality."

"But look at him again. Who does it look like he's talking to?"

"Who…?"

From the side, it looked like the presumed husband of the pair was asking all the questions, the salesman rapidly replying to each salvo. But Suzuno had a different perspective.

"It looks like the merchant is accepting questions from the husband and giving his replies to the wife."

"Right! That's because he knows it's the wife who has the final say on whether the purchase is a go or not. How she feels."

"Like, she's got her hands on the purse strings, that kind of thing?"

Maou sneered as Rika shrugged. She shook her head at him.

"Noooo… You men just don't get it sometimes, do you? A TV is something used by the entire family."

"Oh?"

Maou seemed lost. Ashiya, eyes still on his fliers, tried to elaborate:

"She means that a purchase by a single knowledgeable person, and a purchase with the confidence of its entire audience behind it, can seem like two very different things afterward. If the husband understood everything before his wife and made the purchase by himself, both sides would have had a different impression of the transaction. If the woman is convinced it's a good deal as well, the experience is better for everyone involved. The man appears quite ready to break out his wallet right now."

"Well done, Ashiya! There's your househusband eye in action."

"I appreciate the compliment."

His eyes continued to study the circulars in hand as he spoke.

"But I suppose the haggling you mentioned plays into that as well. If the salesman can bring the wife to his side, then offer perhaps some token discount or point bonus, the deal is as good as done. Everyone involved feels like they came out ahead. And if you have an experience like that, what would you do next?"

"What would I do…?" Maou muttered.

"You would…want to shop there again next time, maybe. Point card or not."

Suzuno picked up on it before Maou could. Rika nodded at them, satisfied.

"Exactly! And if the salesguy remembers them the next time they stop by, then everything's perfect."

Maou looked at the couple again, still not convinced. They were already being led to the delivery-service counter, the negotiations largely complete.

"So haggling, in the end, is all about making the store cut a deal for you so you'll come back next time. The point cards just codify that into an official system. That way, even you guys in Tokyo who're too timid to haggle face-to-face can join in on the fun, sort of. You know?"

Rika pointed to the loyalty card Maou still had lovingly clutched in his hand.

"Mmmngh…"

"'Course, it's not like the store's just showering you with random discounts. They're trying to toe the line, turning visitors into repeat customers while losing as little as possible along the way. Haggling is a two-way street like that. You should see some of the old biddies over in Osaka! People think they're, like, the epitome of cheapness, but once one of them takes a liking to a store, they'll drag the entire family over there. Then they'll do it again and again and again. From the store's perspective, they're willing to bet on shaving their profit margins a little if it means a sales jackpot later on. That's why haggling works so well in Kansai—'cause there's a chance of it making everyone happy in the future."

Maou and Suzuno looked at Rika like she was discussing the mating rituals of an alien race.

"I mean, really, it's the perfect way of shopping. It's a way for both sides to handle things like a business transaction while trying to find common ground on a person-to-person basis. Meanwhile, all Tokyoites care about is getting the price on the tag as low as possible. They can't haggle at all. They see the whole thing as *greedy*. But you shouldn't just stand there and be a passive shopper. You have to do business with the salesguys, too. It makes it feel better for everyone."

"That's…one way of thinking about it, I guess."

Maou paused.

"But that reminds me. When I purchased the fridge and washer together, I think they rounded down everything under the thousands digit without me asking. Was that kinda part of their game?"

"That, or maybe you just had good timing. When was this?"

"Just before summer…"

"Yeah, it's possible, then. Spring's a really busy season for moving, so once that wraps up, kitchen appliances start moving a lot slower. If you were buying two pieces at the same time, I bet the salesguy was doin' a little jig inside his head."

"…Would this be an apt period in time to purchase a television?"

Ashiya's question made it difficult to anticipate what kind of answer he wanted.

"Mmm, it should be fine, I s'pose? I know they wanna push up TV sales as much as possible before the switch to full HD broadcasts. And…"

Apropos of nothing, Rika turned toward Suzuno.

"Mm? What?"

"Wellllll…"

Then she gestured Ashiya to come closer, moving away a bit from Suzuno.

"You two stay close, okay?"

"Wh-why…?"

"Think about it. What was her budget again?"

"Seventy thousand, as she so proudly trumpeted to us all a moment ago."

The gears in Ashiya's mind began to turn.

"Oh! Ah, yes! If the two of us could ensnare a single salesperson…"

"Good luck, man!"

Rika slapped Ashiya before he could finish. His old face, ponderous and irresolute as he pored over the circulars, was gone, replaced with a bright, fog-clearing smile. He took Rika's hand in his reverie.

"Thank you very much, Ms. Suzuki. I am so glad you decided to come with us!"

"Hyah!!! Um, uh, I, uh, I, um, you, um, you're welcome."

This sudden outburst from Ashiya made Rika's face burn red as she stared at her entombed hand.

"I will do whatever I can to extract enough money from our 41,239 yen to purchase a cell phone afterward. We are off!"

"O-o-okay!"

Ashiya flashed another warm smile at the squawking Rika and flew back toward Suzuno.

"Suzuno Kamazuki! We must browse the selection together!"

"Wh-where on earth did *that* come from?! What happened?! S-stop pulling me! Let me go, you ogreish brute!"

"…Look at 'em go."

Maou's gaze shifted between Ashiya, manhandling Suzuno all the way to the TV section, and Rika, frozen and red as a stop sign.

"What'd you say to Ashiya?"

"……"

"Hellooooo?"

He waved a hand in front of Rika's face. No response.

Maou thought for a moment. This happened to him before, just recently.

"…Oof!"

He clapped his hands near one of her ears.

"Aigh!!"

Unlike the previous victim, Rika's response as she came to was far from charming.

"Ughh… Did I…?"

"Hey, uh, can I ask you a question?"

"Agh! Wh-what, Maou? Since when were *you* standing there?!"

"...Since a few seconds ago, I guess. Can I ask a question?"

"Wh-wha-what?!"

"I was just wondering..."

"Y-yeah?"

Maou turned around, watching Ashiya alongside a pouting Suzuno as he peppered a nearby salesperson with questions, before returning his eyes to Rika.

"You got a thing for him, or...?"

"*Prggffh!*"

At that instant, with a sound and a blast of air that seemed like it came from a jet-powered humidifier, Rika collapsed into a puddle of goo on the ground.

"Wh-whoa, you okay? I kinda wasn't expecting *that* reaction!"

Flustered, Maou helped Rika back up and dragged her to a bench situated near the stairwell.

"Devil King."

"Hmm?"

"Why do I have to sit here with you on this bench and drink tea with you?"

"Who cares? It's fine."

"I am *quite* unhappy."

"Ooh, that hurts."

Maou and Suzuno were seated on a bench by the Socket City stairwell.

They were drinking from plastic bottles of barley tea they had filled and frozen in their respective refrigerators before leaving. In front of each of them sat a box containing a brand-new TV.

Hearing that Suzuno and Ashiya each wanted to purchase a set made the salesman considerably more amenable than previously.

Ashiya, without bothering to consult with Maou, bought the cheapest set in the store, a 32,800-yen model on inventory closeout. Suzuno's, while the same size as Ashiya's, included a built-in Blu-ray player/recorder.

The salesman, in addition to rounding down everything below

the thousands digit, even gave Ashiya the points that otherwise wouldn't have been included with a closeout purchase.

Thanks to his mistakenly assuming the pair to be family or lovers, the salesman put his nose to the grindstone to placate the clearly perturbed-looking Suzuno. That paid off in the end.

And since he only spent around 30,000 of their 41,239 yen (plus extra for the warranty), now Ashiya was attempting to purchase a cell phone with the difference.

That was the whole reason Rika joined him today in the first place, and thanks to her, the Devil's Castle joined the TV age for much less than otherwise.

If she hadn't been around, they never would've been clued in on the "go shopping together" trick. Suzuno never would have conceived it.

"Listen, though...what do you think of those two?"

"Those two? Alciel and Rika, you mean?"

Maou motioned toward the two in question as they played around with cell phones in a seemingly random order.

Ashiya's attention was focused entirely on the merchandise at hand, but Rika, her mind elsewhere, kept tossing furtive glances at Maou's direction, then averting their eyes whenever he returned the favor.

Was the odd redness to her face due to the outside air filtering its way into the phone department a little, or...?

"Rika is aloft in her own world," Suzuno replied.

"Ah?"

"When the two of them stand together, Alciel's clothing is far too austere. Everyone likes a tall, dark stranger, as they say, but he really must mind his wardrobe if he wishes to be trusted in society, must he not?"

"Trusted in society? That bad, huh?"

"Of course. He is making Rika look overdressed, right next to him like that."

"Okay, but why did Rika Suzuki bother dressing up at all? 'Cause to me, that just seems like her normal look."

"Why...? It was Alciel who suggested this shopping trip, no? I cannot say how they began to mingle with each other, but Rika has no idea Alciel is a demon. Any woman accepting an invitation from a man would do at least something for such an expedition..."

Before she could finish, Suzuno fell silent, realizing something was off with her assessment.

It was Maou who spoke next. "I don't know if this her way of 'haggling' her life, but you think she'd go firing away guns a-blazin' like that?"

"...Hold it, Devil King. I do *not* like this line of thought."

"You know how laid-back she is with people. When we first met, she had no problem verbally nudging me all the time. Even though I was just a friend of a friend, you know? Why would a girl like that accept Ashiya's invite and dress up for it?"

"Rika... She couldn't be..."

Suzuno fell into a state of bewilderment, the plastic bottle falling out of her hand.

It didn't make a sound, mostly frozen and wrapped in a towel to absorb the condensation. Very little of the tea spilled out at all.

"D-Devil King, is *that* what you mean to say? That...that Rika bears...excessive goodwill toward Alciel?"

"I asked her that earlier. She growled at me like a pit bull and—*gehh!*"

In the middle of Maou's sentence, Suzuno punched him squarely on the jaw.

"Jeez, ow! What was *that* for?!"

"What was that for? I could ask you the very same! Have you no common sense? No decency?!"

"Huhh?"

"Small wonder Rika has been stealing looks at us like a frightened puppy! What did you *say* to her?!"

"This is totally gonna bruise, isn't it? ...I didn't say anything! I was just, like, 'Hey, you got a thing for 'im, or'—*gnngh!*"

The force of the second punch was enough to make Maou's own bottle launch out of his hand.

"This! *This* is why you shall forever be Devil King!!"

"S-Suzuno, you're killing me… P-people are watching us!"

"…!"

Suzuno was all but lifting Maou off the floor by the collar before she finally realized what she was doing.

"I…I just thought we should get everyone on the same page before anything else…"

"And *then* what?!"

Suzuno took a deep breath to collect herself, then plopped back down on the bench, sighing ruefully.

"Then…I dunno, I didn't have any huge plans or anything!"

The flummoxed response made her roll her eyes at him.

She spoke, softly but sharply, so that only Maou could hear.

"This is different from Chiho. Are you trying to force us into rewriting Rika's memory?"

"Hehh?"

Maou yelped helplessly, unable to grasp what Suzuno meant. Suzuno, expecting this, continued hissing at him.

"Chiho knows about both us *and* you. She knew all of it, and yet still she is attracted to you. She is aware, in her own way, that there is every chance all of you will be annihilated sooner or later. That is *not* the case with Rika."

"……"

Having someone else say it to him made Maou admit it was a bit awkward. Not wishing to be murdered by her Light of Iron at the moment, however, he remained silent.

"Falling in love with Alciel guarantees nothing but a bleak, unhappy future for her. If you wish her not to become involved, I want neither of you to see her from this day forward."

"Hey, how do you know it's gonna be *that* bleak for her…? And why are you so sure Chi's gonna have to go to my funeral sometime soon? Who says that's gonna happen?"

"That's…"

Suzuno was about to fire back, but then recalled the conversation she had with Emi the evening they returned from Choshi. That, and

Alas Ramus. She chewed on her words for a moment. "Well. From an impartial point of view, I suppose there is at least a paramecium dropping's chance of your survival."

"That low, huh?"

"But neither Alciel nor Rika would have even that luxury granted to them! Even if you, Alciel, and Lucifer all decided to live out your mortal lives in Japan, it could never happen."

"Wh-why not? I mean, not that I necessarily want to do that, but..."

"How long have you been in human form? Who on this planet could guarantee that all of you will see out your golden years if you stay on Earth?"

"I..."

"Even if your strength is that of an average human—even if you require human medical treatment for your injuries—you are a demon all the same, once you gather enough demonic force. And once you do, even if you have a change of heart and elect to side with the humans, unhappiness will be sure to greet whoever decides to become close to you. As long as your body remains young, that is all but inevitable."

"Huh. Kinda surprised, though—you think we're gonna pal up with humans that much?"

"Oh, *now* you say that?" Suzuno huffed, the question clearly settled to her. "The truth can never be born from bias. If I were to comprehensively evaluate your personal qualities as I've directly interacted with them in this world, 'palling up' is a fair enough inference to make—Ah!"

She stopped midway, glaring at him as if he had killed her family.

"But do *not* take that to mean I have a positive impression of *any* of you! That is strictly an objective analysis!"

"A-all right, all right. Stop standing so close to me. I got it." Maou attempted a smile to stave off the Church cleric who just physically assaulted him in a public place.

Suzuno, eyes still dead upon him, looked over at Ashiya and Rika, who were still near the display of phones. "Even if Rika continued with this affair, the day will come when she has to grieve over her lost love or see him off as he returns to another world. Do you think myself or Emilia will allow that?"

"……" Fixing his shirt collar, Maou picked up his bottle and tried to return Suzuno's glare.

"You know what I am trying to tell you. If possible, I want you and Alciel to cut off ties with Rika today. That would keep the wounds to her psyche at a bare—"

"All right, so why haven't you erased Chi's memories yet?"

"—minimum… What?"

"The only difference between her and Rika Suzuki is that one knows the truth about me and one doesn't. Shouldn't you just erase Chi's memories right now? Isn't she gonna be unhappy, too, otherwise?"

Suzuno's eyes widened, like a deer on the highway.

"I mean, what kinda line are you drawing between Chi and Rika anyway? If you're respecting Chi's wishes as a friend or whatever, then why aren't Rika's wishes worth considering?"

"Th-that is not my intention! I simply mean that—"

"That what?"

"……"

The one-two punch from Maou cowed Suzuno into silence.

"Or how 'bout I give you this One Weird Tip that'll keep Rika from having some huge love tragedy? Church clerics *hate* it!"

Now Maou was in his element. The confidence was written across his face.

"Here it is: We just explain to Rika that we're demons from another world, in a way that she can believe. If that freaks her out enough that she stays away from us, that's perfect for you guys, right? And if Rika still wants to hang out around Ashiya, she'll at least be informed and prepared for whatever happens. She won't be the only one being all sad that way."

"Are you insane?! If you do that—"

"If I do that, what?"

"Then…then you will get Rika involved in all of this."

Suzuno was quickly losing steam.

"Well, wouldn't it be nice if our enemy cared about that?"

Maou didn't need to emphasize the *our* to get his point across.

"'Cause Olba didn't hesitate for a minute to get Chi involved in our little spat. Did you think Ciriatto and all those dudes he brought along cared about all those helpless Japanese people back in town?"

Maou's voice was quiet, but there was a sharp, supreme confidence to it.

"From the moment Emi and I came down here to Tokyo—the central core of human society in Japan—it didn't *matter* how much we cared about getting humans involved in this. So what's it matter, trying to hide our true identities when push comes to shove? Or, what, does Rika strike you as the type of girl who'd let a little something like demonic wars stop her?"

"You... Enough! Enough of your faulty logic! Human relationships aren't as simple as that!"

"Yeah? Well, how 'bout human-demon relationships? Wouldn't those be even *less* simple? 'Cause Chi seems like she's getting along okay with me, isn't she? Besides, Rika's been 'involved' ever since Emi decided to make friends with her. The only difference is that she's not in clear and present danger yet."

"......"

"I dunno how this is gonna turn out, and I'm not saying we should all try to expand our friend base or anything. But I'm already interacting with all kinds of people in my job. And..."

Slowly, Maou stood up, swaying back and forth to stretch out his back.

"I know I don't need to tell you this, but it's boring, living alone. You'll wanna have some friends sooner or later."

Suzuno, the loser of the debate, averted her eyes and put her hands to her knees, shoulders shivering.

She had no logical argument to retaliate with, but it was clear she was in agony, unable to accept it on an emotional level.

Seeing this out the corner of his eye, Maou let out a deep breath from his nose, the day's heavy lifting done.

"You gotta stop thinking in black and white so much. Emi never thinks *that* much about whatever she does. It's worked fine for her so far."

He put a hand on Suzuno's head, watching the hairpin quivering on top of it.

"D-don't touch me!"

The edges of her eyes reddened a bit as she brushed his hand away.

"You and Emilia... Both of you just smash headlong into everything you encounter! What is so wrong about at least *one* of us carefully considering things first?!"

"Nothing. But if your thoughts keep dwelling on bad outcomes or keeping the status quo, that doesn't accomplish anything. As long as we're dealing with other people in this world, it'd be a lot more fun to focus on the *good* stuff that comes out of it. Plus, I'm a King. I have a duty to live that way for my followers."

"King..."

Suzuno tossed the word around in her mind.

"But..."

"Mmm?"

"If you keep such a rosy view of the world, just doing whatever you think is right even when it fails...what then?"

"Simple."

Suzuno intended the question to bite at Maou, pulling the rug out from under him. But Maou had a ready answer.

"Someone else shows up who thinks he can bring everyone in a better direction. He knocks me out. Then he takes the lead."

"Hey, um, Ashiya?"

"Yes?"

"Do Maou and Suzuno get along much?"

"Hmm?"

Rika pointed toward a bench next to the stairwell. Maou and Suzuno were there, yelling and scuffling with each other. From a certain angle, one could conclude they were just having a playful shove or two. Either way, Ashiya doubted they were having an exchange of any major note.

"Normally, it should not be that way at all."

"It shouldn't…? Huh?"

"But…"

Ashiya's face was twisted in pain. His words were the polar opposite.

"Lately, that has not been the case."

"…Oh. Kinda complicated?"

"Yes. Very complicated indeed. I think…"

Ashiya, relaxing his tormented expression a bit, turned his eyes to Rika.

That alone was enough to press the FAST-FORWARD button on Rika's heart.

"The time may come when I will explain why to you, too."

His eyes, the apex of sincerity, were like arrows stunning Rika into silence.

"…Mmm."

All she could do was nod.

Ashiya had some kind of dark shadow, one Rika couldn't begin to fathom. She felt that from the first time they met.

Something about his relationship with Maou indicated they were more than simply boss and subordinate. And even though they acted excessively hostile around Emi, it kind of seemed like they didn't hate her *that* much.

Plus, how did these people run a company if they were so out of touch with things like how to work a TV set? It was all so strange.

She put it aside at first—they were just passing acquaintances back then—but maybe "the Maou Group," the company he told Rika about, was actually a feint to hide some kind of bigger past.

Or maybe it was just her imagination. This was only her third encounter with Ashiya. They were only slightly familiar with each other. If someone asked whether they were friends, she couldn't honestly say they were at that point. She was in no position to pry into his past.

That, and Ashiya was yet again being the perfect picture of politeness.

Each of the men of Rika's age she'd interacted with up to this point would drop the effort within a day's time and act like he'd known her for years. If they made it to a third date, the guy usually took that as a cue that it was okay to unrepentantly fart in her presence. But the wall between Ashiya and her showed no signs of even cracking, much less crumbling down.

I'd love to break it down.

I want to know more about Ashiya, beyond the wall.

That sort of natural desire was starting to sprout within Rika.

Maou and Suzuno, with all the hate supposedly between them, seemed perfectly comfortable with each other. No restraint whatsoever.

It wasn't exactly the ideal relationship, no. But, still, Rika wanted to know more. More about what Ashiya was thinking as he went through his daily routine.

Suddenly, it came to her.

She gave an extra little clench to the bag in her hand, still holding the simmered fish he had gifted her.

"Say, Ashiya?"

I.

"How 'bout we just pick up some spec sheets and think it over for now? It's not like we gotta buy you a cell phone today, right?"

"That is true enough, yes…"

Have fallen.

"I sure don't get a commission if you buy a Dokodemo phone, so don't worry about humoring me there. A little time to talk it over with Maou wouldn't hurt, either, I don't think. But if anything jumps out at you after that…"

In love with this weirdo.

"…lemme know and I'll help you shop some more, okay?"

Ninety percent of that invite was rational. The rest was ulterior:

Ashiya, on cloud nine after the deal he earned on the TV, was having trouble making rational buying decisions at this point.

Rika hadn't checked on what kind of phone plan Maou used. If they could have Ashiya join on his contract, or switch over to some kind of friends-and-family deal, he could get the functions he wanted for a cheaper price. She truly felt she didn't have the info she needed. That much was true.

The other 10 percent was telling her that, as long as she framed it like this, she could easily get another chance to see Ashiya. Thus, the ulterior motive.

She had trouble expressing why explaining her outing with Ashiya to Emi over the phone—to anyone, really—made her so tense. But now that she knew where her heart was, it made perfect sense.

"...Would that be all right with you, Rika?"

It was no wonder that establishing a "next time" made her so happy.

"Oh, totally! They call me the Queen of Connectivity around the office, y'know. You wanna find the best cell phone for your needs, you just come to me! I ain't gonna steer you wrong!"

"I look forward to it."

She hardly knew him, but seeing him smile made her so, so happy. *Ahhhh, this isn't like me at all.*

"Allow me to collect a few more of these pamphlets for now, then. I will need to check Maou's work schedule to be sure, but I should be able to contact you again before long."

"Sure. I've got work, of course, so we can talk about it then. So how 'bout we get those two over there to stop bickering and call it a—"

It was as she was speaking that it happened.

"Yeeeaaaggghhhh!!"

A scream rang out from the floor above them. Ashiya and Rika, Maou and Suzuno—they froze.

The rest of the customers looked similarly confused, looking around to figure out where the scream came from.

"Hey, what was that?"

"Let's go look."

An employee and his supervisor ran up the stairs.

Maou watched them go past his bench, but, suddenly realizing something, he headed toward Ashiya and stated his thoughts. By the looks of it, Ashiya was thinking along similar lines.

"Could you wait here just a moment, Ms. Suzuki?"

"Huh?"

"Hey, did you notice that, Suzuno?"

Maou looked deadly serious as he spoke. Suzuno reluctantly nodded.

"…You watch Rika for me. Ashiya and I will be right back."

Not bothering to hear Suzuno's response, he made a bull rush upstairs, Ashiya following behind.

"Hey! Hey, uh, guys, shouldn't we leave that to someone else?"

Rika, sensing at least a smidgen of the tension in the air, had no one left to address as Suzuno looked up the stairwell warily.

The second floor was where Ashiya and Suzuno had made their TV purchase.

It couldn't have been more perfectly normal back then, but in tandem with the scream, the air now seemed infected by a nebulous miasma.

"…You had best wait outside, Rika. I have a bad feeling about this."

"Um? Uh, okay, but what about them…?"

"They will be fine. They have survived quite a lot, despite all indications."

"Wh-what do you mean…? Oh! Wait a sec, Suzuno, he forgot his TV!"

After a moment, Rika finally succeeded in having Suzuno give her the pair of TV boxes and help her jog for the exit.

Outside, Shinjuku was the same as usual. The scream didn't make it beyond Socket City's walls, the passersby betraying no sign of being disturbed by anything.

Maou and Ashiya, meanwhile, realized something was wrong the moment they made it upstairs.

All the TVs lined up on the shelves, the same ones they so intently studied a few moments ago, were shattered down to the last screen.

The floor was littered with pieces of LCD panel. The customers and staff were stuck dumb, unable to parse the events around them.

The supervisor who climbed the stairs ahead of Maou grabbed a nearby employee—by coincidence, the same one who waited on Ashiya and Suzuno.

"Wh-what happened?!"

"Um, uh, the screens... The floor-model screens all flashed white at the same time..."

"All of them?!"

"Yeah, it was like a camera flash or something. I shielded my eyes for a moment, and then..."

Another employee ran up to them to finish the sentence.

"...the next thing we knew, they were all in pieces."

"Th-that's absolutely crazy! That's... All right, we better get everyone outta here, now! Someone call the cops and the fire department..."

The supervisor, despite his difficulties assessing the situation, still managed to consider customer safety first. *Must be a talented boss*, Maou mused.

It wasn't long before the staff rounded up Maou and Ashiya as well, escorting them downstairs. Taking a final, concerned glance at the TV section, Maou descended the staircase and exited the store.

"Well? What was it?!"

"Are you okay, Ashiya?!"

Suzuno pounced on Maou, as if he had caused the whole thing. Rika was more preoccupied with Ashiya. It wasn't exactly the warmest of welcomes for Maou, but he righted himself toward Ashiya.

"Hey, Ashiya, you should take Rika home just in case."

"Huhhh?!"

"Yes. By my very life, she will be safe."

Rika let out a crazed whimper. Ashiya merely accepted his orders.

"Um... Allow me to see you home, Ms. Sasaki. You mentioned you lived in Takadanobaba, yes?"

"Ummmmm, I, w-wait, I think this is a little fast, I haven't prepared and my room's all messy and— Hey!"

Watching Ashiya head for the station, the hand of the suddenly panic-stricken Rika in his own, Maou gestured toward Suzuno.

"I'll explain this on the way home. We better regroup with Urushihara for now. You get Emi over there, too. Ooh, and I better call Chi and warn her to stay away. It's gonna be pretty rough around my apartment for a bit again."

"Let me confirm one thing first." Suzuno's voice was far more acerbic than before. "That was demonic force, yes? Barbariccian in nature?"

"Dunno. But...and I know this ain't gonna matter to you...this ain't us."

The miasma-like air on the second floor was unmistakably demonic energy.

Nothing of Maou's or Ashiya's doing, of course. And Maou had no idea why the mere presence of demonic force would be enough to destroy several dozen TVs.

The only thing certain: This was no natural occurrence.

"I *know* that."

Suzuno pouted as she accelerated her walking pace. She and Maou were carrying their TVs while walking as quickly as they could, causing beads of sweat to appear on each of their foreheads.

"You and I were engaged in that pointless argument. I don't need further pointless excuses to see it wasn't you. For a king, you act remarkably timid."

"Eating dinner with an assassin sent by your sworn enemy would put anybody on edge, most nights."

The breezy smile was back on Maou's face.

"...Say what you will. We must hurry."

Suzuno, no longer possessing the mental capacity to deal with it, turned her face away and walked on ahead.

By the time they half-ran back to Villa Rosa Sasazuka, Emi and Urushihara were there—the former looking even more peeved than usual, the latter far more serious.

"The Devil King was with you the whole time, Bell?"

"Y-yes...as was Alciel, until a moment ago."

Emi looked relieved to hear that for a moment, but quickly scowled back at Maou.

"Where's Alciel? What happened to you?"

Something wasn't right with Emi. Even Maou could tell.

Her eyes were quivering with anxiety, something he'd never seen before.

Even in the past, when the two of them were slashing away at each other, her eyes constantly burned with a strong, powerful will. Now, they were filled with a dull, unguided glow. No one else in the room had seen that before.

"Part of me wishes this was your fault...but part of me's glad that it's not. I want to be sure on this. You were together with Bell *all* day today? You didn't go out again after visiting the real estate office yesterday? Do I have that right?"

Maou and Suzuno nodded in unison.

"Chiho's been poisoned by a concentrated dose of demonic force. She's unconscious in the hospital right now. Her mom told me she was already acting weird last night."

THE DEVIL AND THE HERO DECIDE TO FOCUS ON MORE IMPORTANT MATTERS

To Maou and Ashiya, who'd been on everything from a Ferris wheel to an ambulance at this point, there was one method of transportation they had yet to try out.

The humble taxi.

A very convenient way of navigating the city, getting you where you wanted to go with pinpoint accuracy (assuming the driver cared enough), its convenience came at a cost. It was the most expensive ride Maou had ever been on.

The base cost alone of catching a taxi within the city center was equivalent to boarding the Keio Line in Shinjuku, taking forty miles or so to the last stop at Mount Takao, then doubling back and going almost all the way back down the line before getting off at Kami-kitazawa.

Besides, Maou had never been in a position where a taxi was a necessary choice. He and his demon cohorts were the kind of Tokyoites willing to walk anywhere within three station stops of their current location, if it meant saving on train fare.

And yet, when Ashiya arrived back home, Maou and crew wasted no time calling for two taxis to their apartment—the Devil King's army in one, the Hero and her servant in the other—and heading straight for Yoyogi.

The scene inside was grim. No one said a word.

Maou, in the front passenger seat, wistfully watched the cab ahead with Emi in it, grabbing the strap above the window with undue force.

Ashiya looked equally pensive. Even Urushihara, ever ready to ruin the atmosphere with one inappropriate quip or another, simply stared out his window.

Before the meter had much chance to tick above the base rate, the two taxis entered the roundabout in front of the Tokyo Hospital, run by the Seikai University Department of Medicine.

Once they stopped, Maou asked Ashiya to handle the fare and flew out of the cab without so much as a "thanks" to the driver.

Emi was already out of her own taxi, Suzuno apparently volunteering to pay.

"This way." Emi motioned toward Maou, then headed on toward the hospital's front desk. "We're here to visit Ms. Sasaki in Room 305…"

"Certainly. If you could just fill out these cards and take them to reception on the third floor…"

The time it took to jot down everything the visitor cards demanded from them seemed a colossal waste.

"I know you want to, but we can't run inside the hospital. Just calm down. Her life isn't in danger right now."

"…Yeah."

Maou took a deep breath to ready himself, face still knotted with concern. Emi, watching on, picked up a visitor card for him.

"Don't lose this. They won't let you see her if you don't give it to 'em."

"Jeez, I'm not a child. Just take us up there."

"Right. This way."

For now at least, Emi didn't bother taking the bait as she took the lead and briskly set off.

Riding the large elevator to the third floor, they each presented their visitor cards to the nurse station.

"All right. You can see her now. It's a shared room, though, so try to be quiet if you could, please."

The staffer, clad in white, pointed out the door to them.

Emi and Maou nodded their thanks to her and headed for Room 305. The door was already ajar.

Inside were four beds, separated by privacy curtains. The plethora of strange and ominous machines installed near one made Maou's blood freeze. Emi picked up on it at once.

"Not that one. This one."

She grabbed his sleeve and pointed out the much less cluttered bed in front of them, a nameplate reading SASAKI poised on the edge of the curtain railing.

"...Sorry to bother you again. It's Yusa."

Emi's reserved voice was enough to summon another familiar one from inside.

"Sure, come on in."

"Thanks."

It was Riho, Chiho's mother, seated in a chair next to the bed. Maou tried to greet her, but something else caught his eye first.

"......"

In the hospital bed, Chiho was asleep. She looked healthy enough, breathing on her own and all. But the fact she was sleeping in a hospital bed at all made Maou lose his voice.

Riho, noticing him, stood up and bowed lightly.

"Oh, hello, Maou! How nice of you to stop by."

Her smile was warm and unpretentious, but it failed to hide a tint of fatigue around the edges.

Maou finally managed to gurgle up a question.

"What...what happened to Chi, ma'am?"

Riho bent her neck downward, troubled.

"Well, if only we knew..."

Her tired smile warped with anxiety.

"She was sleeping on the sofa when I came home around din-nertime last night. I told her to get some rice cooking for me, but I thought she was just having a nap or something instead..."

Riho tried her best to retain her serenity. It wasn't working.

"But... It was the strangest thing. She just wouldn't wake up. I called for her, I shook her… Nothing. It was so weird. I tried slapping her, even though I knew she'd be angry at me…but she didn't respond to that, either."

Realizing this was no ordinary nap, she had immediately called for an ambulance. They had brought her here, to Seikai University Hospital.

Neither the first responders nor the doctor who admitted her could diagnose why Chiho was in such a deep sleep.

Her breathing and brain waves were normal and she had no external injuries, so the hospital decided her life was not in danger and admitted her for observation. That, as Riho put it, was the story.

"And, you know, there wasn't a gas leak or anything. She didn't hit her head. There's just no telling what happened to her…"

Riho turned her eyes toward Chiho, clothed in flower-patterned pink pajamas as she lay there. Emi and Maou found their gazes similarly fixed.

The girl seemed perfectly tranquil. No suffering at all.

But if Emi was so sure this was demonic force poisoning, something grave must have happened.

Suzuno entered, dragging Ashiya and Urushihara behind her.

"Chiho."

"Ms. Sasaki!"

"Dude, you're too loud, Ashiya."

"Oh! I'm so glad to see all of you. I'm sorry it had to be in these circumstances… Um, you're Suzuno Kamazuki and Hanzou Urushihara?"

Riho bowed deeply to these unfamiliar faces.

"I hate to bring this up now, but I do appreciate you watching out for Chiho over in Choshi. She didn't bother you too much, did she?"

Maou stepped up to respond. "Oh, absolutely not. We—Chi's always been a huge help to us. Without Chi…and you…we probably couldn't have the life we have right now."

"Well, make sure you tell her that first thing once she wakes up. I don't think there's much that makes her happier than a compliment from you."

"......"

Riho's casual observation robbed Maou of words all over again.

"So...there's no telling what this is or how long it'll last, so I haven't gotten around to contacting her friends or school yet... Honestly, I'm not sure what to do."

In Riho's hand was Chiho's cell phone, a familiar sight to Maou.

Riho was, by nature, a cheerful woman. That must have been why she tried to hide it. But the fear and anxiety of seeing her daughter stricken by some mysterious...event, or whatever it was, was clear as day, all over her.

But there was no way Maou, or Ashiya or Emi or Suzuno, and especially Urushihara, could find any words to cheer her up.

"Chiho..."

Suzuno's voice was shaky as she took a step forward, grasping the right hand that stuck out from under Chiho's blanket.

"......"

Emi looked on sternly.

"Oh! Actually, Maou..." Chiho's mother began.

"Yes?"

Cheerfully, if a little shakily, Riho placed both her hands on Maou's shoulders.

"Was that...you, perhaps?"

"That...? What's that?"

"Oh, don't be silly! You know I'm not angry or anything. Although I will admit that from a woman's perspective, I'm not sure it suited Chiho very well."

What was she talking about? Riho pointed to Chiho's left hand, opposite to the one Suzuno held.

Not even that was enough to make Maou understand. He looked doubtfully toward Riho.

"You're sure it wasn't you? I wouldn't think she'd go around in public wearing that if you didn't give it to her, but..."

Riho went around the bed and picked up Chiho's hand.

What she revealed made everyone except Emi gasp.

On her left index finger was a ring. If it was any normal ring, one could explain it away as a teenage girl's experiment with accessorizing.

But the stone in that ring sparkled as it reflected the sunlight from outside, transfixing everyone who looked at it.

At that moment, Maou finally realized why Emi knew where Chiho was first.

They had exchanged a few words before she traveled to Choshi, but it seemed hard to believe Riho would contact Emi before even Chiho's school.

Emi was after that ring. And it just happened to bring her here.

There, inside the Seikai University Hospital southwest of Muddraker's in Yoyogi, was the polished Yesod fragment Emi had been guided to.

✳

Each floor of the hospital had a public space, giving visitors a place to rest and the more ambulatory patients a chance to take in some TV.

Urushihara was the one staring glassily at the TV. Maou, Ashiya, and Emi, meanwhile, sat silently in chairs, their faces tormented.

Suzuno, by herself, was using Emi's Relax-a-Bear notebook, and a pen with Relax-a-Bear's friend Yellow Bird perched on top of it, to jot out a long set of what looked like mathematical equations.

To the uninformed observer, a quick peek at her writing would have produced more questions than answers. It would have looked like nothing but a bizarre, seemingly random string of patterns.

She was writing in Holy Vezian, one of the common languages shared across Ente Isla's Western Island.

Holy Vezian saw use chiefly on the continent's western side, where the Church's influence was particularly pervasive. On the eastern side, nearer to the Central Continent, there was a dialect known as Common Vezian. The common tongue saw more widespread use as a spoken language, thanks to the influence it had on Ente Isla's universally taught language of Centurient, but Holy Vezian was the working language of higher education across the island.

This was the language that saw the most use in specialized pursuits, from politics and government to law, medicine, and the arts. If you wanted to participate in any of these fields, a working knowledge of Holy Vezian was a must.

The Western Island was the only one of Ente Isla's major landmasses that the Devil King had failed to conquer. Maou, Ashiya, and Urushihara could understand Common Vezian to some extent, but—from the written language onward—they were wholly unversed in the Holy variant.

Maou tried asking Emi what she was scribbling away at when Suzuno began, but Emi shrugged it off, telling him to "shut up and wait."

Over an hour passed after they'd left Chiho's hospital bed. It was still bright out, but darkness would no doubt be spreading across the horizon soon.

In no part thanks to that, Maou and the gang were the only ones left in the public space.

Right when the TV switched from a quick news update to a series of ad spots for the day's wacky variety programming:

"I have it!" Suzuno finally lifted her head above the notebook.

"You have what? What have you even been doing this whole time?"

"This is the first time I've had to write out all of the formulas from scratch since...my time at the seminary, if I recall. I've found it, Emilia."

"And?"

Suzuno beamed.

"Chiho's body is the perfect picture of health. She is young, and strong. As soon as tomorrow—no later than two or three days—her body will neutralize the demonic force, and she will awaken."

"S-seriously?!"

Suzuno's appraisal made Maou jump out of his seat with a clatter. Ashiya looked dubiously at her.

"How...how are you so sure of that?"

"It would perhaps be easier to demonstrate with an experiment. Give me your hand, Alciel."

"What?"

He extended his arm, eyebrows still arched downward, and obediently clasped hands with Suzuno. Then:

"*Nrrhh!!*"

With a groan, Ashiya's entire body glowed dimly for a moment. The next instant, his hair stood on end, as if he had just stuck a fork in a power outlet.

"*Gnh...nh...* Wha-what are you *doing*?!"

Ashiya glared at Suzuno with unfocused eyes, having trouble articulating his complaint at first.

"That hard on a demon, is it? That was the same level of force as the sonar I probed Chiho's body with."

"...Sonar?"

Maou's eyes came to attention. He hadn't heard that word in a while.

Come to think of it, Suzuno's compassionate caress of Chiho's hand seemed a little too forced to be sincere. She must have been sonar-ing up and down her body then.

"Before one can undertake full training in the holy arts, they use this method to measure your body's core receptiveness to magic. This can greatly affect how one's holy magic affects their body, as you know."

"Y-yeah..."

"A form of holy sonar is run across the body, containing a spell meant to examine its contents. Gauging the reactions one receives from each section of the body allows you to gain a general idea of their receptiveness. The human body can react in a variety of complex ways, so normally you would use specialized instruments for this procedure, but a caster can use their own senses if an approximate calculation will suffice."

Suzuno pointed out the ten or so pages of Emi's notebook she had filled with her mysterious scrawl.

"Of course, even an approximate calculation can take quite a bit of time if you do it by hand."

Maou and the hair-on-end Ashiya pouted ruefully at her. Urushihara was still focused on the TV.

"Look, I don't need the deep-cuts version, all right? Cut to the chase!"

"Before that, I need to ask. Emilia, why did you diagnose Chiho's condition as magic poisoning?"

"I followed this light into the hospital."

Emi extracted the bottle with the Yesod fragment from her bag. It made Maou's eyebrows arch up a bit.

"…That's the piece Camio had, huh? You didn't give it to Alas Ramus?"

"If I fuse it with her, I can't pluck it back out later, you know? I kept it because I thought we'd have to look for the other fragments, sooner or later. I can't go brandishing my holy sword around in public to search for them."

"Oh… Right."

Emi explained her motives—the woman in white at Tokyo Big-Egg Town, the way she healed Alas Ramus, and the Yesod fragment she tried to track her down with.

"I busted it out near the Tokyu Hand in Shinjuku, but I wasn't expecting to find it after less than thirty minutes of walking. And who could've known Chiho, of all people, had it…"

The story of Chiho in a coma at the hospital was shocking enough. But when Emi came to see her, she could feel, clear as day, the residual signs of demonic force.

That, combined with the ring on Chiho's finger, made it impossible for Emi to figure it out by herself—so off she went to Devil's Castle for assistance.

"So why did you not call myself or the Devil King?" Suzuno inquired.

She had a good point. Emi knew perfectly well that Maou, Ashiya, and Suzuno were somewhere in Shinjuku at that point in time. But the reply came from Urushihara.

"'Cause I called her. I needed to talk to her about somethin'…but it kinda doesn't matter now. I wanna hear Bell's full diagnosis first."

His eyes never left the TV screen.

"…So, that's the long and short of it. I saw all kinds of people afflicted by demonic force in Ente Isla, and Chiho reminded me of all of them. That, and there's no way I should detect demonic power from Chiho, of all people. So I figured she was poisoned right off, but..."

Suzuno nodded in agreement.

"Emilia's intuition is half correct, half mistaken."

"How so?"

"Chiho, indeed, suffers from demonic poisoning. But not from an external source. The demonic power was generated from within, due to a dangerous energy imbalance in her body."

"?!"

Maou and Ashiya joined Emi in a clear gasp of shock, striking the point home. Even Urushihara looked back toward Suzuno sharply.

"Generated from within Chiho's body?"

"One might say that Chiho's own spiritual energy transformed into demonic force."

"Uhhh, wait. Hang on a sec."

Maou raised a hand in the air.

"Is that kind of thing even possible?!"

"Assuming my calculations are correct, yes. That, and the equations themselves, handed down from generations of Church doctrine."

"Well, do it over again," Maou demanded.

Suzuno pouted, indignant.

"Don't be ridiculous. I could not believe it myself at first, so I double-checked every calculation before reaching my conclusion."

"But...demonic power from *within*? Chi's a human being. A Japanese girl. She's from Earth!"

"I understand what you are trying to say, but have you already forgotten your past? You regained your Devil King form on more than one occasion here in Japan by absorbing demonic energy from the hearts of mankind."

"I... Well, yeah, but..."

"Regardless. After estimating the remaining demonic force within Chiho's body with my sonar, it is clear that this is a case of poisoning, though not one serious enough to threaten her life. She fell into a coma due to her body consuming its strength in the act of trying to push it back and neutralize it, but the holy force I infused within my sonar should help catalyze the process. Once that is complete, she will wake up naturally."

"So if all the pieces are put together…you're saying that you almost vaporized my person just now?"

Suzuno let the irate jab from Ashiya slide with a smile.

If she was telling the truth, no one had any reason to worry about Chiho's safety. But discovering the cause only led to a completely different problem rearing its ugly head:

Chiho, a mere human, was generating demonic force within herself, and they had no idea what was inducing this. Furthermore, in her comatose state, she was wearing a ring festooned with a Yesod fragment.

Emi racked her brain for some sort of hint.

"This may not lead to anything…but I think Chiho's ring is the same kind as the one that woman in white had on."

"You *think*?"

"Well, I was kind of in a panic, all right? I don't really remember what kind of ring it was. But I think it looked like that."

"Yeah, great. Really useful, Emi. So why's that ring on her finger?"

"Maybe…that woman in white put it on her, for some reason…"

"Oh, come on! Let's worry about where it came from later, okay? The thing we *really* need to be thinking over right now is…"

"The external cause of Chiho Sasaki's body generating that force, right?"

"…Urushihara?"

Everyone focused on the man, whose gaze was still fixated upon the TV.

"Demonic force in her body is weird, dude. Real weird. But judging by how you guys keep on transforming, it's totally likely that humans in this world…you know, just *do* that, right? But either way, someone or something acted upon Chiho to make her do that."

"Could you at least stop watching TV and *face* us?"

Emi was clearly irritated. Urushihara paid it no mind, currently enthralled in a local-interest news story about a regional cook-off in one rural burg or another. "I told you that I called Yusa, didn't I? Yusa, the girl who never saw me as anything besides a breathing vending machine and line wrangler. Why do you think she bothered answering my call?"

Emi scowled.

"Because you said that Gabriel paid a visit to Villa Rosa Sasazuka."

"Gabriel did?!"

The other three in the room were instantaneously stupefied.

"That huge, slimy freak better not have laid a finger on her..." Maou growled.

"Yeah, I wish the story was that simple. He came in on other business," Urushihara replied. "Apparently he's been put on desk duty after screwing up the Yesod-fragment hunt one too many times. Now they're looking for some relic from the Demon Overlord Satan or whoever."

Emi rolled her eyes.

"Desk duty? You think this is some kind of cop drama?"

"A 'relic from the Demon Overlord'...?"

"You know that, Maou?"

"Hope it's worth money. I could use some of that...though the inheritance tax would be a deal breaker. ...Yeah, I think it rings a bell, but I don't see why folks up in heaven would get in a lather searching for it."

"Whoa. Glad to see we're both on the same level, Maou."

"Huh?"

"Nothing. Anyway, I guess Gabriel's searching for that...whatever it is, but there's a chance they've sent another angel down in his place. And if they have, I know who it'll be."

"Yo, Suzuno. If you have even a shred of conscience left as a cleric, go back to Ente Isla and take down the Church as the idol-worshipping fraud it is," Maou grumbled.

"...I have no defense."

Suzuno hung her head down low. Meanwhile, Ashiya crossed his arms.

"My, my, my. Between this lazy shut-in and that girl chaser... Is there anyone at all half decent up there?"

"Dude, don't lump me in with them, Ashiya. I left 'cause I hated it, remember?"

"'Left'?"

"So you're saying that even you, the self-described shut-in, has some self-awareness?"

"Geh..."

Ashiya tipped his head lightly at Urushihara's words, but as soon as all that, Maou thrust in, and Urushihara was only able to get a single word out.

"A-anyway!"

The fallen angel sputtered through his attempt to continue:

"If we're gonna believe Gabriel, they sent the Observer down here to Japan."

"The Observer...? Raguel? The angel who oversees the behavior of all the other angels?"

Urushihara nodded at Suzuno.

"He's not all that high on the ladder, so to speak. Gabriel could probably whip his ass in a fair fight, and he's not a Sephirah guardian, either. Thing is, though, Raguel's been granted certain...powers the others don't have."

"The Call of the End Times...?" Suzuno muttered.

"Good evening. It's the end of the week and time for your Friday evening news..."

The newscaster on TV demonstrated impeccable timing.

"......"

All eyes rested upon Suzuno. She turned red once she realized why.

"Wh-what? A mere coincidence!"

"......"

Then all eyes swiveled their way back toward Urushihara.

"I did not intend to do that! It is not my doing!" Suzuno protested.

Urushihara ignored her.

"I don't know how the Call of the End Times was described in

Ente Islan mythology, but it's nothing all that fancy. Raguel has the power to observe the other angels, judge them as necessary, and announce the results to the rest of heaven. It usually involves booting angels out of the club, though."

"Fallen angels?"

"Yeah. They set that whole system up not long after I left heaven. The Observer levies his judgment, and the Evil Eye of the Fallen carries out his sentence."

"You mean…Sariel?"

It wasn't a name Maou expected to come up.

"Think about it, dude. If Sariel was the sole judge, jury, and executioner when it came to kicking out angels, there wouldn't be a single man left in heaven."

Maou, Emi, and Suzuno exchanged glances. It was an extremely persuasive explanation.

"I know it looks like everyone just does what they want up there, but inside the bureaucracy, you're pretty restricted in how you can use your powers. Not too different in the human world, either, right? The same kinda idea as why the soldier with his finger on the A-bomb button doesn't try taking over the world."

"But why is Raguel in Japan? The way you're putting it, it doesn't sound like he makes all that good of a substitute for Gabriel, given his power levels."

Urushihara nodded at Emi's question. "Well, if you assume that Raguel ain't here to bring Gabriel back to heaven…I'm guessing he's here to lay judgment on someone."

"It might not be 'doves' like me paying house calls any longer."

The warning was clear upon Urushihara's mind.

"What kind of judgment?"

"You don't know?"

Maou's question seemed far less weighty to him than Emi's.

"Neither of you? The King of All Demons and the half-angel Hero over there?"

Urushihara then turned to Suzuno.

"Heaven stood by blithely while the Devil King's army ran

roughshod over Ente Isla. So why's it sending angels down to Japan, on another world, like it's goin' outta style? You ever think about that?"

For Suzuno, a high-level Church cleric who sent many of her sect's knights to their doom while proclaiming all the while that her god's blessings were on their side, the question was enough to crush her.

"…No matter how many Ente Islans lose their lives, it never affects the heavens at all…" she whispered.

"Bingo."

A cruel reply.

"But if they think it's their fault, they'll try to fix it…in the way *they* prefer to do it. You get me? Maou, Yusa, and Ashiya and Bell, too, of course—you're all getting close to a truth the heavens want to keep hidden; you're keeping Sephirah fragments to yourself; and you used your innate powers to dispatch multiple frontline angels. If Raguel declares you to be an enemy of all heaven…"

The newscast, playing to Maou's crew and nobody else, played footage from a civil war in one nation or another.

"*That's* when heaven's gonna start gettin' serious. They'll make Gabriel's Heavenly Regiment look like a bunch of kindergartners."

"…Bullcrap!" Maou hammered an angry fist down on the table. "Then why didn't they just attack us directly this time, too?!"

"Dunno, man. All this assumes that we can believe what Gabriel told me. For all we know, they're after something totally unrelated to us—that 'woman in white,' for example. We have no idea where Chiho Sasaki's ring came from, right?"

"So what do you want us to do? We can hardly just sit here and wait for Raguel to take action. That could lead to more victims like Ms. Sasaki."

"Yeah, about that. I actually got ideas along those lines, so I've been waiting for a bit now."

"Waiting? For what…?"

"*Now for a roundup of the day's top news.*"

The newscaster chose that moment to wrap up his civil-war coverage and launch into a recap of Japan's main news stories of the day.

"Technicians are still looking into a bug that's inconvenienced users across the metro area, one that's preventing TV-compatible cell phones and tablets from receiving broadcasts."

"Oh, that wasn't just Dokodemo?"

Emi, who had spent much of the past few days assuaging irate customers about that exact issue, perked up at the mention.

The screen showed some hapless phone-company executive apologizing at a press conference, bowing down low as he drowned in a blaze of camera flashes.

Then:

"Geh!"

"Whoa!"

"Agh!"

As if thrown off balance by the litany of flashes, Maou and Ashiya fell off of their chairs.

Urushihara managed to grab on to the table in time, but his knees were visibly trembling.

"Wh-what's wrong with you guys?"

"Are you all right?!"

Emi helped Maou up and Suzuno lent a hand to Ashiya, both wondering why they had been suddenly blown aside by nothing in particular.

"Huh?"

"Wha?!"

When they set eyes on the two demons, however, their eyes popped out of their sockets.

Their hair was on end, as if they had been electrocuted.

Poor Ashiya, fresh from Suzuno's sonar probing, had his hair going every which direction, as if he purchased an economy-sized jar of hair wax and figured he better use it all before the sell-by date.

"What is going *on* with you people?!"

"…That's what I want to know." Maou's voice was shaky and cheerless.

"Emilia and Bell didn't notice that? Must be that receptiveness you guys have…"

Urushihara looked unfazed at first glance, but he still sounded a bit pained as he gestured toward the TV.

In the midst of this furor, the news had already moved on to a story about the nationwide heat wave leading to an epidemic of heatstroke cases.

"Wh-what? The TV? Huh? A-all right, all right, gimme a sec!"

Emi, meanwhile, was talking to herself, one finger to her temple. Hurriedly checking to make sure there were no people or security cameras around, she summoned Alas Ramus into the visitor space.

"Teh-bee!"

The child made a beeline for the TV and began banging a tiny fist against the screen.

The LCD screen bent slightly at the force as Emi earnestly tried to stop this sudden bout of violence.

"Wh-what're you doing, Alas Ramus? You can't do that! That's the hospital's—"

"It was all *whoosh*!"

"…Huh?"

Alas Ramus's soft hands continue to bop against the screen.

"All *flaaaash*, then *ziiiiing*, then *dooooooooom*!"

Her right hand was battering the TV. Her left was pointed at her own large eyes.

"'Flash, zing, dooooooom'?"

The barrage of sound effects meant little to Emi. Urushihara, still straightening out his hair with a comb that nobody had realized until now he kept handy, motioned toward the TV.

"Remember what Bell just did to Ashiya, dude? Alas Ramus must've picked up on it. She's really sensitive to that kinda stuff. It's that sonar, except, like, *mega* scaled up. Someone's breaking into the broadcast and firing sonar bolts. Multiple times today! He can trace the TVs that sent back a sonar response, so that's a lot easier than casting a net nationwide. One of them must've done in Chiho Sasaki."

"Sonar? That jolt right now was *sonar*?!"

Maou, his hair still sticking several inches off his head, confronted Urushihara at his seat. Ashiya nodded, glaring at Suzuno as he did.

"It...it was rather similar to Suzuno's little trick earlier, yes..."

"Are you saying that was Raguel just now, Urushihara?"

"Yeah, there's a pretty good chance of that. If it isn't Gabriel, it's gotta be the other guy."

"W-wait a minute. How could they fire off bolts of sonar through TV waves?!" Suzuno exclaimed. "And even if they could, tens of millions of people are watching TV in Japan right now! Surely Chiho would not be the only one affected! Besides, I have never heard of anyone rendered comatose by it..."

The only local expert at the procedure seemed genuinely offended. But Maou, suddenly realizing something, looked upward as he finally got around to straightening his hair.

"Chi's house has already been the site of at least one sonar strike."

"What?!"

"Oh..."

Emi came to the same realization as Maou. It made her mouth hang open.

"You mean Al's—I mean, Albert's sonar?"

That episode had come before Chiho had learned the truth behind Maou and Emi:

Albert, one of Emi's traveling companions, had fired off several sonar messages to warn his friend in Japan that something terrible was coming her way.

Chiho chose Maou to discuss the experience with...which was part of what brought the two closer to each other in the first place.

"You got it. All those untargeted sonar blasts and Idea Links, no particular recipient in mind, pummeling against Chi's body... Hey, Suzuno. A decent caster can change who or what his sonar or Idea Links react to, right?"

"Y-yes. If you are merely seeking out the position of someone or something, the required calculations are quite simple. If you change resonation methods, as I did with Chiho and Alciel, you can use them for a variety of purposes."

That was why Chiho unintentionally picked up on Albert's Idea Link. That ministorm of sonar pulses took place all because Albert happened to find a willing recipient in Chiho before anyone else. The Link was tuned to search for "someone with a strong link to Devil King Satan"—and now, Chiho was the only Japanese person who knew about Ente Isla.

"That's why the sonar that made it through the TV in Chiho Sasaki's house must have sparked some kinda explosive reaction."

"Wait. Why's it matter if the area had a strong reaction to a pulse before now? Are you saying it responded to whatever residue was left from Al and Eme's holy force? 'Cause if that was the case, all the holy power me and Gabriel tossed around Sasazuka would've made the whole town explode whenever a sonar pulse hit it."

"Uh, that holy-power sonar blast just now nearly took our heads off."

"You said it."

Maou's and Ashiya's complaints were not commented upon.

"Y'know, I wasn't paying attention at the time 'cause Maou was too busy kicking the crap out of me..." Urushihara, meanwhile, was back to his usual air of supreme confidence. "But why were Emeralda Etuva and Albert Ende able to fire sonar bolts over to Japan, on Earth, anyway?"

"...What do you mean?"

"Well, Olba, I get. He's the guy who sent Emilia through the Gate after Maou in the first place. But not those two. They shouldn't be able to use Gate magic at all. How'd they manage to take a sonar bolt and transmit it right over to Japan?"

"That was before I arrived here, so I am unaware of the details, but did they not follow your and Lord Olba's paths through space? That was how I arrived here."

"Why're you making me repeat myself, Bell? Emeralda Etuva and Albert Ende *don't know how to work Gates.*"

"But they both made it over here! Like what the Devil King said, they could use that feather pen made from an archangel's wings to summon Gates without using demonic force. Both of them had feather pens from Laila...from my mother. They probably just came over here to send out those sonar and Idea Link transmissions. That's how Chiho was able to pick up on Albert's... Um?"

"...Oh."

Emi and Maou exchanged glances, both picking up on something of their own.

"Yeah, dudes, that's it. You know what Raguel's trying to look for now?"

The blood drained from Emi's head.

How long ago was that phone call from Emeralda?

How could I have been so stupid, this whole time between today and running into that woman in white in Tokyo Big-Egg Town?

"The number one item on Raguel and Gabriel's list right now isn't the Yesod fragments; it isn't the Better Half; it isn't Maou. For now, that all takes a backseat."

I should have known *that angel might be coming to Japan.*

"It's Laila. I don't know why, but they're tracking Laila's trail and they're trying to lay some kind of judgment at her feet."

"All thanks to that idiot Albert sending an Idea Link with Laila's feather pen, huh? Man, lucky thing Chiho's mom wasn't caught in the cross fire, then."

Maou groaned to himself, realizing the situation was far worse than it seemed, but Emi felt the brunt of it.

"What…what happens with Raguel's Call of the End Times?!" She found herself grabbing Urushihara by the collar.

"Garghh!"

"Emilia! That is too strong. And this is a hospital! Calm down!"

"You want me to calm down *now*?!"

Her voice was rising.

"I've never met her… I didn't even know she existed until recently… But…unless I can meet her and talk to her…unless she's safe, she…she's my mother, all right?!"

"Um, is something the matter? Should I call for somebody?"

A nurse had appeared, watching them dubiously, no doubt alarmed by the shouting. Emi returned to her senses and, for the time being, released Urushihara.

"I… Sorry. It's nothing."

"Oh, no? Well, remember, this is a hospital. I'd like to ask you to keep things quiet, please."

The nurse, not looking particularly convinced, quietly padded off nonetheless.

Urushihara, near tears and realizing Emi was done screwing around with him, opted to cut out the back talk from here on in.

"Kahh...nnngh... They're probably gonna kick her out of heaven, I'd assume. Raguel and Sariel work as a team, after all. Or worked."

"Sariel's in on this, too?!"

"Nah, dude. Not at this point. I probably shouldn't dis him too much, but I'm startin' to get the impression he doesn't give two craps about heaven any longer."

Maou recalled the last time he saw Sariel—metaphorically melting into a pile of goo and oozing into the sewer grate after Kisaki, the supreme love of his life, banned him from MgRonald.

"So I dunno how he's planning to do that, really. Banishing someone from heaven doesn't happen all that often, but I've *never* heard of them going to other worlds, interfering with all kindsa crap over there, all so they can lay judgment on a single archangel."

A beat, and then Maou nodded and stood up. "...So we're gonna have to beat up Raguel and make him give us the whole story, huh? If Urushihara doesn't even know, our only option's gonna be to ask the guy himself."

Ashiya remained seated, much cooler to the idea. "Your Demonic Highness, why do we need to, as you say, 'beat up' Raguel?"

"Look, I don't care about how angels deal with humans. Like, not at *all*. But he just took out one of my prime candidates for a Demon General spot in the army I lead. Do I need any more reason than that?"

Ashiya smiled and nodded at Maou's stern countenance. "Not at all, my liege. I would be glad to lend a helping hand to a talented future comrade."

"Urushihara. Emi. Suzuno."

"Mm?"

"What!"

"Yes?"

Maou sized up each one of them in succession.

"I need to smoke this Raguel guy out and make him pay for putting Chi in the hospital. Help me with that."

It wasn't the most politely phrased of requests, but strangely, no one offered any resistance to it.

"Well…sure, dude. I'm free anyway. I guess I owe her for least a coupla things."

"I wouldn't mind if you saved that talk about Demon Generals until after I kill you, but if it's one of my best friends we're talking about, so be it."

"I will gladly teach even an angel a lesson to protect my friends. For this, and only this, I officially agree to cooperate with you."

For the sake of a single girl, the Devil King, his Great Demon General, a fallen angel, the Hero, and a Church cleric stood strong in the hospital waiting room, uniting for a common goal.

"…Hmm?"

Maou noticed something tugging at the sleeve of his pants.

"Daddy!"

Alas Ramus, eyes deadly serious, was looking up at Maou.

"Alas Ramus love Chi-sis, too!"

She seemed proud of this affirmation.

Maou whisked the child into the air, smile just as strong as her eyes.

"Wanna do it?"

"Yehh!"

The five of them, plus one toddler, headed down the elevator and marched out of Seikai University Hospital as a group.

They were seen out by the same nurse who had upbraided Emi for screaming in the waiting room.

Waving something resembling a clipboard in her hand, the nurse headed for Chiho's room.

"Pardon me for barging in, Ms. Sasaki… Hmm?"

Upon entering, she found the young patient's mother gone. Her handbag was still there, perhaps indicating a quick trip to the bathroom or the gift shop.

The nurse gave herself a nod and stood next to the sleeping Chiho's bed.

"Ms. Chiho Sasaki? I think your friends might just help you see the outside of this hospital soon!"

She peered into Chiho's face, a beaming smile painted upon her own.

"You have all these disparate minds focused on a single goal… The mother of a new Da'at, perhaps?"

Several minutes later. Riho, returning from the ladies' room, spotted a piece of paper on the small desk next to the bed—a rundown of the examinations slated for the next day.

The distraction made her completely fail to notice the faint glow that was now present around the ring on Chiho's left hand.

Leaving the air-conditioned hospital interior, the warriors from another planet were instantly assaulted by the stifling heat, which showed no sign of loosening even as sunset loomed.

Several minutes after their solemn oath, all five of them were already starting to grimace under the strain.

"So…if you were willing to give that speech just now, do you have an idea of where Raguel might be?"

Emi set up a no-look pass to Maou. He ignored it.

"Uh, you know anything, Urushihara?" Maou asked.

Urushihara, realizing the ball was headed his way, rolled his eyes at Maou for his clear failure to take initiative.

"Well…I got a thought, anyway. But how 'bout *you* go first? You're *soooooo* good with machines, I wouldn't want to look like an idiot if I got it wrong."

The defiant *sooooo* was still ringing in everyone's ears by the time he concluded the sentence.

"So, what're you thinkin', dude?"

"Two places."

Urushihara's eyebrows arched upward. "Huh. Guess we're in agreement."

Suzuno gave him a poke on the back. "Would you mind sharing it with the rest of the world, please?"

Maou responded with a single arched eyebrow of his own. "What was it that broke apart around us at the electronics store? What's the thing that's been flashing white and screwing up for people all day? What just scrambled my and Ashiya's brains a moment ago?"

"Frizzy-frizz!"

Maou paid Alas Ramus no mind as she played with his hair, still on end even now.

"It's the TVs, right?"

"You... Wait."

Emi's eyes opened wide. Urushihara nodded at her.

"It's not like all the TVs involved were airing the same program every time. He's not targeting a single network—he's working across the entire range of TV signals in the Kanto region. Which means there's only two places I can think of."

"If there's one thing that fancy-pants prick always liked, it's high places. He's like a goat or something. Not that I was one to talk, but..."

A summer evening's breeze lapped at their hair.

"Tokyo Tower and the Tokyo Skytree."

✳

"Hey, did you know, Ashiya?"

"Yes?"

Shiba Park, in the Minato ward of Tokyo.

The Devil King of another world turned toward his faithful Great Demon General and snorted.

"The top of Tokyo Tower is made out of tanks!"

"......" Ashiya sighed and looked at what Maou clenched in his hand. "Is that written in there, my liege?"

Maou was holding a copy of a small paperback entitled *Everything You Wanted to Know About HDTV* (*But Were Afraid to Ask)*. He'd purchased it at a station-side kiosk on the way here.

"The area of the tower that lies above the topmost observation deck is made from steel taken from American tanks that were scrapped after the Korean War," Ashiya concluded. "It was still hard to obtain high-quality steel in the Japan of the nineteen fifties, the US was eager to develop a new generation of tanks, and—as I understand it—their needs dovetailed each other very closely."

"…! …!" Maou look at Ashiya, then his book. "…Y-you knew that?"

"When I was working as a theater stagehand, I had to move props around for a play set in that era. They touched upon it in one scene or another."

Ashiya had a thoughtful look on his face. (The two of them had finally gotten around to fixing their hair earlier.)

"Did you know, Your Demonic Highness, why the tower is painted in white and red? Or, should I say, the shade of yellowish red known as 'international orange'?"

"…No."

"According to aviation regulations, any structures or other objects over two hundred feet above the ground that may interfere with air safety need to be painted in alternating shades of white and international orange to indicate the obstruction. These markings are painted across the entirety of Tokyo Tower, however."

Maou stared at Ashiya, mouth agape.

"But…but the Skytree isn't that color!"

"The pattern is not required if you install high-powered aircraft warning lights or other devices."

A few furious flips through the paperback, and:

"………Whoa, you're right."

He'd found the relevant section.

Ashiya grinned as his master's crestfallen look. "That's what led to the Tokyo Tower we know and love today…but personally, I think a nice shade of pure red would suit this tower the most."

He sized up the tower before him as he spoke. The tower, all one thousand ninety-three feet of it, was used as a central site for radio, television, and other electrical signals, gradually evolving into an architectural symbol for all of Tokyo over the years.

The Skytree, while still under construction, already had it beaten in height. That still wasn't enough to tarnish any of the structure's grandeur, however. Thousands of tourists visited Tokyo Tower daily, and since HDTV transmission duties were now handled by the Skytree, the resulting free bandwidth in the Tower ensured it would be serving Tokyo and its citizens for years to come.

"Y'know, I know I came here on my own volition and stuff...but I'm starting to have cold feet."

"How so?"

"There's too many people. Is there really an angel around here?"

It did not affect Maou and his friends whatsoever, but to most Japanese citizens, it was currently the tail end of summer vacation.

Tokyo Tower was a landmark icon of Japan. In this warm August evening, it was predictably mobbed.

"Meaning that Emi has more of a chance to find our target at the Skytree, you mean?"

While Maou and Ashiya were at Tokyo Tower, Emi had volunteered to head for the Skytree, with Urushihara (at his suggestion) remaining at Yoyogi so he and Suzuno could swiftly reach either building and provide backup should trouble arise.

The fact Urushihara suggested this provided Maou some pause, but his logic was sound enough. From Yoyogi, they could either quickly board the JR Sobu Line to Kinshichou, near the Skytree, or hop on the Toei Oedo Line to Akabane-bashi, the preferred stop for Tokyo Tower sightseers.

Suzuno, whose usefulness in a fight was undeniable at this point, protested the idea of being behind the front lines.

But if an angel *really* felt like a scrap, the fact was that only Emi had the strength to deal with that.

So Suzuno acquiesced in the end. Maou's none-too-subtle reminder that she was incapable of standing up to Sariel at first—and, indeed, helped Maou take Devil King form only because she was outside the field of battle—helped the opposition's case immensely.

"Hey, but can we settle this someplace where I don't have to repair a lot of collateral damage again?"

Maou felt justified in emphasizing this point. This was the Suzuno, after all, who destroyed enough of the train infrastructure around Shinjuku station to bring all JR lines to a screeching halt. But Suzuno's response was arctic in tone.

"Assuming you can collect enough power in said place to turn you into the Devil King."

The potential of another postfight cleanup filled Maou with dread, but he appreciated that Emi and Suzuno were willing to accept that he might have to take demon form before long. That was a huge step forward for them.

"But the Skytree hasn't gone into full operation yet, has it? Wouldn't someone up there notice if some intruder started messin' around with the satellites and stuff?"

The demons certainly noticed by now—their brains were still a bit scrambled by it—but if, as Urushihara thought, this angel Raguel was inserting sonar signals into TV broadcasts, being harassed by Japanese video technicians along the way wasn't a very efficient way to go about things.

"Tokyo Tower, as well, is subject to frequent and, may I say, extremely thorough safety inspections. Things are little different here. Instead of fretting over it, I say we make our move and see for ourselves instead."

Here, on the ground, Maou and Ashiya were just two men stuck at the back of the visitor line.

Given how they needed to investigate this tower as much as humanly possible, their main priority right now was to explore every nook and cranny they had the right to access.

Without a moment's hesitation, they paid the 2,840 yen required for two tickets to the tower's twin observation decks. The fact this was their first visit to the site since touching down in Japan added to the lack of pause.

It was, in its own way, a sign of how large a presence Chiho had grown to become in both of their lives: 2,840 yen was, yes, worth *that* much to them.

"Your Demonic Highness, we will be going upward by elevator from this point..."

"Uh-huh?"

"But Tokyo Tower can also be climbed by stairs, I understand."

"...Um?"

"I think this to be rather improbable, but if an angel like Raguel was on the staircases..."

"Whoa, whoa, hang on, are you saying we should...?"

Maou looked up at the illuminated red tower looming above.

In the back of his mind, he recalled having to climb up the entirety of the Tokyo City Hall building to rescue Chiho, clad in nothing but a pair of boxers.

"...Are you *kidding* me?"

Emi, meanwhile, could just Heavenly Fleet Feet up from the roof of a nearby building to conquer the Skytree. Dressed in a black sweatshirt, pants, and boots to keep her from being spotted in mid-air, she was on comparative Easy Street.

Wearing a long-sleeved shirt, by itself, almost drowned her in her own sweat when she tried it on at the UniClo in Shinjuku. At nearly two thousand feet above sea level, however, the wind was howling hard enough to give an unprotected human being hypothermia in no time flat.

"Maybe I should've put on another layer..."

The muttering was all but drowned out by the sound of her hair flapping in the gale-force breeze. But unless she was willing to shell out serious cash for mountain gear or the latest winter fashions just as the season was ramping up, she'd have to make do with this.

Despite the late hour, the Skytree was still packed with TV staff and technicians, thousands of people running to and fro down on the ground. Instead of trying to dodge them all and enter from below, it was far easier to begin at the very peak and work her way down.

Inspectors, of course, were still doing their work up high. The Tokyo Skytree wasn't fully built yet, but the news reported earlier about the daily test broadcasts radiating from its antennas. Maintenance and inspection work was more likely to happen at night than any other time.

This was because, if you approached an antenna unprotected during the afternoon or evening hours when the most electricity was coursing through it, you risked being literally cooked by the high-frequency waves running through you.

Emi landed above the observation deck located about 1,500 feet above the ground.

She checked the emergency supply of 5-Holy Energy β she had in her chest pocket, then carefully gauged her surroundings.

She was wary of bystanders, of course. But if the angel actually *was* in this tower, he had probably noticed the holy force Emi had used to reach this vantage point.

In the worst case, Emi could expect an incoming barrage from within the tower at any moment. But, for now, she felt nothing but the cacophonous wind against her face. It puzzled her.

The vast Tokyo cityscape spread out beneath her eyes, the mountains that formed the westernmost boundary of the Kanto Plain hazily visible in the night air.

Taking a quick look at the the high-powered aircraft warning light nearby, Emi carefully began to walk across the roof of the observation deck, taking care not to let the wind throw her off balance.

"So…no dice?"

Except for the heavy wind, the brightly shining warning light, and the sturdy walkway she was currently on, there was nothing.

"Maybe I should look around a bit more, then head for Tokyo Tower…"

She took out her cell phone, almost dropping it in the wind, as she attempted to contact Maou or Suzuno about her failure. Then:

"!"

The wind suddenly carried a clearly out-of-place noise with it. On cue, Emi crouched low and scanned her surroundings.

No one was visible in the scaffolding.

That was what made it seem so eerie to her. What she had heard just now…

"A sneeze?"

"Ehhhh-*choooo*!!"

It was clear as day that time. A man, sneezing, in vastly comical fashion. And she recognized the voice, too.

"Mommy! Up there!"

Alas Ramus pointed him out from within Emi, an odd trace of frustration to her voice.

In the scaffolding, fifty or so feet above her, was a figure that could only be described as bizarre.

Emi was expecting a fight—with this angel Raguel, even, should the need arise. That was what made this man's outfit all the more ridiculous to her.

It was too dark to make his face out too well, but he was curled up in a ball, arms over his shins.

"Ehhhh-*choooaahh*!!"

Another sneeze. Emi gazed at him, unsure what to do next. But:

"Ah!"

The curled-up man noticed her.

Then he stood right up, in an apparent panic. The force was enough to make his foot slip right off the railing he was perched upon.

"Look out!" Emi shouted instinctively, still not knowing who this was. But the man's possible fate 1,500 feet below was extinguished in the next second.

"!!"

Emi, looking on, did not hesitate another moment to materialize her holy sword.

It was because the man, just as he fell off the railing, spread his glowing wings into the air.

Beyond any doubt, it was an angel lying in wait for Emi.

Maou was right to finger the TV towers the whole time. But now that the truth was thrust before her, one question remained:

Why didn't the angel engage Emi in combat when she first approached him?

Emi had energized her holy-force banks to their limits, preparing herself for any potential opponent she could picture. But the angel, wings in the air, found himself foundering around like a kite on a windy day, plopping slightly in front of Emi like a squashed toad. Then he went still.

Once again, Emi wasn't sure how to react. She took a step forward to investigate further.

But Alas Ramus, in her sword, stopped her.

"Mommy! That's Gabwraell! Don't!"

Emi, realizing after a few moments that the jumble of syllables she just uttered were meant to mean Gabriel, leaped back and brandished her holy sword without a second thought.

Urushihara told her that Gabriel was back in Japan, but running into the angel as she was snooping around for holy-force sonar clues was totally unexpected.

She had defeated him once before, but he was still a powerful archangel, the symbol of all that was holy up in heaven. Emi stared him down, ready to react to so much as a single twitch.

"You *scaaaaared* me, girl!"

The first reaction Gabriel made was to warble out that shaky-voiced whine.

"I, like...*totally* didn't notice, mm-kay? S-since when were you bumpin' around down there?"

He glared sullenly at Emi, hands crossed at the elbows, his lips a clear shade of blue.

"It, it, it's *collllld* up here!!"

"...Well, don't look at me."

Emi found it hard to think of anything else.

In a remarkably inspired fit of fashion coordination, Gabriel's toga—right at home at a summer party in ancient Greece—was paired with a T-shirt with an I LUV LA logo on it. His legs were bare, the sight of which Emi did not appreciate very much, and he wore his sandals without so much as a pair of insulating socks.

All of his garments, except for the T-shirt perhaps, naturally held untold powers that Gabriel could wield at will against his foes. The power of warmth, sadly, did not seem to be among them.

"I-I mean, E-Emilia? What're *you* doing here? Th-the Skytree isn't even open yet! It won't be up to full two-thousand-eighty-foot mode until later!"

His teeth chattered a bit as he complained at her.

"I-I-I guess the humans sure did one on me, huh? Yeah, I ain't *ever* seen nothin' like this in Ente Isla. Or h-heaven, even! Like, *maybe* the Devil's Castle was T-Tokyo Tower height, but…I didn't think it'd be so cold and windy up… *Grphhoo!*"

The archangel's unhygienic sneeze spread particles of spittle across the city sky. Emi was unimpressed, pointing the tip of her blade at him.

"I'd like to know why *you're* here. Weren't you fired from your Yesod-fragment job?"

"Yeaaaah, about that. You got any t-tissues or something? Like, p-premoisturized would be nice right about now."

If Gabriel felt any danger at Emi's presence, he was doing a good job hiding it. But there was no reason to treat him with kid gloves. Not after what he'd tried to do to Alas Ramus.

In a flash, Emi ran up to Gabriel, bringing her sword's tip to his chest as she had done once before.

"You haven't forgotten about earlier, have you? I was never a very patient woman."

"Oh, c'mon! You treat angels and demons the exact same way, girl!"

The wind was starting to make Gabriel tear up.

"Look, I… Y-you know, I told Lucifer, but I don't care even in the *slightest* about you or the Better Half or those silly little demons, 'kay? Cross my heart, I'm serious! I'm just here on a bit of a business assignment, so as long as you guys keep all bein' good little boys and girls for me…"

"Sorry, not gonna happen. That's why *I'm* here. Did you fire off those sonar bursts?"

"……"

Emi, the wind to her back, chose her words carefully. For now, she had no clear signal that the angels, as Urushihara theorized, were after Laila.

"Do you remember the girl who knew all about us? That sonar put her in a coma."

"Huh? Really?"

Was that an honest expression of surprise, or just Gabriel being Gabriel? Either way, the natural-born class clown of heaven's face betrayed sheer dismay. He opened his mouth and took a deep breath.

"Hehhh-*choooo*!!"

Rather a lot of force behind that one.

Then, at that moment, Gabriel vanished from Emi's view, her sword left jabbing at emptiness.

"...!!"

"Mommy! Not there!"

Following the holy force, Emi whirled her sword behind her back.

"'Bzzzt'!"

Then she felt a finger against the back of her head.

"Bang! I win."

"......"

The Better Half's blade sliced through nothing but the fog of holy power Gabriel unleashed as a decoy. The real Gabriel was behind her, upside down in the air, putting his finger against Emi's head like a pistol.

"Maybe I don't have much of a chance with your sword from the front. But I can always skin this cat another way, right?"

She could sense the holy energy surging into his finger.

"...You gonna kill me and take Alas Ramus?"

Emi's voice was almost lost in the high-altitude wind.

"Oh, of course not! Now why would I do that when I don't even know how that child's fused with you? I'd be super *double* screwed if I killed her, too!"

Suddenly, the holy force rapidly dwindled, the murderous rage she sensed behind her head disappearing.

"Instead...can you tell me more about that girl in the coma?"

"Huh?"

"'Cause all *I* did was make sure the test broadcasts from this tower didn't interfere with what Tokyo Tower was transmitting. Didn't want that to dilute our sonar's accuracy. I don't know how Raguel was actually firing that stuff off, really. He didn't say anything about it knocking the people of *this* world unconscious."

Emi turned her head, never letting her guard down for a moment. She tried her best to stare down Gabriel, although she found it slow going, considering his current inverted state.

"It's *that* girl, huh? Chiho Sasaki? That cute girl who's gone all 'teen romance' for the Devil King? She works at the same place he does, doesn't she? I think Sariel mentioned that."

"Why do you care about that? Are you gonna kidnap Chiho and treat her like a lab animal? The way Sariel wanted to?"

"Uh...? He was trying to do *that*?"

Gabriel wiped his nose, then used the momentum to feverishly shake his head, arms wide open.

"Did you honestly think *I'm* that depraved, too? 'Cause that really hurts, my dear. I just wanna know what that girl's suffering from, is all."

"...Why do you want to know so badly?"

Gabriel scratched one of his cheeks awkwardly.

"Wellllll... Maybe I don't wanna get so directly involved the way Sariel did, but I guess we both wanna know a little, y'know? I mean, you know how folks on Earth research stuff like evolution and genes and all that, right?"

Something about Gabriel's phrasing disgusted him. She was leaning over his face now, not bothering to hide her frustrated rage.

"You expect me to tell you after saying *that* to me?"

"...Is that a 'nah'? Though given everything we've done to you guys, I guess it's a bit much to sit down and have a nice chat over coffee at this point, huh? So how 'bout we do a little business instead, pray tell?"

"Business?"

A particularly strong gust of wind blew Emi's long hair into the dark sky.

"I'll even pay in advance! I'll leak a couple of particularly tasty tidbits to you first. Then you can decide for yourself whether you wanna talk about Chiho Sasaki or not."

"...Like you can prove you're not lying through your teeth. I'm not gonna sell my friends over some story the enemy plants into my brain."

"That's why I *saaaaid*, you can decide for yourself! Talk or not, it's all good in the 'hood! I've got a sneakin' suspicion you'll consider it, though, once I'm done."

Finally taking the time to put himself right side up, Gabriel gave his wings a light flap as he landed on the roof of the observation deck.

"For example, what if I told you that your father...that Nord Justina is still alive?"

"Wha...?!"

The unexpected angle the words took on the way to Emi's ears made the shock clear upon her face. The reaction seemed to cheer Gabriel up noticeably. He chuckled a bit from deep down in his throat.

"Wanna hear more?"

"...ah."

Emi wasn't allowed the time to formulate a response.

"Oh, wait...wait, get away from me, get... *Geh-shooo!*"

His entire head twisted in pain, no longer able to stem the tide rising from his chest, Gabriel sneezed heartily upon Emi's face.

"............"

The gusting wind chilled the completely unwelcome liquid particles that now covered Emi's cheek.

"*Hngh!*"

The young woman lowered the butt of her sword onto Gabriel's head.

"Gahh! Ugh, my eyes... They're pounding..."

"Keep it short, and I'll listen to you. But if Alas Ramus thinks you're lying, I'll help your head kiss your ass good-bye for you."

"Oh, *jeez*, lady...! Why d'you have to treat both me *and* the demons like we're some kinda plague...?"

A quick glance at Gabriel's blubbering countenance gave her all the reassurance she needed.

"I show my foes zero kindness. And that goes double for Alas Ramus's foes."

The archangel raised both hands up in a surrender posture.

Five minutes later, the two of them were inside the freshly constructed observation deck.

The lack of wind made things blessedly warmer for both.

Masking sheets were draped here and there on the walls and floor. The space was still clearly a work in progress.

"Hey, I think it's gotten a lot warmer. You want some?"

Gabriel took a can of coffee out from somewhere within his toga. He showed it to Emi.

"Mommy, no drink! He's mean!"

Alas Ramus, her animosity for Gabriel clearer than ever, was now materialized and hovering around Emi's legs.

Emi didn't need the warning. There was no telling *what* Gabriel used to warm that can up.

"Oh, come onnn! I didn't spike it or anything, okay?"

Gabriel tried to defend himself. But poison wasn't the issue to Emi.

"Sorry, but I'm not interested in accepting food or drink from people outside of this world. Tea's fine by me, so just say what you're gonna say and get your ass back to heaven."

"Jeez, what a slave driverrrr! Y'know, it's funny, though. That myth about 'oooh, no, don't eat anything from the afterlife, you'll never come baaaaack!' The same thing in Earth *and* Ente Isla, huh?"

Gabriel, not looking particularly offended, popped the top off his can of low-sugar coffee.

"Oooooh, this hits the spot..."

He remained unhurried, as always. She knew this was all part of his strategy, but she found herself tapping her fingernails against the wall regardless.

"I'm not here for light conversation, Gabriel. If you want anything from me, talk about my father *now*."

"Oh, you'll listen?"

"If I think you're lying, it ends. Right there."

"Don't lie to Mommy!"

Being accused of deceit in stereo by a mother-daughter pair was enough to deflate even Gabriel's monstrous ego.

"...Well, like I said, you can listen to me, and then *you* decide what to do, all right? I've got things to tell you about besides Nord Justina, anyway."

Gabriel held the coffee can lovingly in both hands.

"So, listen. Heaven's, like, about *thiiiiis* close to being pretty well cut in two, yeah? It's like nothing ever before... Well, okay, not nothing *ever* before, but we're talking, like, *maaaaybe* once every thousand years or so. And your mom and dad...and where *you* came from, too...plays a *huuuuge* role in it."

"...I don't need reams of exposition, okay? Just cut to the chase. I get that this guy Raguel is pursuing my mom Laila, for whatever reason. ...Did my family do something to piss you guys off, or...?"

"Oooh, not exactly that, but I *do* think y'all kinda went out of your way to make life difficult for us."

Gabriel smiled weakly, taking great care not to let his true thoughts come to the surface.

"But really, Laila and Nord are just one facet of it all. I mean, if you don't mind a little angel straight talk for a sec, there's you, there's the Devil King Satan, there's that Yesod fragment... And why stop there, even? There's Lucifer, there's that cleric chick in the kimono, there's Satan's ever-faithful lapdog... And Chiho Sasaki, too. They're *all* involved now. And, eesh, you could *also* say that for everybody else on Earth, huh?"

"Didn't I just tell you to keep it short?"

Emi remained peeved.

"All right, all right! What, you got a plane to catch or something? I'm just tryin' to set everything up so you realize how mind-blowing it all is when I open the curtain."

Gabriel's eyes turned down toward his can of coffee.

"But first off... Just to be sure we're on the same page and all, we angels...we're not exactly strangers to this world."

"Huh?"

"Our job descriptions, you know, they can be summed up pretty easily. If something poses a danger to heaven, we do whatever it takes to avoid it. Simple, huh? I know it's extreme, but we really don't care how many people the Devil King's army kills down on Ente Isla. As long as it doesn't put heaven in danger, *hakuna matata*, baby. Do a poll around heaven—they're all gonna say that."

It was a candidly worded statement, but it had the power to send any religious man or woman on Ente Isla into hysterics.

"So, like, when the demons got pushed out of Ente Isla, you got blown all the way to Earth, right, Emilia? And once that happened, you officially became a certified, bona-fide danger to heaven."

"How delightful to hear. Why?"

"Aw, don't you remember, lady? Like, when I told you to think again a little about what you really are?"

It was true. It had been one of his parting shots after nobly fleeing their first battle over Alas Ramus.

"What I really am?"

"Yeah. Ummm… This might not really be the best example, but maybe it'll help you understand a little more. Like…you know how people and chimps can't interbreed, right?"

"Huhh?!"

Emi's eyebrows arched high upward. It wasn't the sort of question she expected.

"Well… Yeah. Of course not!"

"Why not?"

"Why… Well, why do you think? They're different types of animals."

"They're both primates, right? Like, humans are really close to monkeys that way. Different breeds of dogs and cats mate and produce offspring all the time, right?"

"That's because their genes are a lot closer to each other! I mean, there's still some debate about the structure of human and chimp genes, but the theory that there's only a few percentage points of difference between them's still just a theory!"

"Ooh, you're a lot better read up on genes than I am. Nerrrrrd!"

"It…it was just something I saw on TV a while ago!"

"Wow! The Hero goes channel surfing, huh? Wait'll I tell the folks back home about that!"

Gabriel eyed Emi for a moment, as if silently gloating over his little jab.

"But anyway, what you're saying, Hero, is that humans and chimps can't produce children because they're too disparate from each other."

"Yes! What are *you* getting at?!"

"So why are a human and an angel any different?"

Time stopped.

It was the perfect—really, the only—way to describe that instant.

"…What…are you…?"

"You're the daughter of Laila, an angel, and Nord Justina, a human. That much I guarantee is true, so don't start doubting that on me, too, all right? That's the whole reason you're a danger to heaven right now, besides."

"H-how so…?"

"…Y'know, I think you put it best just a second ago. There's nothing that disparate about them. You're totally right."

Gabriel spread his arms out wide. The sudden flourish made the remaining content of his coffee can spill out a little, staining his toga.

"In the realm of creatures, which do you think it is—are humans angels, or are angels humans?"

"Which…? What do you…?"

Are angels…humans?

The wings folded behind him. The overwhelming aura of holy force. The blue-tinged silver hair and deep blue eyes. As long as she ignored the coffee stain, Gabriel clearly wasn't human.

But.

"You guys… For whatever reason, you just decided that heaven and the angels were these crazy, supernatural things, no? And as an angel, I'm not gonna *deny* that, exactly. But supernatural? No. I mean, if anything's supernatural here…"

Gabriel looked at the small figure in Emi's grasp, her eyes still transfixed upon him in a hostile glare.

"It's her."

The girl just labeled by an archangel as "supernatural" stood up in Emi's arms, trying to protect her mommy with her own body, and gave her best attempt at a threatening snarl.

"Ooo..."

Her challenge wasn't that threatening.

Emi, still attempting to process everything, realized her legs were shaking. Gabriel wasn't prepared to wait for her.

"But really, that's just the opening act, y'know? The *real* meat of it comes after that. And the fact we angels don't take action unless heaven's in danger has a lot to do with it. We got two sides kinda fighting over how to define that, if you follow me, and so Raguel's stepped up to make everyone march to the beat of a single drummer again. And the way Raguel decides to settle that little question... Well, he's got a lot of stuff to consider."

Gabriel seemed to enjoy this now, directly addressing the colorless Emi.

"Like, for one, I'm pretty sure your dad's here on Earth, along with your mom. And depending on Raguel's judgment, *he* might face the long arm of heavenly law before long, too."

✳

The lights were out in Room 305 of Seikai University Hospital.

The only illumination came from the crack under the hallway door and a flashing LED that indicated the location of the NURSE-CALL button.

That—and another, dimmer light, deeper inside. It was purple in color and had an odd warmth to it. Only the snores of the nearby patients greeted it.

"Mommm... You *know* I don't like it when you put peas on top of my pork dumplings..."

Chiho, voice clearly still half asleep, sat up in bed. She tossed the covers aside, the last memory she had still fresh in her mind. "Ah! Sorry, Mom! I kinda fell asleep so I forgot to turn on the...rice...?"

She blinked at the wholly unfamiliar walls, the ceiling, the window. Then she turned around, sensing someone whispering something into her ear.

"Huh...? A hospital?"

Then she noticed her cell phone by the bed. The battery must've run out on it. The back panel wasn't displaying the time.

Chiho puzzled over this for a moment. Then it came to her. She had had this whispering experience before.

Carefully, she sized up her surroundings. The voice sounded like it wasn't even two feet away from her. But there was nobody nearby. She didn't expect a response, but Chiho went ahead and asked anyway.

"Um...Albert? Or is it...Emeralda, maybe?"

Suddenly, the phone she thought was dead lit up in a dazzling pattern, something Chiho knew she never configured herself.

This wasn't a call, or a new text. But *something*, to be sure, was accessing her phone.

Gingerly, Chiho picked it up and opened it. The screen was jet-black. She brought the phone to her ear, doubting her sanity as she did.

"Uh...hello?"

She was rewarded with a female voice on the other end. What it had to say defied expectation.

"Oh, what do you mean, don't be so picky?" Chiho replied. "I mean, whoever decided to pair up pork dumplings with peas must be some kind of devil spawn! Maybe the demons like it, but I'll take shrimp or corn any day!"

She had commented on Chiho's half-awake murmurings. There were two occasions that Chiho would voluntarily eat peas: If someone cooked them into a dish without knowing any better, and if all food except for peas was eradicated from the planet.

The voice didn't seem to be making fun of her, but Chiho's face reddened in the darkness anyway. She had let a total stranger know about her childish food hang-ups.

Then the voice directed Chiho to look at her left hand. Only then did Chiho realize she was wearing an unfamiliar ring.

"My left hand? …Oh, wait, is this one of those things? A Yesod fragment?"

She chuckled to herself a little. With everything that had been happening to her lately, her shock threshold was pretty high. The voice seemed suitably impressed.

"…Satan? Oh, you mean Maou… Huh? Oh. Where in Tokyo? … Okay."

The conversation continued for a few moments. The tenseness in Chiho's voice gradually disappeared.

"All right. I'll try and help you out. …Huh? No, not scared, really. Kinda nervous, but…"

She smiled.

"I mean, all the demons and angels and Ente Islans around me… They'd all deny it, but they really get along pretty well, so. …Hmm? Oh, not really. Like, what would trying to trick me accomplish for anyone on *that* world? If that's what the game is, it'd be a lot quicker and easier to just kidnap me like Olba did."

The light from Chiho's ring flickered a bit, as if tittering to itself.

"…Weapons? Well, I don't know if I'd really call it a weapon…"

Chiho made a fist in the air, demonstrating her resolve to her invisible partner.

"But I've been doing *kyudo* for a while, so I think I'm pretty decent with a bow!"

✳

"Hey… You think he's really here?"

"Don't ask me."

Maou and Ashiya made their way down yet another Tokyo Tower stairway, the fatigue starkly written across their faces.

It being the dead of summer vacation, the entire tower was crawling with visitors. The trauma of his experience in Tokyo City Hall was fresh enough on Maou's mind that he successfully convinced his cohort to start by taking the elevator all the way up, then running back down the stairs to conduct the search.

But even the journey up to the observation decks was enough to nauseate Maou. The crowds seemed to ripple and undulate around him, and every square inch of the observation space was filled with people, people, people.

It was impossible for the two of them to check up on everyone present. And there wasn't a speck of holy force nearby, either.

Since they had no idea who, or what, was generating those holy sonar pulses, they went through the trouble of standing in line for each and every one of the coin-operated binocular stands. They studied the in-room displays intently, knowing they were getting in the way of other people as they did, trying to find some clue as to how the tower's TV equipment was connected to the sonar.

Their efforts were fruitless on both decks they examined. And from the one stand that offered a view of Tokyo Skytree, they saw no sign that Emi was waging any sort of battle over there.

"If he's eating dinner at the ground-floor restaurant or something, I'm gonna make him inhale soda up his nose."

Maou and Ashiya, grumbling in a sort-of threatening, sort-of ridiculous manner, trudged their way downstairs. The little signs showing the calories you'd burn based on how many steps you've taken were proving to be too much irritating trivia even for Maou's tastes.

Unlike the Skytree, Tokyo Tower was lit up at all times, making it all but impossible to hide in a convenient shadow. And there was no sign of anyone suspicious trying to hide in the scaffolding around the observation decks, either.

Which meant the only possibilities were that their target was even higher up than what the observation deck allowed, or posing as a figure in the wax museum perched underneath the tower.

"If you think about it, my liege, this sonar signal isn't something that is being constantly broadcast... The chances of this Raguel remaining here at all hours of the day might be rather low, actually."

Ashiya's theory seemed to make sense.

Even if he could keep himself in Devil King form, not even Maou was too willing to hang out in this maze of metal beams, exposed to the elements, unless he had some damn important business.

"Yeah, but…what *now*, then?"

"I am afraid we have little data to work with, but if the sonar truly is the culprit behind that incident at Socket City, that means the two sonar events today occurred five or six hours apart from each other. Which means…"

"The next one's coming at midnight or so? I can't wait that long!"

"Why not, Your Demonic Highness?"

"Um?"

Maou was puzzled at Ashiya's confusion.

"Assuming we can trust Bell, Ms. Sasaki should be safe for the time being. And while I hate to make Socket City lose any more inventory for our sakes, there won't be quite as many TVs on at midnight. As long as we can find a way to convince Ms. Sasaki's parents not to turn on the TV tonight, I think it safe enough to wait it out."

Maou looked reluctant to accept this. "Whether Chi's fine or not… If we let them launch another bolt and that gets certain other things involved, that's gonna be bad for me."

"Hmm?"

"I…I want to hear him out. What he's got to say. Now that I'm Devil King and Ente Isla's already slipped outta my hands… If I let heaven get a leg up on me like this, I'll have even less of a chance than before."

"My liege?"

Ashiya failed to follow Maou's concern. Maou ignored his servant's puzzled face as he took out his cell phone and called Suzuno.

"*Kamazuki speaking.*"

"Yeah, we did the rounds around Tokyo Tower, but we didn't spot anyone. How's Emi doing? She tell you anything yet?"

"*I cannot say. She has yet to contact me. …Hmm? What?*"

"What is it?"

"*Lucifer is… Here. I'm putting him on.*"

Maou heard some scuffling about, followed by Urushihara's shrill voice: "*Nothing, dude?*"

"No. We're startin' to think maybe he's not in the tower right now."

"Yeah, guess he wouldn't have to be there all night."

"'Maybe' is the key thing. I mean, if we just sit here, he'll have a chance to fire another sonar bolt. I dunno what to do."

"All right. You try calling Emilia yet?"

"No. I was just about to. But as far as we could tell through the binoculars, it didn't look like there was a fight goin' on or anything. Plus, if she was duking it out right now, I could probably feel the holy force all the way from here anyway."

"Okay. I'll see what kind of plan I can hatch. You mind staying where you are for now? I'll call you later and letcha know if we see anything."

"What kind of plan? Like, what are you... Hey!! Ugh, the bastard hung up on me!"

"What is wrong, my liege?"

"I dunno. It sounds like Urushihara's got some kind of wacky-ass idea in mind that he's not telling me about."

"That is certainly unsettling. Hopefully it does not involve dipping into our bank account again."

"What, you think he's gonna call a detective or something? ... Ugh. Let's give him fifteen minutes. If I don't hear from him by then, I'll have everyone group back together somewhere or other."

Maou dropped his cell phone back into his pocket and began trudging back down the stairs, Ashiya following closely behind.

✳

Suzuno, following Urushihara, ran down the streets of the Yoyogi neighborhood.

The moment Urushihara hung up, this was what he said to her:

"I'm gonna lure the angel out. Give me a hand."

Then he ran off. No further details.

"Lucifer! Where do you intend to go? We're drifting away from the station!"

The pair of them were stationed at Yoyogi precisely because it was a quick train ride from both Tokyo Tower and the Skytree. Without a handy station nearby, they had no easy mode of transport unless they tapped their supernatural powers—which they needed to conserve in case a fight broke out.

"Hey... You and Emilia, you guys can refill your holy force, right? You got some kind of method handy for that?"

"...What do you mean?"

A capped bottle of 5-Holy Energy β was at the ready somewhere in Suzuno's kimono. But she had little intention of revealing the secret to the Devil's Castle.

"We can't find Raguel. We have to, before he can fire off more of that sonar. But we can't. And we got no time to call Emilia back here. So you do it."

"Do what? What are you even bidding me to do?"

Suzuno looked up into the air once Urushihara finally stopped.

There was a needlelike tower before them, dark and smooth as an obelisk. It loomed large in the dark cityscape, the moon framing it from behind as four red warning lights flashed on each corner of its roof. It bore a company logo that Suzuno was familiar with.

"You know, I never really wanted a TV in the first place. Who needs it? If you got the Net and *maaaybe* a cell phone, that's way more than enough."

"This, this is hardly open to the public at time like this, is it?!"

Urushihara brushed off Suzuno's flustered hesitation.

"Startin' to see what I wanna do yet?"

"I do, but if you break something or cause any other problems, the entire city will descend into panic!"

"Yeah, dude. That's why I'm having *you* do it. Not Emilia or Devil King–mode Maou. We don't need to kill an archangel. Your power's *juuuust* weak enough for the job."

"...I do *not* like your tone of voice. ...I, er, that is not the problem, but... Ah! Lucifer!"

Urushihara, unwilling to let Suzuno gripe at him for the next few minutes, made a beeline for the building entrance.

A security guard attempted to stop him. As he should have. A young man in a wrinkled, sweat-stained T-shirt did not fit the profile for this building's usual clientele.

But, in a single glint of light from the purple eyes lurking underneath his long, unkempt hair, Urushihara completely disappeared from the guard's sight.

In front of the guard, stopped cold at this guy suddenly vanishing before his eyes, Urushihara turned around and motioned Suzuno to follow. Then he strode right into one of the landmark buildings of the Yoyogi neighborhood of Shibuya—the Yoyogi Dokodemo Building, usually referred to as the Dokodemo Tower.

Suzuno followed behind, hesitant at first. But, remarkably enough, nobody lifted a finger to stop this dirty-T-shirt-wearing man and kimono-wearing woman, one of the oddest couples this building had likely ever seen.

"If there's a company that does as much high-frequency transmission as a TV network, it's gotta be a cell phone company, right?"

"W-wait, are you... Are you telling me to do what Raguel did...?"

Urushihara nodded and smiled.

"Yep. Fire a sonar bolt on Dokodemo's cell phone frequencies. Use it to look for someone with more holy power than anyone in Japan'd normally have. One of the blips has got to be our angel."

"Wh-why did it have to be this...?"

Suzuno shivered, hugging herself to stave off the cold.

It was blisteringly hot at ground level, but up here, at the top of the 902-foot-high Dokodemo Tower, the base of the building's microwave antenna was in the midst of a powerful, punishing gale.

A kimono was a singularly inconvenient garment to wear in high winds. The flapping cloth was all but useless in keeping her skin insulated.

"Okay."

Suddenly, Urushihara's head popped out from an antenna maintenance corridor below, one usually restricted to company servicemen. A large map of Tokyo was in his hands, covered in frequencies and color-coded ranges.

"I've tracked down the frequency that'll reach the biggest chunk of greater Tokyo. Fire your sonar at the antenna and I'll make sure it hits that frequency. But don't touch it. It'll burn ya."

Suzuno wondered blithely if Urushihara planned to put that map back where he found it after all this was done. Judging by the state of his computer desk, the answer was probably no.

"And...and doing this won't destroy some important computer somewhere, or somesuch?"

"No, dude, it'll be fine. I just suppressed part of their bandwidth to make room for your sonar, so hurry up before customers start bitching, okay?"

"...All right! Let it be, then!"

It was hard to tell exactly what Suzuno meant by it. But there wasn't enough time to ask for clarification.

Boosting the holy power within her body to its limits, Suzuno shot it at full force toward the antenna.

"Holy Seeker!!"

The moment the power flowing out of Suzuno's hands fused itself with the microwave antenna, it shot in every direction outward, as if invisible electric lines spidered out from the installation. It formed an enormous ring of light, growing larger and larger, until its edges were several hundred feet away from Dokodemo Tower. Then it dissipated into the air, disappearing quickly.

But even if the wave of holy power was impossible for a person to see or feel, just like the signals transmitted by their cell phone, it was definitely flying off, farther and farther away, and soon it would catch something.

"Hn...nnnnh."

Holy Seeker, essentially a long-range method of detecting enemy positions, wasn't a fire-and-forget weapon. Launching the wave was little more than taking some holy force *here* and tossing it over *there*. The trick was waiting, seeking out the responses that would wing their way back from the expanding wave. It was Suzuno's job to keep her detection range as broad as possible, making sure the flow of power never stopped until she picked up something. But even though Suzuno wielded superhuman powers, that was still only compared to a normal human being. Her stores of holy force were like a can of baked beans compared to Emi's fully stocked zombie apocalypse survival bunker.

"I…I can't…"

If she kept letting the holy force pour out of her like this, she'd run dry in a matter of moments.

"Nh!"

With a groan, she thrust her hand into a pocket and took out her bottle of 5-Holy Energy β. With a single thumb whip, just like in the TV ads, she uncorked the cap and downed the entire contents on the spot.

"Whoooaaa, *that* thing, huh?"

Urushihara, right next to her, grinned in wonder, like a squirrel discovering a new acorn.

Suzuno was expecting to use the Light of Iron to jump down off the building once the job was done. That was on the back burner now. She had to use her recharged power to hang on until she picked up a response.

"…There!!"

Finally, the ring of Holy Seeker light came through for her.

Running through the wave of holy force, an unseen sensation, like a mild electric shock, shot across the Dokodemo Tower antenna and into Suzuno's body.

At that moment, she let her concentration break, heaving a mighty sigh as the sweat poured down her face.

"There's one about four miles southeast of here…two about nine miles east-northeast…one very faint reaction just southwest of here."

Urushihara eyed the map in hand disapprovingly as Suzuno gasped out her report.

"Southwest of here is Sasazuka. I don't know why it's so weak, but that's gotta be Sariel. Four miles southeast would be Tokyo Tower, I'm pretty sure, and nine miles east-northeast is near the Skytree. If Emilia and Alas Ramus are one of the Skytree blips, then… Yeaaaah, better call Maou. Someone's gotta be in the—"

"And...one more..."

"Huh?"

The sweat streaming down her body, Suzuno deftly extracted the large pin holding her hair in place. With a flash of light, it transformed into a gigantic hammer, settling into Suzuno's graceful hands.

Urushihara reared back for a moment, fearful that Suzuno's patience for being ordered around without explanation had finally wore a little too thin. But she paid him no mind as she approached the edge of the antenna installation.

"Here."

"Dude?!"

"Brace yourself, Lucifer. Something, I know not what, is approaching."

Suzuno probed the night scenery of Yoyogi below with her eyes.

There was a light among the cars, just slightly stronger than their headlights. With a flicker, it zoomed upward, following the contours of Dokodemo Tower's outer wall.

"It's coming!"

"Wh-what is?!"

Urushihara was about as unprepared to battle as any demon could be. Suzuno reared back from the edge and steeled herself, ready for whatever this attack could bring, ready and able to bash whatever confronted her in the head with everything she had as she focused her remaining holy force.

Her foe was closely hugging the building's wall. She might have to prepare for aerial combat, given that.

Then, the whooshing of the wind changed in tone.

"...!!"

Suzuno was left speechless.

Urushihara was similarly frozen, his frenzied panic now a thing of the past.

Someone they weren't expecting in a million years was now floating in front of them.

The wide-open eyes of the figure, surrounded by a faintly glowing golden light, were also a change of pace from usual.

They were purple, like Urushihara's or Sariel's.

But any otherworldly mystery these deep-violet eyes might have projected to the viewer was somewhat ruined by the flowery light-pink pajamas and the green slippers with faded golden lettering on them that read SEIKAI UNIVERSITY HOSPITAL.

"Ch-Chiho?!"

"Dude, what the hell?!"

It was Chiho, right where she really shouldn't have been.

"Oh! Hi, guys!"

The two "guys" were shocked, to be sure, but Chiho didn't seem to anticipate running into them, either. With a hand to her ear, she began talking to…someone.

"This isn't the right place! …Huh? Oh, uh, really?"

They had no idea who she was addressing. Urushihara began to wonder if Chiho, clearly enveloped in holy force, had unlocked some latent magical ability he didn't know she had.

"An Idea Link?"

"Huh? Oh, not that! I got some earbuds from Socket City with a mike attached to them. It was kinda weird going in the store in this outfit, but…"

"…Oh."

Urushihara, finally noticing the black cord wending its way from Chiho's pajama pocket to her ears, fell to his knees. Suzuno, now agitated to the point where she was spitting out her words, addressed Chiho.

"That doesn't matter! Chiho, what on Earth has happened to you?!"

"Um, I don't really have time to explain! Was that you who fired that sonar shot from here, Suzuno?"

"Y-yes."

Suzuno barely managed a nod. Having Chiho glowing a radiant gold as she asked the question was causing both of them serious confusion.

"Okay, uh, I guess you probably shouldn't do that? Like, it's kind of bad, apparently?"

"Huh?" Suzuno replied.

"She's saying you shouldn't rock the world's balance from one side only, or else everything'll get all messed up."

"Dude, Chiho Sasaki, who're you *talking* to?" The sharp-eyed Urushihara focused squarely on Chiho. "There's no way you should know about that. Who's on the other end of your line?"

This question, oddly enough, made Chiho rear back a little, obviously reluctant to answer—almost in tears about it, it seemed.

"Um, she…she told me to tell you 'take a hike, you total dimwit.'"

"Huhh?! What the hell?!"

"It-it's not me! She's, um, she's telling me what to do through this thing…"

The rare sight of Chiho half-hysterically trying to defend herself against Urushihara brought order back to Suzuno's mind.

Between Chiho's ring and what Emi had said earlier, it was clear that whoever overloaded Chiho's power with all this holy force without any ill side effects couldn't have been on Gabriel's side.

But the Chiho who greeted them wasn't under anyone's control. She was Chiho Sasaki, the same one Suzuno knew well by now.

So she, along with whomever she had on the phone, must be here on some sort of mission. But instead of asking for an explanation, Suzuno lifted her hammer, and in the blink of an eye, brought it down.

"Wave-Rending Light!!"

"Eek!"

A shock wave whizzed past Chiho as she balled herself up out of fright. Suzuno, following her own salvo, leaped off the Dokodemo Building into the night sky. The wave released by her hammer, so deftly handled by her dainty arms, flew in from the darkness…and effortlessly blew away the four balls of light that were, just then, rapidly advancing upon Chiho's back.

"…The Heavenly Regiment!"

"Ohhh, yeah, guess Gabriel *was* coming and all, huh?"

Urushihara and Suzuno glared upward at the four shadows in the air, in the direction the balls of light came from.

"None of you move!"

The Regiment, the soldiers of heaven and servants of Gabriel, had their swords at the ready, floating defiantly in the air as they tried to deter their opponents.

"...Chiho. Once you do what you must here, you may safely leave these men to us."

Suzuno's hammer remained at the ready.

"Oh, uh, but..."

"What mission brought you here, and granted you that power? ...I suppose we have no time to discuss it in detail, however. And I doubt you have gained the powers of a first-tier warrior in the course of a single evening. The Devil King and Alciel are at Tokyo Tower. Emilia is at the Skytree."

"Um... Okay!"

Chiho, glowing gold, brought both arms in front of her.

The area between her palms lit up for a moment, and then Chiho spread them out to her sides.

She pulled her right hand all the way back behind her ear, bringing her left out front at just about the same height, pointer finger extended.

Urushihara noticed that the ring on her left index finger was glowing the same shade of purple as her eyes.

Then, from thin air, Chiho produced a silvery bow of light.

Her pose, the *kai* stage of traditional Japanese archery that signified the final moment before the arrow was released, would remind onlookers of a lunar goddess from mythology if it weren't for the flower-print pajamas and slippers she had technically just stolen from the hospital.

"Maou's at Tokyo Tower, you said?"

She was turning to Urushihara for confirmation. He nodded. A small smile found its way to Chiho's face.

"Seelku etulo louseetoh!"

In her voice, in a language she couldn't possibly have understood, Chiho fired an arrow of light toward the Dokodemo antenna, just as Suzuno had done a moment prior.

It was the light of Holy Seeker, one infused with enough holy power to make Suzuno's seem like a children's game. She had spoken in Holy Vezian, using words that meant "Holy Seeker" in the sacred language.

Arcing streaks of gold light, each retaining a clear shape in the dark landscape, spread out from the Dokodemo Tower into the sky.

Unlike Suzuno's, the light streamed out across the heavens, never losing its luster or brilliance as it radiated across the Tokyo nightscape.

"I'll explain everything later! Just be careful for now!"

And with those parting words, Chiho shot like a comet east-northeast toward Tokyo Skytree.

"Halt!!"

The Heavenly Regiment attempted to give chase. They did not get far.

"You are here to fight *me*!"

In the air above the Yoyogi Dokodemo obelisk, Suzuno stood strong against the four pairs of wings.

"You aimed those spheres of holy light toward Chiho, did you not? And your eyes, as you even now attempted to give chase, were nothing I would ever call angelic. What are you possibly doing?"

Suzuno, a ferocious grin on her face, looked up at the "angels" she once prostrated herself before.

"If you act against mankind, wearing the mask of all that is holy... then it is time for me to correct this!!"

"Uh, Bell, if I could, uh, say something..."

Suzuno stopped Urushihara before he could continue from his perch next to the antenna.

"I know," she said. "But if you attempt to lead a flock doing only what you are told to do, you never truly feel the pain of your errors. You cannot regret your mistakes in any true fashion."

"Uh, what?"

"Their actions hurt innocent people and caused untold damage to other worlds. This is an error that no angel would ever dare commit. Thus, I must correct it."

The four angels in the Heavenly Regiment, clearly ready for battle, couldn't help but look confused at this.

"Sheathe thy weapon, human! We are the Heavenly Regiment, in the service of the archangel Gabriel! Thy foolish behavior goes against the will of our God and the teachings of the holy—"

"Silence, vulgar philistines!"

"…?!"

Being called "vulgar philistines" by a human clearly agitated the Regiment.

But one didn't have to be Suzuno to break out that sentiment. They looked suitably angelic during the previous visit to Villa Rosa Sasa-zuka, but now, with their T-shirts and hoodies clearly visible under their togas, the way they were half-acclimating to Japanese culture presented a less-than-divine image.

Perhaps the angels knew it. Perhaps that was what agitated them the most.

"Do not speak to me about the will of our God! Our God speaks of loving thy neighbor! How would he dare allow an innocent girl, and the peaceful land she lives in, to face this pointless violence? And you, so freely using the divine as an excuse to hurt someone…"

Then, Suzuno planted a foot on the obelisk and flew into the Shin-juku night.

"Who do you think you are?!"

Hammer in hand, her internal holy power burning, the former Death Scythe of the Council of Inquisitors all but overwhelmed the four angelic servants facing her.

"Fall back, Heavenly Regiment! Your judgment begins now!"

She pointed her hammer straight toward the angels ahead, her long hair shining dully in the air.

"One! Thy master's behavior has hurt innocent people and prop-erty. By the values of justice the Church is rooted in, I beseech thee to take proper atonement! Two! Provide one good reason why you have attempted to harm sensible, God-fearing Church members without warning! I have laid these two sins bare before the face of our God as I shall attempt to make you atone for—Hoh!"

The Regiment did not bother to listen to Suzuno's oratory to the end.

Wordlessly, they drew the same swords they had challenged her with once before and lunged forward.

Not panicking, in full control of herself, she stopped the swords with the hilt of her Light of Iron.

These were not that same as Emi's holy sword, Sariel's great scythe, or Gabriel's Durandal. These were made of simple tempered steel, completely normal in nature.

Urushihara, watching from the Dokodemo Building roof, whistled his admiration.

"Dang. Pretty intense."

"You? The child of a human, laying judgment upon the servants of heaven? You make me laugh!"

"Oh, do I? An archangel, one formerly of your ranks, came begging to me for confession, for holy mercy! But, regardless..."

Suzuno grinned as she swung her hammer to deflect a sword away.

Using the resulting recoil to spin her weapon around, Suzuno aimed it squarely at the back of one angelic soldier.

"Star-Rending Light!"

"Krahh!"

It did not send the soldier flying. Instead, the explosive force from her body sent him up in the air, eyes lolling lazily as he fell on to the roof where Urushihara was standing.

"Let your guard down, and even the child of a human can defeat you."

Suzuno swung her hammer three times in the air before letting it come to rest on her shoulder.

"I am using my holy force to overload my physical form. I created this move in the hopes of quelling the demon hordes, originally... but so be it. Who will be next? Or will you instead meekly accept my judgment and admit to your mistakes with—Oh, I suppose not, hmm?"

The remaining three soldiers attacked as one, the gist of the question already clear enough to them.

Their swords, coming from three different directions, were all blocked by the round edge of Suzuno's hammer. Then:

"Wha!"

"Yow!"

The soldiers and Urushihara let out a simultaneous cry of surprise.

She wrapped up the blades in her kimono, grabbing them all with her bare hands, then kicked them with the heel of a sandaled right foot that brimmed with holy power.

Her assailants found their allegedly galvanized swords, along with most of the bones around their right wrists, thoroughly shattered.

"We had best take our garbage with us. Sharp fragments falling from this height could cause serious injury."

Suzuno looked almost serene as she deposited the now-useless blade and scabbard shards into a sleeve.

"Now. I have given you two chances to relent. There will not be another one. The great Buddha that is found here is willing to forgive people's sins three times. Myself, I am not so patient. Twice is all I have time for."

She readied her hammer with both hands and let out a small breath.

"!!"

The angels had no time to react.

A holy-power-infused heel kicked through the air, making a sound like a mortar. The noise took them by surprise, drawing their attention away from Suzuno. While it did, the kimono-clad cleric in front of them suddenly veered behind their backs.

The next instant, after alighting behind them, Suzuno leaped once more, showing her own back to the soldiers in the blink of an eye. Her foes, expecting a hammer strike, blinked helplessly as they felt nothing more than a passing wind against their bare skin.

Suzuno, slicing the wind with her hammer as she used her free left hand to wrangle her hair back into a recognizable shape, returned her Light of Iron to its hairpin form like a samurai returning his sword to its sheath. Then, with a caress of her hair, she clicked it back in place.

"Dance of Light: Phoenix Transcending."

Everything changed.

Three shock waves of holy light echoed across the Shinjuku night sky.

The three angels, unable to withstand the wave of force from within, were knocked out instantly, just as the one before them was. As a group, they fell to the Dokodemo Building roof, directly next to Urushihara.

"Do not take humans lightly. Taste the pain of living."

"Ooh, scary."

Urushihara was very unironically shaking.

Ignoring him, Suzuno wiped the sweat of battle from her brow. She extracted a piece of debris from under her sleeve and examined it.

"But...how am I to think of this? What *are* angels, in the end?"

There was no Holy Silver gilding the swords these warriors of heaven wielded. It was not some mystery supermetal beyond human reckoning.

It was plain old iron. A metal Suzuno interacted with on a daily basis.

"Hey! Bell! Is there something else coming?!"

Suzuno turned, puzzled.

"...?"

She looked up, folding a sleeve so that its contents did not fall out.

Something was drawing toward them, from the faraway edges of the sky.

It looked like one of the bolts of light Chiho had unleashed a moment ago. But something was accompanying it.

What Chiho unleashed differed in appearance from Suzuno's, but it was a sort of sonar all the same. Then, perhaps, this was the "reaction"—a signal that the caster had found to indicate what he or she was looking for.

But was the signal it carried...within?

"*Ngh...!*"

Suzuno instinctively steeled herself. It couldn't be.

Chiho had fired a bolt of holy force just now. That was undeniable fact. And yet.

"Demonic force?!"

The belt of golden demonic power extending above the dumb-founded Suzuno's and Urushihara's heads flew southeast.

"...Huh?"

As the streak passed them by, Suzuno felt something small—trivial, perhaps, but clearly malicious—lift itself from her body.

✳

"What in the hell did Urushihara just do?"

Maou and Ashiya were standing in front of a bathroom mirror inside Tower Leg Town, a shopping complex spread out underneath Tokyo Tower, around the main elevator to the observation deck.

Ten or so minutes after Urushihara hung up on them, Maou and Ashiya felt an ominous premonition as their hair stood on end once more, as if someone was playing some static electricity-oriented practical joke on them.

"Any messages, my liege?"

"No, nothing."

Neither of them were vain or greaser-y enough to carry a tub of gel around at all times, so the two of them were now in the john, trying to wet their hair down to socially acceptable levels.

Nobody knew what was going on. That went double for Ashiya, who had been struck by Suzuno's sonar twice in the course of a day.

"Eesh. Emi isn't calling me, Raguel's nowhere to be seen... Why did we even come here?"

The two of them moaned at each other as their hair finally calmed down a little. Gloomy, they left the bathroom as they looked back at the Tower, which they had just spent far too much time going up, then back down, to no avail.

The masses around the tower still showed zero sign of dissipating. The idea of having to find someone in this crowd without knowing what he looked like filled them with fatigued irritation. Then:

"...Hey, Ashiya, do you sense that?"

"Yes... I have a bad feeling about this."

The pair exchanged uneasy looks. It was just like the last time their hair went all pointy—a sense of dizziness mixed with dread, not unlike unrelenting seasickness.

Then someone from the crowd pointed at the sky.

"Whoa, what's that? A shooting star?!"

Maou and Ashiya joined the rabble as they all looked upward. A single streak in the sky was coming in from the south. Maou's Devil King experience helped him spot it right off.

"Holy energy... Was that what made me go all tingly? Emi?"

"Your Demonic Highness, if Emi ever heard you say her presence made you 'all tingly,' it may very well be your head. Besides"—Ashiya pointed his own finger upward as he enigmatically chided his leader—"I think the source of our consternation might be behind that, actually."

Maou knew what he meant well in advance.

A streak of gold was coursing along behind the shooting star, zooming downward as if ready to envelop all of Tokyo Tower.

As it eddied around the tower, it gradually formed itself into an enormous circle of light.

This was nothing natural. Yet, there couldn't have been any spellcaster left in Japan capable of unleashing it.

"W-wow! What kinda trick is that?!"

"The northern lights?!"

"There aren't any northern lights in Tokyo! Maybe it's fireworks or something!"

Maou steeled himself, ready either for a fight or for the crowd to erupt in panic. But despite this cataclysmic turn of events, the sheer beauty of it all kept anyone from acting remotely concerned.

"Dahh, did Gabriel try pulling something stupid again?"

"Hrgh?!"

Maou spotted it. Someone in the crowd around them said that, while the rest were pointing at the sky. He looked around in a panic.

Then he realized there was a man behind him in sunglasses and a punky Afro.

"Agh! You..."

"Hmm? Oh, what a coincidence! The man from the udon shop."

Maou was stopped cold at the sight of the familiar man, dressed like some relic from the American 1970s but now, oddly, speaking perfectly fluent Japanese. Before he could react, Ashiya stepped in between them protectively.

The man tilted his sunglasses a bit, sizing up the pair. He had, for some reason, a toothpick in his mouth.

"My liege, his eyes..."

The low growl from Ashiya made Maou take a closer look.

"Purple...?"

"Mm? Something up with my eyes?"

The man's toothpick bobbed up and down as he spoke. Then he removed his sunglasses, giving them an up-close-and-personal look at his eyes.

"The udon at the ground-floor cafeteria here, y'know...not too shabby! And I think I'm startin' to get the hang of those stupid chopsticks, too!"

"Uh... Wait, you're...?"

Maou began to quiver. It was hard to tell whether it was out of anger or due to the mystery ring of light approaching them.

Taking a closer look at the man, he could see that his Afro wasn't fully black after all. There was one shock of purple, as if he decided to get a bit fancy with the hair coloring in the shower.

"*You're* Raguel?!"

"Ohh? I'm not sure I quite remember stating my name to you..."

The Afro-bedecked man's eyes opened wide in abject surprise.

"Oh, for eff's sake, you really *were* eating at the *ground floor*?!!"

Just as he spoke, the ring made contact with Tokyo Tower's antenna, bathing the structure with an enveloping shower of light.

"...Oh!"

"Huh?!"

"Oooooh! Ahhhh!"

Maou, Ashiya, and the man who was apparently Raguel all voiced their exclamation.

The moment the exploding particles of light made contact with the Tokyo Tower floor, now filled to the brim with onlookers, the glowing dots suddenly swirled together and made a beeline for two young men.

The shower made a direct hit on Maou and Ashiya. The Afro man covered his eyes at the resulting shock wave.

The sense of discomfort that greeted them instantly afterward, along with the job it did on their hair—making the guy's Afro look like amateur hour at the hotel nightclub—were both things the pair had no time to comment on.

Instantly, the transformation took place.

Within the whirlpool of gold, a darker, more sinister light was welling up from the two of them.

"Ohhhhhhhhhhhhhhhhhhhhhh!!"

The scream absorbed the golden shine, shattering it to pieces among the jet-black rays of darkness and instantly dispelling Tokyo Tower's subdued illumination.

The red-and-white tower, a constant watchman over a mighty age in human history, found itself with a seemingly endless flood of darkness emanating from beneath its chandelier of light.

A bloodcurdling voice of evil made its way out from the darkness. What it had to say, however, was not quite as foreboding as its sound.

"If you were on the ground floor, you could've *told* us, man! We had to waste so much money going up there!"

The world was now filled with a green hue, emanating from underneath the Tower.

The next moment, the green light covered all of the area around Tokyo Tower, freezing everything within.

Just like the demonic barrier that was triggered over Sasazuka once, all people and things in the green light were both there and not there, in another realm and protected from all destruction taking place within the sphere.

From afar, the aurora-like barrier probably made it look like Tokyo Tower was all done up for St. Patrick's Day.

The lone demon behind this phenomenon, his eyes brimming

with enough anger to put anyone they gazed upon into cardiac arrest, glared at the Afroed man.

"I'm gonna make you inhale soda up your nose!!"

At that moment, the Devil King Satan and his Great Demon General Alciel descended upon Tokyo Tower, the demonic force tucked inside the golden light firmly ensconced within their bodies.

"What are you talking about, man?!"

The Afro man tossed his sunglasses aside and returned a snide stare. But, when he opened his mouth, he did not address the demons.

"Eesh, Gabe, did you know *these* guys were in Japan?"

"!!"

The Devil King Satan's UniClo T-shirt, stretched beyond all reasonable limit, opened up a new tear as he turned around, quickly growing as battered and bruised as his one missing horn.

"Yeah, sorrr-eeee. Didn't think they'd get involved, all right?"

Since when was *he* here?

There, within the Devil King's barrier and looking none the worse for wear from the demonic force flowing around him, was the proud angel who once tried to take Satan and the Hero's child away from them.

It was Gabriel, the "shooting star" who had chased the streak of light all the way to Tokyo Tower.

✳

"...Mommy?"

"......"

"Moooommmmyyy..."

In a corner of the Tokyo Skytree observation deck, Emi was balled up on the floor, hands on her knees.

Alas Ramus tugged at her, her face wavering toward tears as she steadfastly refused to let her alone. Emi did not respond.

Emilia's father was alive.

She remembered when they were separated, five years ago. The sight of her father standing before her, hazy through the tears. It transformed in her mind into sadness and anger, and it was what kept her fighting.

Compared to that, the story of how angels were not supernatural beings at all seemed like a mere triviality. Nothing about Lucifer or Sariel, certainly, suggested they were supernatural at all. If anything, it made it clearer what heaven really was—a powerful organization that saw her as its enemy. Nothing more, nothing less.

But more important than that, her father was alive.

It should have been ample cause for joy and celebration, something she hoped and wished for more than anything.

But her legs were too jittery to prove much use.

There was little chance Gabriel was lying about it. He had nothing to gain personally by deceiving Emi about Nord's health.

One of the issues that made heaven "pretty well cut in two," as Gabriel put it, no doubt stemmed from the fact that Laila and Nord had a child in the first place. It had the potential to muddy the waters so deeply, to rob heaven and the angels of their invincible holy aura, that they probably saw that as a danger.

Heaven, and its denizens, were the target of worship and adulation precisely because people believed they were supernatural, beyond human comprehension. If they realized they were just another race, of sorts—a culture with a different civilization from theirs—that would be the end of the gravy train, so to speak.

Ente Islans, after all, were capable of miracles just as astonishing as those in heaven could conjure. The only difference, really, was the scale involved.

No, if Gabriel wanted to lie, he would've said Nord was dead, no longer part of this or any world.

Then he could have manipulated the world's image of her father, the father of the Hero Emilia, any way he wanted. He could have revealed to Ente Isla that Nord was a simple wheat farmer. He could say that he enjoyed a place in heaven, or was appointed an angel. Anything. It would have been twisting the knife.

And before that, it was only natural to hate someone for killing your parents. Emi was hardly friends with Maou at first. If Gabriel had confirmed that Nord was dead, it would have made Emi hate the Devil King Satan all the more. In fact, it could have even helped heaven quash two annoying mosquitoes at once.

But Gabriel hadn't said that. He'd said Nord, her father, was alive.

That, in itself, enshrouded the road ahead in fog. She turned her head up a bit, only to find Alas Ramus's pained expression sizing up her own.

"Mommy? Are you okay? Your tummy hurt?"

"...No. I'm fine. I'm fine, but..."

She smiled weakly and buried her face back between her legs.

"...I'm just trying to...you know, figure out what I should do."

"What do you want to do?"

It was something she was fully aware of from the first time she stood on the battlefield as a Church knight, but the one reason she savored the most, the single greatest inspiration she had to defeat the Devil King's army, was in order to exact revenge for her father.

Since arriving in Japan, she had admittedly gotten rather chummy with the Devil King—purely because of circumstances beyond their control, certainly nothing voluntary about it—but not once had she seem him as anything other than an enemy she must slay sooner or later.

But.

"Is this someone who shouldn't matter to me anymore? Just because my father's alive?"

A man of the land, her father certainly had muscle, but he couldn't have had much in the realm of battle training. Seeing the strength and cruelty of the demon hordes for herself, seeing the charred remains of what was once her village, all she could imagine was that Nord died a helpless, ignoble death. It was the only conclusion to make.

So she spent the next five years contemplating the idea of having the Devil King taste her father's pain, her father's bitterness. It was always on her mind.

The fact he was now alive, of course, didn't make all of that hate disappear like a candle flame.

He might be ill or injured, for one. And there was no wiping away the pain and anger of seeing her peaceful upbringing destroyed before her eyes.

Not even as the Hero, but as just another Ente Islan, she could never forgive any of the pestilence and tragedy the Devil King's army had exacted upon her native land.

But with one of the larger gears in the clockwork that drove her to set off against the Devil King now popped out of its socket, there was no denying that her heart was now beating to a different rhythm.

And the gears that remained were clueless as to how they should mesh together any longer.

All that remained in the room was the can of low-sugar coffee Gabriel had left on the floor as a souvenir.

Around the point that he suggested her father might be in Japan, Gabriel started pressing her for payment—in the form of how Chiho was doing.

Emi was shaken. She had zero intention of divulging anything about a friend as precious as Chiho, but now a part of her heart was literally playing devil's advocate for her, suggesting that spilling the beans might get her that bit closer to her father.

But time did not allow Emi to waver.

Below her, as her mind foundered between her desires and her conscience, an enormous mass of energy zoomed by.

"Ah, crap crap crap *crap*."

The easy grin on Gabriel's face disappeared. He finished off the remaining coffee.

"Okay, that's all for now. I kinda gotta cover my ass for the time being, so this little confab's over. Let's call that info I gave you a freebie, all right? Feel free to pay me back next time. With interest!"

"W-wait a—"

"Though I s'pose it ain't easy for you, but..."

His face had an uncharacteristic somberness to it. Then he used one magic or another to float right through the walls and windows, and then he was flitting outside the observation deck.

"...it's not like everybody in heaven uses their job title as carte blanche to do anything they want, y'know? We just don't wanna die, like everybody else. And maybe I don't, like, show it off much, but I know full well that folks down there are worshipping us."

And soon, he left, flying toward the mystery blob of energy. Both of them traveled south. *Something must be happening at Tokyo Tower, where Maou is.*

But it still couldn't make Emi move.

Who should she be fighting? What reason did she have? What did she have to protect? It was all chaos in her mind.

"Hey...Alas Ramus?"

"Oo?"

"I think this Hero stuff's too much of a load on my shoulders. I used to be a simple farm girl, just like all the others around me. Maybe if I had some better schooling from a younger age, I could've had some more resolve. Like, forget about the little details, just slay the Devil King! That kind of thing."

"No Hero? You don't like it?"

She couldn't understand some of the loftier concepts, but it was remarkable how Alas Ramus grasped at the crux of it, beautifully encapsulating what Emi wanted to say.

"I used to. I did. But if I was never the Hero, I probably never would've run into you, so I don't think it's so bad now."

"Nee-hee!"

"Alas Ramus?"

"Yeahh?"

"What do you want to be when you grow up?"

Alas Ramus blinked a couple times at the question. *Must be too young for that talk*, Emi figured.

"I wanna be Rewax-Berr!"

Or not. Her eyes twinkled as she raised two triumphant arms in the air.

Emi wasn't expecting an actual occupation, but the response she earned threw her for such a loop that silence reigned for a few moments. Then, a soft smile came across her face.

"You want to be Relax-a-Bear, huh?"

"Yehh! And, and..."

Alas Ramus climbed up on Emi's body. It was an effective debating tactic.

"…cuwwy!"

"Huh?"

Emi furrowed her brows. She had never fed curry to Alas Ramus before.

The Devil's Castle promised they were feeding her age-appropriate food as well. Curry would've been out of the question. So why was it her favorite thing now?

"Mommy love Rewax-Berr and cuwwy! I love Mommy, too! When I grow up, Alas Ramus, Rewax-Berr! Cuwwy!"

"…Oh."

When she grew up, she wanted to be the things Emi loved.

Emi could feel the tears coming. She hugged the little girl close, in order to distract herself.

"I'm sorry. Guess Mommy's turning into a wimp, huh?"

"Eat cuwwy?"

"Once Chiho's all better, let's all go eat some together."

"Okeh!"

Alas Ramus shot her right hand upward in approval.

"Mph."

And hit Emi in the nose.

"…Heh. Maybe I needed that, huh?"

The tears came back, for a different reason this time. Emi finally found it in her to stand back up.

"Not like it's the first time I've decided to procrastinate large decisions. Right now, I've gotta take action to protect what's in front of me. What happens later…I can think about then."

For now, as long as Raguel was clearly hurting Chiho, Laila, and Japan in general, he was undoubtedly Emi's foe.

Gabriel had just let slip that he was trying to avoid interference between Raguel's sonar waves from the Tokyo Tower and the digital test broadcasts from the Skytree.

Which meant that the main field of battle was clearly going to be Tokyo Tower—Maou, Ashiya, and Raguel, all in one place.

And if they were going to take on Gabriel or Raguel in combat, they had zero chance of winning. Beyond that, there was the danger of the Devil King being taken back to Ente Isla, as Suzuno suggested.

"I still don't know how to deal with this…but I can't have him that far away from me!"

She felt safe in exclaiming it out loud. Nobody from the ground was going to pick on her about it.

So she retraced her steps, running through the same service corridor to reach the observation deck's roof. It was right when she focused on her legs in preparation for a full-strength leap that she was interrupted.

"Ooh, not right now. Tokyo Tower's shut away in Maou's demonic barrier. If you try to force your way in, that'll break the barrier and probably hurt a lot of people and stuff."

"…*Ngh!* Wh-who's there?!"

Nobody should have been in the Skytree except for Emi and Alas Ramus. And Alas Ramus was fused within her.

"I sure am glad to see you, though! Good to see everybody's still here in Japan, too."

The light was streaming down from above Emi's vantage point on the roof.

The form within it continued speaking to the speechless Hero.

"Let's go together, okay? I'll make an entrance for you."

"Ch-Chiho… Why are you…"

"Are you ready, Yusa?"

Chiho, bathed in a holy golden light, didn't wait for Emi's response as she loaded a holy-force arrow into the silvery bow of light she summoned out of thin air.

"…!"

Then, with a sudden release of concentration, the silver air penetrated the night sky, sending Chiho and Emi southward through the air on its light trail.

Their forms were lost in the dazzling light. All that remained to break the silence was the blustering wind beating against the scaffolding.

✳

"Oooh, things're getting fun now, huh?"

Gabriel defiantly looked down upon the two demons within their world of green light. The Afro man, between Satan and Alciel, sullenly glared at his heavenly partner.

"No. Not at *all*, they're not! Why'd you come all the way here from the *other* tower, Gabe?! Sonar's all about precision! You're gonna screw it all up!"

Behind this man, roughing it in his Afro, preworn denim, and T-shirt, two unexpected and rather out-of-place wings emitted a soft, glowing light.

"Yeah, well, Emilia distracted me. But we don't need sonar any longer, no? No way any normal guy could make that energy wave just now. We could find it right now if we looked a little."

"Look, did you think that *didn't* occur to me or something? Think about it."

Raguel and Gabriel locked eyes for one uncomfortable moment.

"You think *this* guy's gonna let me go anywhere right now? I mean, look at those eyes. They're demonic."

"Would you expect anything else?"

The dark voice seemed to rumble upward from beneath the ground. Its power, like the guttural growl of a death-metal front man, was enough to keep both archangels riveted in place.

"You bastards better not even *think* of taking one step outside this barrier."

"……"

Devil King Satan, accompanied by the Great Demon General Alciel.

Two angels and two demons, facing off at Tokyo Tower, locked into a proverbial steel cage of demonic force.

"That, and… Come *onnn*, I thought there wasn't any demonic force in this world! This is *totally* Devil King Satan right here, isn't it?! I dunno who that muscly weirdo next to him is, but…Gabe, could this *be* any different from what we first talked about? Huh?"

"Yeah, yeah, sorr-eeeee. I wasn't really lying, though! I really didn't think they'd bother getting involved at all. Pinky swear! It's just… It's all that *thing's* fault."

Gabriel used his hands to simulate the events of the past few minutes—the hail of light, along with Satan and Alciel's sudden appearance.

"Pretty cute light show, but the ending needs some work, no? If you ask me, Laila must've stumbled onto something we don't know about."

"Uggghhh… Look, can we just make this simpler for all of us? She's kicked out of heaven anyway. We deploy the entire Regiment, we wipe out anyone who knows anything about this, bada-bing, bada-boom. Like we care about what happens to this nation anyway—"

"*Not* gonna happen."

"……"

Gabriel shot a look at Satan's face. But before he even had time for that, Raguel had already fixed his ire upon the Devil King.

"And what's with *you*, besides? Transforming into a human, all struttin' your stuff and showing off your English skills to everybody… You completely tricked me! And why are you messing with us, anyway? You coulda just sat there and slurped up your udon, like a good little boy! I know you and Gabe have kind of a past, but I didn't even *do* anything to you guys! You mind butting out of heavenly affairs a little?!"

It was a full-on diatribe. Bits of spittle flew out the edge of his mouth as he ranted. Gabriel, watching on, grimaced in awkward embarrassment.

"Uhh, Raguel? I know that's, like, the case and everything, but if you say that to them…"

Jets of black flame shot up from behind Satan and Alciel.

"…See? I knew you'd piss them off. I knew it!"

"Your inane squabbling with each other… It hurt one of our friends."

The darkness advanced, the light edging backward.

"If you've changed your doctrine so it's okay to rule over the world with violence now…well, hell, I could've still respected that. That was kind of my plan when I invaded the human world myself. I'm evil. I force people to do my bidding under the threat of violent harm. So when I see anyone like you two… It makes me want to pummel you."

Satan was now within point-blank range of Raguel. Then, the next instant, he sent a fist sailing toward the side of his slack-jawed face.

"Oghh?!"

With an eerily off-putting groan, Raguel was thrown against the Tokyo Tower scaffolding.

"Nhh… That was fast…"

"His Demonic Highness never hesitates to land the first blow."

"You were too slow, all right?"

It was becoming unclear whose side Gabriel was on.

"Trampling all over people like it's your prerogative, acting like it's all for some great cause… You won't find anyone that low, even in the demon realms. You know what we usually like to call ourselves… Gabriel?"

"…'Demons,' right?"

Gabriel sounded oddly proud of himself, although he took care to remain poised for battle.

"Yes. We are demons. We are evil itself. We cannot live without preying upon someone. The lowest of the low!"

Satan, King of the Demons, sounded like he was at a confessional.

"And if you aren't prepared to live with the sins you commit, then stop bitching about it to other people! This is the world of humans! A world where you have to live with everything you've ever done! It's all weighing upon your back!!"

"…Uh, so are they gonna fight us, or what, Gabe?"

"Kinda lookin' like it, yeah."

Satan's fist had about as much permanent effect on Raguel as his tirade just now. Despite how far he had been blown, there wasn't a single bruise on his face.

The scaffolding he was thrown into was similarly unscathed, protected by Satan's demonic barrier. There wouldn't be any repeat of the Shuto Expressway near-disaster of time gone by.

"You take 'em, Gabe."

"Oh, I *knew* this would happen..."

"You were expecting something else? Combat wasn't really in my job description. I *told* you that right at the start! That I'd have my hands full tracking down Laila!"

Not pausing to hear Gabriel's response, Raguel flew up toward the topmost antenna of Tokyo Tower.

He was trying, in other words, to break Satan's barrier. The border between himself and the sky above him was closer than the boundaries covering the ground at either side.

Then several things happened at once.

Satan chased behind Raguel—who made it up to Observation Deck 1 in the blink of an eye—at supersonic speed, attempting to land a dark, flame-infused punch on his body.

Gabriel, traveling even faster than Satan, flew between him and Raguel's back to stop him. Alciel, watching on from his original position, released a telekinetic wave straight toward Gabriel.

But as Gabriel stopped the Devil King's attack cold:

"*Syahh!*"

Using nothing but his eyes and sheer force of will, he brushed off Alciel's beam attack.

The Great Demon General, who had the power to effortlessly move countless gigantic boulders around during the Battle of Sasazuka before, didn't even make the guardian angel of Sephirot break a sweat.

"Guyyyys, don't you remember? Even during the Devil King's heyday, he *still* probably couldn't have beaten me, all right?"

Satan attempted to pull his fist away. Gabriel refused to let it budge an inch.

"I've got a job here myself, y'know. It's not like transdimensional combat is my hobby or something. And I really feel for that girl, too. Seriously! It's just... Maybe it all seems totally nutso to you all, but to us, it's kinda life or death."

"!!"

Satan, feeling the holy force well up from Gabriel's palm, boosted his own body's demonic power.

"Ooh, perceptive of you. Bit late, though."

An alien form of energy penetrated through the demonic force and under his skin.

It was the all-time mother of sonar bolts, packing an untold amount of holy power—far more than what Suzuno jabbed into Ashiya for fun at the hospital.

The holy force within Gabriel's vessel coursed past Satan's demonic life energy, rankling his body as it robbed him of strength like snake venom.

There was nothing flashy to the attack, but it was enough to make the King of All Demons' vision blur.

However, Gabriel had no follow-up attack in mind, it seemed. Satan made a mighty leap backward, away from his foe, his breathing labored from the excruciating pain.

"Head on out, Raguel. You can probably sniff out Laila's trail once you're outside. I can take these guys alone."

Gabriel pointed at the ceiling. Raguel flew off without another word.

Like any wall, if a force was applied to Maou's barrier that outclassed his demonic force, it would crumble apart. A single hole wasn't enough to bring the whole thing down. But it had to hold. It had to keep the battle from leaking to the outside world, and it had to cage up two archangels at the same time.

But if Gabriel gained the upper hand all by himself and Raguel escaped, all was lost.

"Ashiya! Stop him!"

Alciel was already in motion before Satan bellowed the command. Approaching from Gabriel's blind spot, he fired six simultaneous shots of telekinetic force at Raguel—two from his eyes, two from his hands, and two from his dual-tipped tail.

"Try again!"

A blast of wind raked across Alciel.

Gabriel, facing Satan until just a moment ago, now had something resembling a sword in his hand, using it to shrug Alciel's telekinesis away.

The blade must have been quite a bit longer once. A closer look revealed that, considering the size of the hilt, the blade was astonishingly short.

"Durandal..."

Alciel angrily spat out the name.

It was Gabriel's sword, spoken of in legends but shattered into pieces by the Better Half once Alas Ramus fused with it.

"Mm-hmm! Never really could rematerialize the end of it, though. It looks *so* lame, doesn't it?"

Now the sword, which looked like it was chopped in two about halfway down its length, was zooming its way toward Satan, Gabriel lunging behind.

"!!"

Satan, feeling something silently swoop toward him, tilted his head a little.

Despite the distance between them, there was now blood oozing out of a scratch on his cheek.

"Funny thing is, though, it still cuts just as good as it always did! And I don't care how good the material on your UniClo wardrobe is—it ain't gonna put up much resistance to this, you know?"

"...So try it." Alciel refused to falter.

Flying toward Gabriel, he began to launch a flurry of strikes with his tail and the claws on each hand.

"Wh-whoa, whoa, look out! You're gonna get your fingers chopped off with this... Huh?"

Gabriel, not wanting to permanently maim Alciel, prepared to strike him with the butt of his sword. But something seemed off. It was strangely heavy in his hand.

There was no room to swing Durandal between the attacks.

"Oh? Oh? Ohhh?"

"...! ...! ...!"

Gabriel had one sword. But Alciel had three methods of attack. And while it took time, the silent barrage of strikes with his claws and the hook-like spikes on his tail gradually began to swipe against Gabriel's body.

"Ow! Dahh! Jeez, that tingles!"

"That stoic act isn't just for show, man. He means it."

Gabriel, unable to handle Alciel's bombardment, now had Satan behind his back.

"Gehh?!"

He noticed a moment too late, as Satan took his enormous hands and grabbed his head from behind.

"Who do you think put up with the humans' incessant resistance until the very end?"

"Agh! W-wait, wait a—!"

"Ashiya—the Great Demon General Alciel's body is the toughest in the Devil King's Army. No greater defensive genius out there. You could hit him with Emi's sword, and he still won't get hurt that easy."

"Die!"

"Nnhh!!"

Alciel's claws dug their way deeper into Gabriel's flesh, penetrating skin. Even an archangel could find its match against the strength and demonic force of the Devil King and his right-hand man. Or, for a moment, so it seemed.

"Still, nice tryyy!"

Despite being all but disemboweled, Gabriel shed not a drop of blood as he vanished like a white vapor, his head disappearing in Satan's hands. The two demons were left bewildered.

"I love fighting you guys. Emilia, too. So direct and to the point!"

The voice came from behind Satan.

There was no time to turn around. The edge of Gabriel's palm thudded against Satan's back, with what seemed like no great force.

"Bang!"

"Gaaaahhhh!!"

But even that was enough to send Satan flying. Even barreling into Alciel didn't stop him from tumbling helplessly to the ground, fully vulnerable.

"Wh-what…?"

"Eesh. You don't have to look *that* surprised, guys. It's nothing that world ending. Just a little trick with afterimages, all right? This whole time, ever since I deflected that telekinesis Alciel threw at Raguel, you guys have been fighting my stunt doubles, so…"

Then, apropos of nothing, Gabriel put his hands together in prayer.

That seemed to signal a group of angels to materialize in the air like popcorn, each the spitting image of a simpering Gabriel.

"So basically, the two of you put together can juuuuuust about take on one of my fakes. So just knock it off, all right? Nobody's gonna criticize you for it. I'm not gonna do anything bad to you, either."

"You…you think we'd actually say yes to that, you bastard…?"

Satan glared at Gabriel as he arduously brought himself back to his feet.

"Did you do something to Emi?"

"Hmm?"

"That 'girl' you talked about," Satan continued. "How come you know something happened to Chi?"

"…Uh, hello? Anyone home? You just said we hurt one of your friends, bro."

"That coulda been Urushihara, it coulda been Suzuno, it definitely coulda been Emi. How'd you know it was the one girl least likely to be involved in this?"

"Oh. Yeah. …Okay, guilty as charged, I heard it from Emilia. We met over at Skytree a sec ago."

Gabriel shrugged his shoulders, plainly ruing his mistake.

"But all I know is that Raguel's sonar knocked her out, all right? She didn't tell me about anything else. Boy, I had all kinds of juicy info I coulda leaked out to her, too…"

"What?"

"'Course, what I *did* give her kinda made her lose the will to fight, maybe, soooo… But you really oughta thank me, don'tcha? There's *one* enemy of yours outta the picture, at least."

"*What* did you do to her…?"

"Hey, whoa, whoa, nothing! Nothing *that* much. I just told Emilia her dad's alive somewhere, that's all."

"!!!"

The first reaction from Satan's brain was to recall the Hero Emilia pointing the Better Half at him, screaming about revenge. After that came Emi Yusa, scratched and bruised after falling down his rickety staircase, condemning Sadao Maou through teary eyes about what he had done to her family.

"My liege…?"

Alciel, ever sensitive to his master's behavior, noticed something was off. By now he had at least a vague sense of what lay at the root of Emi's deep-seated, monomaniacal hatred for Satan. But why would that bother Satan at all? It never had before.

"Gabriel…has anyone ever told you you really suck at picking up on social cues?"

"Yeah, I seem to remember *someone* in here calling it a 'B-movie act' not long ago, no? I'm not gonna say no to that, though, so… yeaaahh, maybe."

"Is that fun for you? Taking people's emotional supports and swiping them out from under them?"

"Oh, totally! But not as fun as it is watching *you* worrying about your sworn enemy Emilia, though!"

"…Lowlife."

Gabriel's smile weathered the hateful assault Alciel spat at it.

"Ooh, quite the honor! But if I could get in a word here real quick, I think it'd be nice if she'd knock off that boring 'slay the Devil King' mumbo-jumbo. Take a broader view of things, y'know? The big picture. Whatever crutch she's leaning on… That's just getting in the way, if you asked me."

"…?"

Satan stopped for a moment, unsure what to make of this. He didn't have long to ponder over it.

"Gaaaaaaaaabe!!"

Raguel interrupted the proceedings from his perch far above the fight, near Observation Deck 1. As he did, a powerful light burst forth from Tokyo Tower's antenna.

"Aww, this was just getting fun, too…"

Gabriel dejectedly resented his supposed friend and partner's appearance.

"A sonar bolt come in, or what?!"

"I dunno, man, I don't have a TV…"

Satan and Alciel, helplessly pinned down by Gabriel, had no idea what Raguel was trying to do.

"Okay, uh, Gabe, I think we got trouble!"

"Huh?"

"I can't flyyy-y-y-y…"

"Huhh?"

The voice zoomed by, falling past Gabriel's, Satan's, and Alciel's astonished eyes.

"……"

There, on top of Observation Deck 1, like a duck shot by a rifleman, Raguel lay sprawled on the roof.

"Still safe, huh?"

Another voice came, this one from above where Raguel had fallen from. Craning his neck, Satan saw a familiar sight—in a way, that was. Compared to an angel falling from the sky like an artillery shell hitting him, almost anything seemed normal. Especially her.

Emilia, eyes of scarlet and hair of blue-tinged silver, looked down upon the two demons, a perplexed look on her face.

But everyone—Satan, Alciel, even Gabriel—was transfixed by the person next to her instead.

"Ch-Chi?!"

"Ms. Sasaki…"

Her hair, already saddled by bed head, tore about wildly in the wind, framing her pink flower pajamas and green hospital slippers.

She was supposed to be in a hospital bed, in fact. But now Chiho Sasaki—enveloped in an aura of shining holy energy and holding a bow made of silvery light—was standing alongside the Hero of another world at the peak of Tokyo Tower.

"Maou! Ashiya! Are you okay?!"

"N-no, uh, I mean, I don't…? Are, are *you* okay, Chi?! I mean, what's 'okay' even mean anymore?! What happened to you?!"

One could look up *flabbergasted* in the dictionary and see a photo of the King of All Demons, shot at this very moment.

"Devil King! We'll talk later! Just stop Raguel, now!"

Emilia still made sideways glances at Chiho from the corner of her eye as she attempted to stir Satan into action.

"Just save all your stupid questions for after this and figure out a way to get those meddling angels out of the picture!"

With a kick against the antenna, Emilia was instantly between Gabriel and the demons. Her back was turned to Satan and Alciel.

"Wow. Pretty quick recovery. I figured you'd need to see a therapist or something, no?" Gabriel's attention was still chiefly on Chiho as he spoke.

"…Look," Emi snapped, "with all this ridiculous crap going on, I just decided that I can save the thinking for later!"

"Ooh, that's gonna bite ya later, I think. I mean, saving all the hard stuff for tomorrow? That's pretty much Lucifer's philosophy, isn't it?"

"I don't care right now! Ashiya! Let's stop Raguel! I don't want to blow this like I did with Sariel! Once the Gate's open, I'll toss him halfway across the universe!"

"By all means!"

It was clear from their last meeting that Gabriel couldn't beat Emi in a fair fight.

The demons knew what they had to do. One, leave Gabriel in her capable hands. Two, keep Raguel from launching any more sonar bolts.

They surrounded Raguel as he shakily got back up, each taking one side. The sight set Raguel off on another trademark rant.

"What is *with* you pricks, anyway?! Is Laila *that* important to you?! Would you mind not sticking your necks into human-world affairs for a change?! Just go away and take over the world or something! The entire future course of events in heaven depends on whether we catch Laila or not! So butt *out*!"

"Y'know, I don't remember her being all that much of a big-shot angel. Not exactly the guardian angel of Sephirot or anything, right? Just a single mom with kind of a fancy job title. What's got you so riled up over her?"

"I'm not touching that question with a ten-foot pole! If I answer that, you'll know exactly what I *don't* want all of you to know! These are heavenly affairs! No outsiders allowed!!"

"Ooh, that's not going to work."

An arrow of light landed near the raving Raguel, triggering a small explosion.

"Whoa?!"

They looked up to find Chiho, bow still at the ready after firing her initial salvo.

"That was a warning. Your behavior is disrupting the balance of power in this world. Stop using your sonar and leave at once!"

Satan, for the first time, noticed the glowing ring on Chiho's left hand, the one currently holding the bow.

Raguel looked down where the arrow struck, gnashing his teeth.

"Silence! I don't know if you've possessed that human girl or learned how to control her from afar, but now that you're here, it's time to earn my salary! Once I trace your trail of holy energy, my job here is done!"

"They have salaries up in heaven?"

"……"

"…Hey, say something."

Unlike Shirou Ashiya, Alciel in demon form never bothered reacting angrily to Satan's terrible jokes. It disappointed the Devil King a tad.

"*Seelku etuloo*—oooohhh?!"

Raguel attempted to lob something at Chiho, who was above him. Satan and Alciel reared back in a panic, but Chiho refused to budge.

Not even the bow in her hand moved an inch, as if she were expecting the attack the whole time.

It sounded as if Raguel chanted some kind of magic…but he gave up midway. Suddenly, he fell to his knees, like a puppet with its strings cut.

"Wha, wha, what is…"

Staring at his hands, Raguel stammered in utter confusion. But struggle as he did, he no longer had full control of his body. Even standing was too much of a challenge now.

"Why do you think your wings disappeared just now?"

Chiho breezily floated down to the observation deck roof, joining Satan and Alciel down below.

"This Yesod fragment may not be the whole thing, but the next time it strikes you, I can't guarantee you'll function as an angel ever again. So just go home before that happens, all right? You are not my enemy. In a world far, far away, we are friends."

"Kah...hah..."

"Wh-what on...?"

Even Satan could see it. The stream of holy force leaking out from Raguel's back.

The flash that occurred when Emilia and Chiho appeared must have been the light from Chiho's first arrow striking Raguel's wings.

"Ai yai yai, that ain't good... *Hooph!*"

Gabriel, attempting to take on Emilia as he watched Raguel, brought his hands together. The next moment, a ball of light enveloped him, and he disappeared from Emi's sight.

"?!"

Following her sixth sense, Emi spotted Gabriel, now next to the curled-up Raguel. It was nothing short of instant teleportation.

Satan and Alciel immediately took flight to separate themselves from him. Even Chiho kept a respectable distance. But Gabriel just stood there, showing no sign of wanting a fight.

Then, for reasons only he was aware of, he removed the T-shirt from under his toga and began waving it above his head. The rippling upper-body muscles he exposed to the world as he did would send any would-be bodybuilder into fits of jealousy.

"'Kay, I'm out! *No más!* Fat lady's sung! This is gonna have to pass for a white flag, all right?"

"Huhh?!"

"Agh, Gabe, what're you—*Gahh?!*"

Gabriel placed his palm on the head of Raguel, curled into a ball but still willing to fight.

"What are you...?"

That was enough to cut the strings for good. Raguel was now sprawled on the roof.

The shocked Emilia and demon crew to his side, Gabriel tossed the languid, likely unconscious Raguel on one shoulder. Emilia, watching this bizarre act, had trouble figuring out what to do next.

"What're you trying to do?"

"Ummm, well, how to put it? Now that Emilia's in the picture, I'm startin' not to like my chances so much, y'know? That other girl's some kinda phenom, too, apparently. But you know Raguel's not gonna listen to a word of it. I mean, I'm not really in a position where I can go double-crossing heaven all the time, but that doesn't mean I wanna die fighting for 'em or anything. Although..."

He turned his eternally simpering grin toward Chiho, floating in the air.

"Watching you and everyone else on Earth... I'm startin' to want to see my own world change, too, you get me? So here's hoping you can keep everything going smoothly over here. Betcha do it too, huh?"

"......"

That last sentence was aimed at Chiho.

"...But anyway. Me and her, we got to that conclusion via two completely different paths, so no funny ideas about *that*, are we clear? Just have fun chewing over all the little hints I've been dropping at you. I bet Raguel's gonna be pissed later, but don't worry—I'll make sure him and the Regiment get ferried back home safe, all right? Adios!"

"Agh! Hey!!"

"Wait!"

Emilia and Satan had no chance to stop him.

The ball of light covered them in an instant. In another, they were both completely gone from sight.

Satan expected another strike from some unexpected blind spot. But, after several seconds of silence, no attack seemed forthcoming.

The fact that the faintly glowing, green demonic barrier that protected everyone and everything inside had not even the slightest scratch on it was, if anything, a blow to Satan's pride as a warrior.

That was because, although he'd constructed it to keep the pair of angels from escaping, Gabriel had just revealed that he could teleport himself out of it anytime he wanted.

"...*Deh*. Treating me like some kind of idiot..."

Satan clenched his teeth, along with his fists. Emilia's eyes arced downward as she stared at the space Gabriel and Raguel had previously occupied.

"What was Gabriel trying to do...? If he wanted to, he could've helped Raguel finish his mission long before any of us were involved."

Alciel's eyes were elsewhere.

"...Our enemy's gone. I don't feel them anywhere nearby...and there's something more important on my mind, too."

Satan and Emilia found themselves following his gaze.

"Yeaaah, um..."

The three of them were sizing up the even greater enigma that remained. Chiho, somehow blessed with a new and massive power, was in front of them.

The aura of holy force, easily the equal of Emilia's, still surrounded her. A blast of demonic force had put her in a coma before, but none of the evil power tossed around at the base of Tokyo Tower seemed to faze her now. This sudden, rapt attention from the others caused her to fidget and blush a bit. She bowed meekly.

"I-I'm sorry! I don't think this'll last much longer..."

The apology, and the body language, were both classic Chiho.

"H-hey!"

"I know I kind of ragged on Raguel and Suzuno about it, but I had to throw the world's energy balance off a lot to build up demonic force for Maou and Ashiya, too. It sounds like I have to rebalance it pretty quickly, so... Uh, uh, okay! All right, I understand! I'll be right there!"

Chiho put her hands to her ears and shut her eyes, like someone was shouting right next to her.

"Wh-what's going on?"

"Um, she said she doesn't know, and that's the bad part about it!"

"*Who* said? Chiho, is there someone talking in your...?"

Then Emilia realized it. There was a pair of black earbuds, with mike, in her ears. Chiho wasn't being possessed or controlled by anyone. Right now, she was moving by her own free will, borrowing someone else's power as she did. And there was only one person she could have borrowed it from.

"...My mother?! Is it my mother?!"

"Uh, uhm, Yusa, I'm really sorry, but the way she's putting it, we're really, *really* short on time, so..."

Emilia's probing query flustered Chiho a bit. Quickly, she readied her bow again.

"Maou, Ashiya, get back down to the roof of the deck! It's too dangerous for you!"

"Dangerous? What is?!"

"Ch-Chiho! What're you doing?! Please, could you lend me your phone for a—"

"*Nngh*, I'm sorry...!"

Chiho grimaced at the group's disparate reactions. Still, with a light kick of her own against the Tokyo Tower antenna, she propelled herself yet higher into the night sky.

"Chihoooooo!!"

"I'm sooooorrrrryyyyyy!!"

The divine presence of Chiho, coupled with her not-at-all-divine apology, fired a silvery arrow straight down at the antenna below her.

"Whoaahh?!"

The moment it struck the spire, the whole process began anew.

Sadao Maou's transformation into Satan took place in total reverse, as if some god up above was rewinding the tape on him.

The green demonic barrier melted away, while Satan and Alciel felt the demonic energy ebb from their bodies.

Emilia was unaffected, but still had to steel herself to keep the gushing flow of force from blowing her skyward.

"Ah!"

"Argh!"

Once the barrier was fully gone, Satan and Alciel were back to Sadao Maou and Shirou Ashiya, lying on the roof of Observation Deck 1.

Chiho must have focused all their energy back upon a single point. Emilia could see that much. The demonic force concentrated itself upon the antenna, and then:

"Rain, rain, go *awaaaaaayyy*!!"

With Chiho's signal, a long, thin belt of light shot out in all directions from the tower, bathing Tokyo in an aurora-like glow.

Now that no demonic barrier was stopping them, the crowd at ground level continued to marvel at the festival of light.

The fallen angel and cleric on top of the Dokodemo Tower in Yoyogi joined them, as did the King of All Demons, his Great Demon General, and the Hero of the Holy Sword atop Tokyo Tower.

The teenager in pajamas, growing more self-conscious by the moment, gradually sidled back down toward Maou.

"…! Chi!"

"Chiho!"

"Ms. Sasaki!!"

Emi and Ashiya hurriedly ran up to her.

A smile erupted upon her face as she fell into Maou's arms and passed out.

"Uh, hey, Chi? Chi? What's up? Are you…um."

The cold wind was beating upon them once again, but not even that was enough to muffle the sound coming from her.

"…She's asleep."

Chiho was happily snoring in Maou's grasp.

Her expression was one of pure contentment. The overwhelming presence that had stunned the warriors of another planet into silence was now replaced by a warm, baby-like smile.

EPILOGUE

"Um… Hello, Maou."

It was not the most enthusiastic of greetings from Chiho, as her cheeks glowed red and she attempted to hide her face underneath her hospital-bed comforter.

"Hey. Uh, your mom said you were gonna be discharged tomorrow, so…where is she, anyway? She gave me a call."

It was a bit awkward for Maou, being alone here without Riho present. He looked around the room.

"I-I think she'll be back in a minute. She said she had some shopping to do…"

"Oh? Well, all right. Here, um, I got you some flowers."

"Oh! Thank you very much."

Chiho shyly brought her hands forward.

"So, um…"

"…Yes?"

Chiho and Maou sized each up for a moment, trying to read each other's minds. The silence got to Maou first.

"Do you…remember last night at all?"

Chiho lightly, but clearly, nodded. Slowly, she began to recap the events of the previous night.

"After I helped you with the move, I went home and watched TV. Then the screen lit up all white…and then I don't remember anything. Not until I woke up in here. Then, yesterday… Well, my phone should've been totally out of power, but it rang anyway, and this ring on my finger lit up…and I guess I figured out I could do all that stuff after that. But that was really all me, pretty much. I just, you know, I was hearing all these things on the phone, and I felt like I had to do something."

Maou moved on to the question he wanted an answer to the most.

"Who was on the line?"

"Um...well, it was definitely a woman, and I think she was from your world..."

Anxiety and hopefulness coursed across Maou's mind for a moment. But Chiho shook her head.

"But she didn't give me her name. She said to just brush it off if anyone asked me. That was apparently her condition for lending me all that power..."

"...Man. So you believed her after she gave you that story? You practically surrendered your whole body to her."

It was Maou's honest appraisal. The idea made him break into a cold sweat.

"Well... I dunno," Chiho replied sheepishly. "I just figured she wouldn't be talking to me if you or Yusa were her enemy. I mean, look at all the power she had. She could've taken me hostage or controlled me like a robot if she wanted to, but she didn't. So I figured she wasn't a bad guy, anyway."

"...Y'know, I've been thinking this for a while, but wow, Chiho, you've *really* got a thick skin for this kinda thing."

"Well, that's thanks to all my new friends keeping things exciting all the time." Chiho let out an easy laugh. "Besides, when Gabriel first showed up...that really frustrated me."

"Oh?"

"Remember how you told me that I shouldn't go near your apartment until everything was worked out with Alas Ramus? I mean, I was glad to see you worry about me, and I know I'd just get in the way during a fight, but it was...you know, just a little frustrating, still. I wished that I had enough strength to fight like you guys. To protect everybody I knew. And then..."

Chiho picked up her phone, then looked up at Maou, an apologetic look on her face.

"The woman on the phone offered you her powers?"

It certainly wasn't a good example of thinking ahead—giving

your physical body over to a total stranger over the phone. Very un-Chiho-like. But Chiho shook her head briskly at Maou's stern tone.

"Oh, it wasn't that simple. She heard me talking in my sleep, so she gave me this lecture about how I shouldn't be such a picky eater. Then she talked about why I fainted at home, and how you and everyone else came to visit me in the hospital, and how you and Yusa might be fighting over in Tokyo Tower or the Skytree right this moment, and how it'd be against Gabriel and this other angel I didn't know, and how Sariel wasn't involved at all, and how a lot of other people with vast holy powers were joining in as well, and how despite knowing all of that, she wasn't in a position to go out in public and handle it herself, and stuff."

"……"

Maou fell silent at Chiho's astonishing verbal checklist.

"So once she told me all of that, she got really serious with me, like, 'I'll protect you if it gets dangerous at all and I'll repay you afterward, so please, help me protect the people I hold so dear for me' and so on. That's what made me think, 'Okay, I guess I can trust her.' Like, if I could pitch in and help you and Yusa when you're really, really in trouble…"

Chiho looked up again, gauging Maou's countenance.

"…The idea made me kind of happy, to be honest. And it felt great, too. Flying in the air and all. Pretty cold, but great."

Nobody on Earth was more aware than Chiho of her relationship with Maou and the other Ente Islans, and where exactly she stood with all of them. She would never be one to let her emotions carry her to the battlefield uninvited. That would just make Maou and Emi's job more difficult.

That was why she was so willing to endure the pain of feeling helpless around them. It wasn't hard to picture that. She was, after all, still just another teenage girl.

"Well, if that ever happens again and you think the lady's willing to listen, don't sell yourself out so easy, okay? You know, talk to me or Emi first. No guarantee it'll work out so well next time, besides."

Chiho nodded sincerely—enough so for Maou to accept it. He relaxed his face a little.

"So does your body feel different at all?"

Chiho found it difficult to answer.

"...In a way, yes. But in a way, no, too. I mean, I feel like everything's back to normal, and I'm not in pain at all. But...I've got memories, now, that I know don't belong to me."

"Don't belong to you?"

"I don't know if I should call them memories or just...really strong emotions, or something? Like, at first, I thought I saw it in a movie or something and my brain decided to stick it into my dreams one night. But...but I really think they belong to you. Or, I mean, they belong to Satan."

"...Me?"

"I see this really tiny demon."

Maou gulped nervously.

"He's crying his eyes out, and he's covered in cuts and bruises... He looks like he might die unless someone helps him out. So then I came in and nursed him back to health, and I talked about all these different things while I did. And, soon, you and I were friends. I don't know, it's like I really wanted to help you out, or..."

"Chi?"

The pronoun shift threw Maou for a loop.

"But I was so busy trying to save you from the brink of death that I didn't tell you about the most important thing of all. I kept wanting to apologize to you about it."

Chiho's eyes were squarely upon Maou.

"...Who are you? *What did you do to Chi's body?*"

Now he knew. He sat forward in his chair, his voice stern and low.

"I suppose I was pretty immature back then, too. I was so lost in my ideals that I wasn't able to see the big picture. That's why I guess I made you go wrong in the end. But...what I'm doing now, it's to the point where I can't go back to you any longer. I'm truly sorry about that."

The voice, and the body, was Chiho's. But the atmosphere, the way she spoke, wasn't.

"You haven't forgotten about me…have you, Satan Jacob?"

That, finally, was enough to make Maou leap backward out of his chair.

"Listen to me for a moment. I promise it won't be long."

"What… You… How are you…!"

"I apologize for getting this child involved in this, but I had no other choice."

Chiho's possessor, ignoring Maou's shaky voice, continued unabated.

"My mission is to bring Ente Isla back…to bring heaven, and the demon realms, back to what they need to be. If I wanted to do that, I needed a vast amount of support. And I have to admit it—in a way, I rescued you then because I thought it would help me out later on. I thought you'd grasp the truth I was trying to reach."

"Chiho" turned her gaze toward the window.

"You, being here in this world right now…that's no coincidence," she said.

"What?"

"This is the closest Land of Sephirot to Ente Isla. You, and that child… It was rather like you simply moved a few doors down, in the grand scheme of things. It makes it easier to bring people and things back and forth…and more than anything, this Land of Sephirot is full. Complete. Its seed shall be carried on to the next generation. Neither tilted toward the holy nor the demonic…and yet, it holds both elements within it. Truly, a miraculous world…"

The unspoken *but* was clear in her voice.

"Now, our actions have dragged down the 'inheritance' process. If this continues, Ente Isla will face a disaster on the same level as the Demon Overlord Satan's rise once again. I…I simply wanted to stop that…but I couldn't. That's the kind of people they are. All they care about is what's in it for them. That's why I took action."

"I don't understand what you're saying! Just get to the point!!"

"That child holds one of the keys…as does its father."

Maou deliberately avoided pondering over which "child" she meant. *He* was talking to *her*. He needed to focus on that.

"Where are you right now?"

"My memories being copied into this child's mind was a total coincidence. I never took her over, or possessed her. Not for a moment. Her brain will do away with them soon enough—they're too much of a mismatch with the rest of her experiences. I wish I could have given her the power to protect herself, but…alas. However, I did give her one piece of information she needs to know for my goals. I hope you will forgive me for that."

"Chiho" softly extended a hand to Maou.

"So please… You must find the Da'at of Ente Isla… That key will bring both father and child…to…ing the…en…"

"Whoa! Whoa, what's up?!"

The voice grew scratchy, like noise in a radio transmission, gradually clouding up her speech.

"…the same…an…somehow…is all…"

A pained expression on her face, "Chiho" still mustered a smile.

"Bring the world back to what it needs to be. I wish you the best of luck, Devil King Satan!"

And, the next instant, Chiho was back.

"…Yeah, it's like I'm remembering this stuff from back when you were a little kid, Maou, so I didn't know what I should… Um, Maou?"

"…Oh. Sorry."

Maou gave Chiho a light shake of his head, put his chair back in place, and sat down.

The purple stone on Chiho's ring remained there as always.

"Eesh. Here I am in modern-day Japan, and I *still* don't have anything to record audio with…"

"Huh?"

"Never mind."

Maou smirked, mostly to himself, and shook his head again.

"So did whoever owns that ring tell you anything about what's going to happen? It's not like you can handle that Yesod fragment by yourself, right?"

Chiho took a glance at the ring on her left hand, her face perplexed.

"I think she did...or maybe she didn't? I'm pretty sure that there's something or other that I need to tell Yusa, though."

"...Oh?"

The girl herself seemed fine with it, but Maou fretted nonetheless about what, if any, effect these otherworldly forces would have on her long-term health.

"Well, the way Suzuno put it, I don't think you'd be able to store all that much holy force in your body anyway, Chi. It's probably better that you don't think about trying to harness it too much. It'll make your mom get all worried."

"Yeah. I know. An amateur like me, learning a little about these supernatural forces... That's still not enough to let me fight by myself, huh?"

Maou nodded, satisfied.

"That's what I figure. Our enemies aren't gonna dial it down for us. If anything, they'll dial it up."

"Should I maybe let you or Yusa have this?"

Chiho's eyes were still on the ring. Maou fell silent for a moment, unable to reach a conclusion. Then:

"Nah, you can keep it, Chi. A kind of lucky charm, you know?"

None of the archangels—Gabriel, Raguel, definitely not Sariel—demonstrated much of an appetite for Yesod-fragment collecting at the moment. That ring no doubt triggered Chiho's performance last night, and whoever owned it had already guaranteed Chiho's safety going forward. Having her take it would provide at least a bit of extra insurance, anyway.

That was how much of an indispensable presence Chiho had grown to become, to both demon and Hero. Anything that kept her safe was welcome.

"But... Oh! Maou!"

"Hmm?"

"*You've* already got an enemy like that, Maou! Someone who dials it up for you!"

"Huh?"

"Yusa, I mean! The Hero! That's how she and the Devil King work, right?"

"I don't think she's really doing that just for me, Chi..."

"Maybe I'll keep some some power after all! I'll fight like her!"

"Wh-where did *that* come from?"

"What? I want to, that's all! I can't lose out to Yusa!"

"This isn't about winning or losing, Chi...and, jeez, stop flailing around! You're still technically in recovery, you know!"

The argument over Chiho's potential battle prowess continued unabated, until Riho finally returned from the grocery store.

＊

The Hero of the holy sword, meanwhile, was at her cube.

"Yes. I very much apologize for that, sir. We'll be happy to apply a credit to your bill for the period of downtime you experienced..."

"You can expect an apology to be sent to each of your customers in text and written form within the day..."

"Texting, Internet, and voice... Yes, sir. Absolutely. I deeply apologize for the inconvenience..."

The three women, sitting adjacent to each other, ended their calls and together let out a remarkably well-synchronized sigh.

"I-I was expecting this the moment I heard the news this morning, but..."

Maki Shimizu, the college student part-timer, looked ready to burst into tears.

"Yeah... Man, this is one serious workout."

Rika Suzuki was uncharacteristically lifeless and pale herself.

"................."

And Emi Yusa, for her part, remained doggedly silent.

The phone network at the Dokodemo Customer Support Center was breathing its last.

That was the sort of thing that happened when every Dokodemo phone within the twenty-three central boroughs of Tokyo lost all functionality for seventy-five or so minutes in the middle of the evening.

The complaints started streaming in the moment the morning shift began. The customers asking to be refunded for the outage were, if anything, among the kinder, more accommodating ones. Businesses and civic departments calling to demand reparations for the outage, on the other hand, were beyond anything Emi and her coworkers had the power to handle.

The cause of the outage, reported as the lead story of every early-morning TV news show, was undoubtedly the twin sonar blasts Suzuno and Chiho bounced off the Dokodemo Tower antenna during their little skirmish the previous night.

She couldn't berate the idea, at least—fighting TV signals via a high-energy transmission sent through cell phone bandwidth.

But, due to some miscalculation on Urushihara's part or Suzuno firing a stronger pulse than she intended—or maybe just the general interference dominating the skies over Tokyo that evening—the blasts took over Dokodemo's entire mobile spectrum for what seemed like an eternity.

That made it impossible to connect to certain Dokodemo phones, and the resulting cascade of failures led to the quagmire Emi faced today.

Every chair in the room had a call handler sitting on it. From early morning, the team leader had been texting out desperate pleas to unscheduled staff to sign on for an extra shift or two over the next couple of days.

So Emi was back at work the day after. Her conscience wouldn't allow anything else. This time, at least, there was no shunting the blame over to the demons.

And she needed a distraction anyway. She still hadn't sifted through everything she'd experienced the night before.

The shocking truth Gabriel revealed to her was more than enough to send mighty waves of stress crashing over her heart.

Her father was alive.

Thinking about what that meant, and what effect it would have, filled Emi with a tormenting fear that made her feet stop in their tracks.

So this was good for her, dealing with irate customers, not given so much as a millisecond to dwell on her own thoughts. As she told herself, she needed to focus on handling customer issues as quickly and efficiently as possible. *Her* issues could wait.

"Think we'll get a lunch break today...?"

Rika's exasperated complaint, voiced between the endless barrage of calls, made the blood drain from Maki's face.

"Uggghhh... I stayed up late watching TV last night and felt kinda sick this morning, so I haven't eaten yet today..."

"TV...?"

Emi, remembering something, addressed her coworkers on both sides.

"Hey, guys, um..."

"Mm?"

"Yes?"

"Did you guys see anything weird when watching TV last night? Like...any kind of flashing, like everyone's talking about?"

Rika nodded. It sounded familiar to her.

"Oh, yeah, it affected more than mobile video this time, didn't it? I wasn't really in any shape to watch TV last night so I wouldn't know, but..."

"Me, I haven't bought an HDTV yet. I'm still on analog, but I didn't see anything."

"Oh..."

Rika and Maki didn't run into any trouble. It was a relief to Emi.

"What were you doing, though, Ms. Suzuki?" Maki asked Rika. "Wasn't one of your favorite dramas on last night?"

"Aaaahh!!" Her observation sent Rika into a panic. "I *tooootally* forgot..."

"...Do you maybe have a guy now or something?"

Straight down the middle.

"Oh, c-come *on*, Maki! He's not my 'guy' or anything yet..."

"......!"

Emi grabbed her head.

Maki's face brightened at Rika, who was rapidly digging her own grave right under her own feet.

"Not *yet*? You said not *yet*, didn't you?!"

"Uh, ah, n-no, I, ughhh! Maki! Take a call already! We're at work!"

"Well, I'm expecting a full report later!" Maki shot back. "Thank you for your patience. This is the…"

Rika turned her exasperated face toward Emi for emotional support.

"Sorry. Can't help you this time."

"Aw, that's *mean*, Emi!"

Emi returned to her calls. She had a headache of her own to deal with.

Not even the fact that Rika clearly had feelings for Ashiya was enough to make Emi's mind budge from the subject it was currently obsessing over.

Thinking over why she went through all that effort to demolish the Devil King's Army… If she trusted what Gabriel said, it could make her doubt everything she lived for, in the end.

But something still tugged at her.

"Can't turn back time now, I guess…"

Whether she doubted herself or not, as long as she was alive, she had to keep moving forward.

In fact, maybe she should be happy. She finally had a goal in life aside from slaying the Devil King.

"No point beating myself up pondering over it. That'd just be spinning my wheels by now."

She could start by doing what she could, right this moment, fully gauging what life had in store for her.

Just as she felt her resolve start to firm up, a voice in the back of her mind addressed her.

"Mommy, Chi-sis's lucky charm going boom-boom?"

She must have woken up.

It was highly questionable how much Emi could focus on her work while trying to keep Alas Ramus entertained. She had to smile at the absurdity of her situation.

Once she escaped work today, she was due to visit Chiho at the hospital, giving her a chance to both listen to her side of the story and teach Alas Ramus how to say *Get well soon* to people. She began to write a mental list of sweet shops on the way home that she figured Chiho might like. Alas Ramus caught on to it.

"Senbei! Senbei! Wice crackuhs!"

She was always ready to pitch in her two cents.

＊

"Welcome back, Your Demonic Highness. How is Ms. Sasaki faring?"

Suzuno, for some reason, was waiting alongside Ashiya when Maou made his return.

"Ah, you've returned? Anything happen to you?"

"Nah, Chi's just fine. Couldn't be healthier, in fact. And no, nothing happened to me; what's that question supposed to mean?"

Even if the threat wasn't explicitly targeted at Maou and Ashiya this time, Suzuno still hesitated to see Maou venture outside alone. But today presented a vastly different picture from yesterday. Nothing about Tokyo seemed unsafe at all.

Having Suzuno accompany Maou without Ashiya tagging along would create its own raftload of misunderstandings, so Suzuno instead fretted by herself at Villa Rosa Sasazuka, awaiting his return.

"N-nothing, but..."

She stopped. This sounded suspiciously like she was worrying about him. She raised her voice. Enough of that.

"Enough of that, Devil King! The television! We have the television on!"

"Hah, really? Welcome to the fifties, I guess."

"...Yes. Thank you..."

Something about Maou's sarcasm embarrassed Suzuno a little.

"Thought you'd be more excited than *that*, dude. You're the one who wanted it," Urushihara added in.

Maou shrugged at his griping.

"Yeah, dealing with those two bastards kinda cooled me to the whole thing, I guess. I'm glad we got another tool to let us know if something's going haywire, but it's not like they're dumb enough to try the same trick on us twice, so..."

By modern standards, the TV screen was miniscule. But within the current Devil's Castle, it was more than enough.

"Oh. Hey, Ashiya, I got this."

Maou tossed a wad of paper out from his pocket.

"Hmm? What is it?"

It was a receipt from their bank.

Ashiya carefully unwadded it. Then his eyes expanded into saucers. *Deposit: 50,000*, it read.

"Y-your Demonic Highness?! What on earth is this deposit?!"

"Well, after we screwed up Ohguro-ya, I've been outta work, right?"

Maou opened the refrigerator door and chugged what remained of their barley tea supply straight from the bottle.

"...Pahh. I still got a little bit before MgRonald starts back up, but with Ciriatto back in the demon realm, they might decide to send a Barbariccia squadron or two back over here. We could be in serious danger, for all I know. I figure it wouldn't be a good idea for me to go off somewhere far away for day-labor crap. We probably better stick together more."

Suzuno stole a glance at the receipt from the side, her own eyes popping out of their sockets at this highly irregular deposit.

"There were more jewels embedded on the scabbard of Camio's magic sword than just the Yesod fragment, y'know. So I plucked one of 'em out—nothing too big, you'd never notice it if you didn't know what to look for—and I pawned it over at the Mugi-hyo in Shinjuku. That way, we can budget the TV for next month and you can actually buy a decent phone with what's left, okay?"

"My liege..."

Ashiya's reaction went beyond astonishment and entered the realm of blissful ecstasy.

"Why just one, dude? Might as well just cash 'em all in, no?"

Maou scoffed at Urushihara's sensible suggestion.

"Oh, yeah, a guy in his early twenties dressed head to toe in closeout UniClo gear carrying a box full of precious jewels with him? You think I'm in *that* big a hurry to arouse suspicion? That's more than enough right there. We'd get taxed out the ass if I sold it for too much, besides."

Maou rinsed out the bottle, refilled it with water, stuck a barley-tea packet inside, and placed it back in the fridge.

"Once work starts back up, I'll have to deal with Sariel across the street again. If everything goes to hell, I suppose I can try using him to save my own ass...but until then I figure, hey, why not enjoy some time off for the first time in a couple centuries? All work and no play, and all that."

With that, he picked up the TV remote and instruction manual on the table, referring to one as he tapped away at the other.

Watching him as he crouched over his new toy made Suzuno whisper:

"...So. He *is* thinking about matters, yes?"

Ashiya didn't acknowledge it. He was too busy admiring every digit, every contour of the words *Deposit: 50,000* in front of him.

※

Gabriel, sitting in the CyberSafe Net café he was currently using as his main base of operations on Earth, spotted a familiar face.

"Satou! Hey, someone's lookin' chipper today, huh? You find some decent work for a change?"

Satou, ever-present glass of oolong tea in hand, waved as he took a sip.

"Hey, Greek! You been hearin' about all the trouble they've been having with TVs and cell phones and whatnot?"

"Oh? Uhm, yeahhhh. Yeah. Sorta."

Gabriel, the chief cause of said trouble, found it difficult to reply coherently. Satou, beaming, paid it no mind.

"Well, the phone companies are all staging top-to-bottom maintenance inspections of all their equipment! You wouldn't believe how many traffic guides and security guards they're hirin' for the thing! I'm gonna be up to my eyeballs in work for at least the next two weeks!"

"Oh? Oh. Ohhhh. Well, good?"

"My heart goes out to all the phone companies 'n' all, but I tell you, this is *really* gonna put me back on track to my dreams, y'know? It's like God's rewarding me for all my hard work or somethin'."

"Oh, you...think?"

The archangel had little to add on that front.

"But, hey, you're lookin' pretty happy, too. Find yourself a decent paycheck?"

Satou was fully convinced Gabriel was in the same financial boat he found himself in. There was no need to correct him, but on the other hand, Satou seemed to have a natural-born gift for reading people's minds at times.

"Mmm, I dunno if it'll wind up working out or not, really..."

The burly denizen of heaven filled up his own glass of oolong tea and smiled.

"But I think we *miiiight* just see someone step up to save the world, if you know what I mean."

"Huh?"

Satou paused a moment to think.

"You working for one of those goofball stunt shows down at the amusement park or somethin'?"

Gabriel's scarlet eyes, studying Satou closely, sparkled with the shine of a child basking in the glow of his own epic prank.

THE AUTHOR, THE AFTERWORD, AND YOU

Tokyo Skytree, the official new landmark of Japan, surpassed its old man Tokyo Tower's height of 1,093 feet in late March 2010. The observation deck was completed three months afterward, and a mere year later, in March 2011, it attained its full height of 2,080 feet. Nearly a thousand feet of growth in the space of a year. All hail the glories of Japanese construction firms and hefty budgets. It's grown up so big and strong!

Alongside that, Japan—with the exception of a few areas—switched over to digital-only TV broadcasts in July 2011.

This book will see its original publication in June 2012, so by the time you read this, it'll already be nearly a year after the fact and the Skytree should be open for business. Time flies when you're spending all day writing at home.

I suppose I've gone on in assorted places about how *The Devil Is a Part-Timer!* couldn't exist without depicting Japan as it really is, as if I'm some kind of literary genius who knows where the story's going two pages ahead of the one he's writing. But I've made it this far without explicitly stating which year it is in the Japan Maou and Emi live in.

That ends with Volume 5, though. Between the under-construction Skytree and the rest of the events in this volume, if we assume *Devil* fully complies with time in the real world, the story is officially set in August 2010.

But!

If you look over the whole series, dating back to Volume 1...let's just say that Maou and friends have had an *extremely* busy summer of 2010.

Every volume I've written tends to be a reflection of the time I live in at the moment I put fingers to keyboard. When I was first writing this story on the Web, under a different title—the story that eventually won me a Dengeki Award and this gig—construction hadn't even begun on the Skytree yet. Contradictions abound across the story's world as a result.

These are just novels, of course, so I could just shrug it off and defiantly tell my readers not to sweat the details. But that isn't the problem. Now that it's set in a definitive time period, everyone involved with this series has a very specific issue they need to deal with.

In Volume 1, the Hero Emilia's friend Rika Suzuki discussed her experiences with the Kobe earthquake of 1995, an experience no one in Japan could ever forget.

Nor should they, really. But her memories, too painful for her to talk about with most people, were pretty much taken verbatim from those of a personal friend of mine.

And if the Japan Maou and Emi live in is really going to be the Japan of August 2010, that means there'll be an event in seven months that will ultimately carve its place in the annals of world history. And when this book is released, it's doubtful that any of the ensuing memories or effects will have faded from anyone's minds.

So as someone who used Rika Suzuki's memories as a central piece of character development, I have an announcement to make to my readers.

In the world depicted within the *Devil is a Part-Timer!* series, I am not going to weave the Tohoku earthquake of March 2011 in any way, shape, or form into the story.

The Devil is a Part-Timer! is a story, and like any story, it has to end sooner or later.

I can't say how far past August 2010–ish the story will proceed, or if these guys are going to even bother staying within the confines of Japan, but either way, the "real Japan" of *Devil* is a Japan free of the Tohoku quake.

This is not a case of me attempting to weigh the importance of one natural disaster against another.

It's just that the quake, as I write this, is an event of the *now*, not of the *then*. It is too early to treat it as a memory, or as a completed piece of history. In my opinion, it is not a matter that a novel series that saw its original launch in February 2011—one whose primary aim is to entertain—should be blithely tackling.

The Japan of *Devil* is one where the disturbing memories of the Kobe earthquake continue to reside in people's minds. It is one where the Skytree has only just begun to outgrow Tokyo Tower, where the government is switching everyone over to digital broadcasting, where smartphones are beginning to take over for flip phones, and where even a Devil King needs to work to keep a roof over his head. Nothing more, and nothing less, than that.

It may resemble the Japan you and I see with our own eyes at least superficially, but it is also a Japan traveling down its own unique path in history.

So, going forward, I will continue to not explicitly mention when this story takes place in the real world. I plan to have the characters age in real time, of course, and given the material I cover, I can't help but pin a time frame to many aspects of this tale. But this is their own story, their own history, and one I hope you will continue to keep close at hand well into the future.

But regardless of how I feel about it, this volume still tells the story of the Devil King and his cohorts, normally struggling to keep food on the table, engaging in a rare bout of consumerism.

It may be nothing they need, but having it around expands their perspective on things. I'm just another joe on the street, myself. Instead of having the bare essentials around me in perfect shape, I like having a hodgepodge of things around me as I work. If there's a little dust on it, that only adds to the character.

Though maybe I should at least have them purchase a couple of futons for themselves. I can tell Emi won't abide by that for much longer.

Regardless, as always, I hope that I see all of you who took this book in hand over in the next volume, and I hope all real-life bums will forgive the fallen Demon General for his misguided diatribe on bumming.

Until next time!

CONGRATULATIONS ON RELEASING VOLUME 5!
MY NAME IS AKIO HIIRAGI, AND I DRAW THE ART FOR THE
DENGEKI DAIOH MANGA VERSION OF *THE DEVIL IS A PART-
TIMER!* IT'S BEEN GREAT FUN FOR ME TO DRAW ALL OF THE
CHARACTERS, BUT THIS TIME, I DEFINITELY WANTED TO FOCUS
MY EFFORTS ON ALAS RAMUS, WHO'S ABSOLUTELY NUMBER
ONE IN MY BOOK! I CAN'T WAIT TO SEE HOW SHE'LL AFFECT
MAOU AND TEAM'S DAILY LIVES—IT'LL NO DOUBT TURN INTO
A FAMILY SITCOM BEFORE LONG! (PROBABLY NOT...)

AKIO
HIIRAGI
APRIL 2012

SPECIAL
GUEST 01

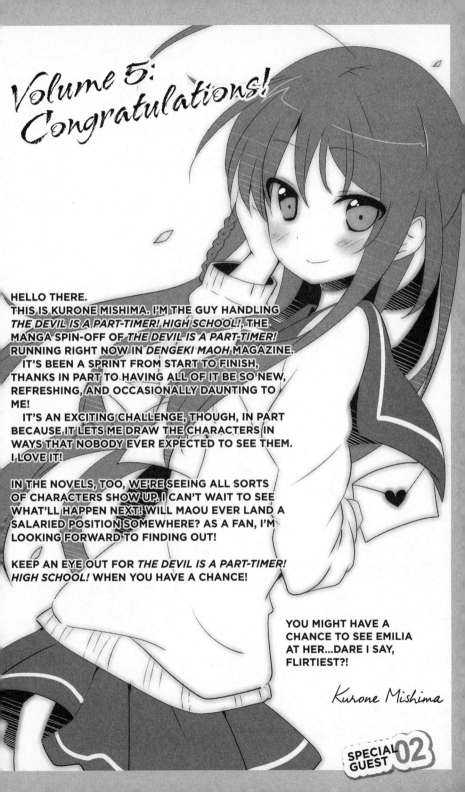

Volume 5: Congratulations!

HELLO THERE.
THIS IS KURONE MISHIMA. I'M THE GUY HANDLING
THE DEVIL IS A PART-TIMER! HIGH SCHOOL!, THE
MANGA SPIN-OFF OF *THE DEVIL IS A PART-TIMER!*
RUNNING RIGHT NOW IN *DENGEKI MAOH* MAGAZINE.

IT'S BEEN A SPRINT FROM START TO FINISH,
THANKS IN PART TO HAVING ALL OF IT BE SO NEW,
REFRESHING, AND OCCASIONALLY DAUNTING TO
ME!

IT'S AN EXCITING CHALLENGE, THOUGH, IN PART
BECAUSE IT LETS ME DRAW THE CHARACTERS IN
WAYS THAT NOBODY EVER EXPECTED TO SEE THEM.
I LOVE IT!

IN THE NOVELS, TOO, WE'RE SEEING ALL SORTS
OF CHARACTERS SHOW UP. I CAN'T WAIT TO SEE
WHAT'LL HAPPEN NEXT! WILL MAOU EVER LAND A
SALARIED POSITION SOMEWHERE? AS A FAN, I'M
LOOKING FORWARD TO FINDING OUT!

KEEP AN EYE OUT FOR *THE DEVIL IS A PART-TIMER!
HIGH SCHOOL!* WHEN YOU HAVE A CHANCE!

YOU MIGHT HAVE A
CHANCE TO SEE EMILIA
AT HER...DARE I SAY,
FLIRTIEST?!

Kurone Mishima

SPECIAL
GUEST **02**

THE DEVIL IS A PART-TIMER! 5
SPECIAL END-OF-BOOK BONUS

RÉSUMÉ COLLECTION

NAME
Rika Suzuki

DATE OF BIRTH	AGE	GENDER
March 3, XXXX	21	F

ADDRESS
Comfort Grandile Waseda 205
X-X-X Takadanobaba, Shinjuku-ku, Tokyo

TELEPHONE NUMBER
080-XXXX-XXXX

PAST EXPERIENCE	
March 20XX:	graduated Kobe Hakuryu-dai Middle School
April 20XX:	entered Hyogo Sugaya High School
March 20XX:	graduated Hyogo Sugaya High School
June 20XX:	call center consultant, Dokodemo Group Home Services

QUALIFICATIONS/CERTIFICATIONS
EIKEN English Text level 3
Bookkeeping certification, level 3

SKILLS/HOBBIES
sewing (clothing, kimono), dining adventures

REASON FOR APPLICATION
Saving money for college!!

PERSONAL GOALS
To make my family business more revved up than ever!

COMMUTE TIME	FAMILY/DEPENDENTS	NAME OF GUARDIAN
30 minutes	None	

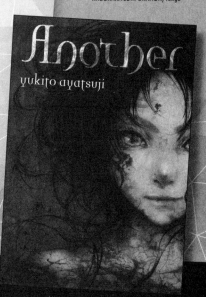

CONTENTS

THE DEVIL IS A PART-TIMER

5

SATOSHI WAGAHARA

ILLUSTRATION BY
029 (ONIKU)